BEAUTIFUL
BROKEN RULES

ALSO BY KIMBERLY LAUREN

Beautiful Broken Mess
Beautiful Broken Promises

BEAUTIFUL BROKEN RULES

KIMBERLY LAUREN

Text copyright © 2013 Kimberly Lauren

Published by Montlake Romance, Seattle

www.apub.com

Amazon, the Amazon logo, and Montlake are trademarks of Amazon.com, Inc., or its affiliates.

ISBN-13: 9781477821589
ISBN-10: 1477821589

Cover design by Mumtaz Mustafa

Library of Congress Control Number: 2014954303

Printed in the United States of America

To my husband, who keeps me sane.

BEAUTIFUL
BROKEN RULES

- ONE -

One thing I know for sure and have come to terms with: I'm the school slut. I hate that word; but sometimes it is what it is, or in my situation, I am what I am. I like guys, all kinds of them and lots of them. College has been the perfect setting for being able to meet so many. I have no desire for a relationship whatsoever, so I sleep around. Sleeping with one guy consistently is too permanent; it gives the impression that I want more than I actually do. I definitely don't want one guy sticking around me on any kind of consistent basis. I would be a terrible girlfriend anyway.

Don't get me wrong; I'm not one of those girls that just goes around sleeping with any guy, without a care for anyone's feelings. I have three rules: Never sleep with someone that a friend has feelings for; never sleep with someone who is in a known relationship (when this isn't disclosed to me, it is not my fault); and, finally, never sleep with someone more than three times. I had to add that last one after Devon Ryan. Man, it was a shame too, because he was fantastic in bed and we got along really well. When we were dangerously close to relationship territory after four nights together, I added Rule Number Three. He wasn't happy about it, but I'm not a girlfriend to anyone. This way, if I come across someone who knows what he is doing, I can stick around long enough to enjoy, but not long enough for him to become attached.

These rules have helped me avoid becoming one of the most hated girls on campus. I don't sleep with anyone's boyfriend, and I try my hardest not to sleep with any of my friend's ex-boyfriends as well, but sometimes that's unavoidable. Nevertheless, I can't please them all. I'm very open about who I am: I don't pretend not to sleep with guys and I don't deny when I have done just that.

I've accepted who I am: the girl who will never become serious about anyone, who will enjoy life, have fun with guys along the way, and never get her heart broken. The one thing other girls count on me for is to never lock one guy down, because they know that sooner or later I'll move on to the next one.

That's why I hope that when Sophia finds out that I slept with Micah last night, she'll understand that I don't plan on actually keeping him. I had no idea that she'd been hoping he'd ask her out, until Quinn texted me this morning with a code red.

Quinn: FYI Soph was gushing this morning about Micah at the gym.

Well, shit. This was news to me. Last I heard she was interested in Mason Lee. This is why rule number one gets broken more often than not; girls can never make up their damn minds!

When the text alert for my phone went off this morning, I rolled over to grab it, only to be hit by the solid chest that belonged to Micah Woods. He was snoring in my face with whiskey still heavy on his breath. Last night was Sigma Alpha's first get-to-know-the-fraternity night of Rush Week. I loved it when a new school year started; it brought in a bunch of new guys. Micah was in Sig Alpha and lived in the house. I usually tried not to stay the night at any of the Greek houses because I hated waking up in them. The next morning, the magic of the party wore off and all you were left with was beer cans, vomit, and a guy asleep in the bathtub. For some reason, there was always a guy asleep in the bathtub; I could never understand how they got themselves there.

This morning was definitely a sign that I should never stay the night again. I had no idea where my clothes were, and it seemed as though all of Micah's clothes were disgustingly dirty in piles on his floor. I sent Quinn a text to see if she had any idea where my clothes were, and she told me to check down by the pool. So apparently, I was in the pool last night. I guess that would explain why I was only wearing a bra and panties. It was actually Quinn's bra and my panties. I'm guessing we thought it would be a brilliant idea to switch last night. Not so brilliant now, seeing as Quinn is two cup sizes smaller and I was having a hard time keeping it all in. I grabbed my phone and my purse—thankfully, I'd had enough insight to bring them upstairs with me last night—and quietly walked toward the door. Before I could reach the doorknob, I stepped on a beer bottle cap and yelped. Micah sat straight up in a huff from under the covers.

"What! Are you okay, Em?" he asked me in a voice that was scratchy and deep from sleep and too much whiskey.

His eyes were squinting at the brightness of the morning. He was attractive with a smooth, broad chest and bright golden-brown eyes. He was fun last night, but sadly, it was night number three with him.

"Crap. Sorry, Micah! I didn't mean to wake you. I just stepped on a bottle cap and cut my foot," I said, bouncing on one foot while holding up the other. "Go back to sleep, I'm just heading out."

He laughed a little bit under his breath and eyed me up and down. "You're going to leave the frat house with no clothes on? You're practically falling out of Q's bra." He got up, walked over to me, and knelt down to examine the bottom of my foot. "I think you'll be okay, it's not even bleeding." He gave the bottom of my foot a quick kiss and then started rubbing his hands up my legs leisurely.

Before he could skim higher up my thigh, I stepped back. "Micah, I have to get to class," I warned him as he scooted forward toward me.

"Please don't follow that stupid 'three times only' rule you have. We're good together, Em. You don't even have to be my girlfriend. Just come back over tonight and I'll remind you what we do so well," he said, still kneeling on the ground and looking up at me with his fingers wrapped around my waist.

"Micah, I don't break my rules. I made them for a reason," I said in a barely audible whisper.

As good as it would've been to come back to Micah, I did not intend to get serious with him, and that's where it would lead. It always does. It's the gradual way of humans. We become comfortable with one another and then we're married and someone's cheating on the other one. I was purely trying to prevent this from ever happening.

He gave my waist a small squeeze, nodded his head in defeat, and slowly stood up to look down at me. "Well, it was fun, and you're welcome back in my bed anytime, babe. Please take one of my shirts before you leave, though. The walk of shame is one thing, but the walk of shame in *that*, Em?"

"Micah, your shirts are disgusting. I can't even walk out of here with one of those on without getting nauseated from this hangover. I'll be fine. Besides, Quinn thinks my clothes are out by the pool anyway. I'll just run down there and put them on. You know none of those guys are anywhere close to waking up anytime soon. See ya!"

Micah shrugged, not even attempting to defend his gross pile of clothes, and was already pulling the covers back over his head in bed, grunting out a good-bye. Must be nice not to have classes until later in the day.

I snuck down the creaky old stairs as quietly as I could, but this house was really old and had more groans than a ninety-year-old man. Besides, my one-legged hobble wasn't helping with my stealthy escape, either, since my foot was still throbbing. Thankfully, no one woke up to see me streaking through the house.

When I made it out back, I decided I was going to have to murder someone that day. I just didn't know who it was going to be yet. My clothes were definitely out here, but they were hanging from a tree branch, and there was no way in hell I was going to be able to get them down. Even if I found a ladder, I wouldn't be tall enough. My flip-flops were floating in the middle of the pool. Fantastic. Thankfully, I remembered I had a change of clothes in my car, so I only needed to get to them, and I wouldn't have to drive home practically naked.

Please, please, please, don't let anyone be outside. I mean, this was Frat Row. No one should be up before seven a.m., especially after a party night. I crept back through the house, tiptoeing over the passed-out bodies on the floor. The majority of them were wearing Sig Alpha shirts, although I noticed there were a few other fraternities present. God, this place was a wreck. I felt bad for the pledges, because they would more than likely be the ones cleaning up this filth. That is one reason I never rushed a sorority. I had no interest in being on the bottom of the food chain; I just enjoyed their parties.

I stepped out onto the front porch and turned to pull the old, heavy, wooden door closed when I heard a familiar voice burst out laughing. Damn. I lowered my head and groaned; I took a deep breath and shut the door all the way, while I exhaled. I turned around to face my humiliation that was my best friend, Cole. But it wasn't just Cole. It was Cole and Mason talking to another guy on a motorcycle whom I'd never seen before.

Okay, so I was going to have to work with this. I would not be humiliated. Pretty much everyone on Frat Row has seen me in my bra and panties before; it was just different when you had liquid courage coursing through your system versus when you didn't. That nasty sweat-stained shirt of Micah's was looking better and better right now. I straightened my shoulders and tried the best I could to hide my limp. My car was parked right in front of Motorcycle Boy, so I had no choice but to walk right up to them.

"Good morning to you too, Giggles. Is that any way to greet a lady?" I asked Cole, nudging him in the stomach with my elbow, while he was still trying to catch his breath from laughing at me so hard. I glared at Mason, who was also laughing. Motorcycle Boy was just smirking at me. I smiled sweetly at all three of them, praying my cheeks were not as red as Quinn's bra.

"I'm sorry, love. It's just that I've seen you do the walk of shame before, but never with so little clothing. If more girls walked out of frat houses like this in the morning, I guarantee you none of these guys would be late for class anymore," Cole stated, wrapping his arm around my shoulders and giving me a quick kiss on my temple as he squeezed me into him.

Quinn and I picked up Cole at orientation our freshman year. Quinn thought his messy, dirty-blond hair and football player's body were hot. When she expressed that a little too boisterously behind him in the school auditorium, he turned around with a huge grin on his face.

"Well, well, well, hello to you too, ladies," he had said in his pleasing Texas accent.

I think Quinn and I both sighed out loud at that. Being from Southern California, we don't have any kind of accent, and neither do any of the guys, usually. He's been with us ever since. None of us ever hooked up and that's probably for the best, because I doubt we would be as close to Cole if either of us had. I love Cole like a brother, and he's pretty protective of Quinn and me. Although clearly he has no qualms about me showing off my goods to complete strangers or drooling idiots like Mason.

Currently, Cole lives in the Sig house, but his best friends from Texas were moving out here to join him at school, so he's moving out to get an apartment next to Quinn and me. We were all pretty excited when the apartment right next to us became available over the summer. He has slowly been moving all his stuff in the last couple of weeks. We'd been trying to get him to move out of the frat house since he moved in; it's annoying to come visit him outside of a party. These guys are fun to take to bed and have drinks with, but when you have to study or have any kind of civil conversation, it's basically impossible at that house. Someone is always yelling, drinking, or breaking something.

"Well, I thought I would try something new today. Spice up your life a little; keep you on your toes. Besides, someone thought it was a genius idea to throw my clothes in a tree out back. All of Micah's clothes smell like sweat, sand, and I don't even want to think about what else. So here I am, trying to get to my car for more clothes with my dignity intact. Obviously that's working well for me," I indicated, gesturing at all three guys. Mason and Cole continued laughing while Motorcycle Boy kept that frustrating smirk of his.

"Damn, Em, you're killing me. Please come over to visit tonight. I'll go buy your favorite beer," Mason said while ogling my way-too-small bra. Mason and I had hooked up in the beginning of sophomore year. It was the worst minute and a half ever. I certainly don't have to worry about breaking Rule Number Three with him. It's not happening with us ever again. I usually just ignore his advances.

Cole shoved Mason back and smacked him on the back of the head with his palm. "Emmy, this is Jaxon Riley, one of the guys I've been telling you was transferring out here from back home. I'm sure you'll meet his brother, Jace, later. They're both moving into the apartment with me."

7

Great . . . so we'll be neighbors. Wow, do I know how to make first impressions. I started getting uncomfortable under this gorgeous guy's penetrating, blue-eyed gaze. He was hands-down the most attractive person I'd ever seen in my life. I rarely get embarrassed, but all of a sudden, I wanted to be anywhere other than here, meeting Jaxon Riley in Quinn's bra and my panties. At the dentist, the gynecologist, in advanced statistics taking a final I didn't study for that was written in German—anywhere besides where I was right now.

I shifted to lift my aching foot off the ground. "Okay, well it was nice to meet you, but hopefully you can forget that this was your first impression of me and we can meet again while I'm clothed. Seeing as we'll be neighbors and all."

Man, my foot was really bothering me, standing on this concrete. I bent my knee and brought my foot up behind me to rub the bottom of it. Jaxon watched my foot come up and my hand rubbing circles on it. His penetrating gaze seemed to pierce through me, as he intently focused on my foot.

"I sure as hell will never forget this moment, meeting you like this. It's nice to know I'll have a hot neighbor."

And cue the blush. Not only did he have that mesmerizing southern accent as Cole does, but he just called me hot. He has also said all this while still balancing himself on his motorcycle. That was my signal to get out of here.

"All right. Well, Cole, don't forget we have journalism in thirty minutes. Don't be late and if you get there before me, please save me a seat, and don't let one of the sorority bimbos take it this time," I pleaded with him.

I'm usually a pretty outgoing person when it comes to meeting new people, but I hated that awkward first-day dance you do, walking into a new classroom, when you have no idea where to sit. It throws me off and makes me feel not in control. Cole and I are both majoring in journalism, so we typically have the majority of our classes together. He understands me and tries to save me a seat, but a pretty face easily distracts him.

I waved them off and hobbled to my car, walking on tiptoe with my injured foot. When I got to my trunk, I popped it open and, thank the heavens, found a sundress, which I hastily threw on. I breathed a sigh of relief at feeling comfortable again. As I rounded my car to open the driver's door, I glanced back at the guys. Cole and Mason were already stepping up onto the porch to head inside. Jaxon was still balancing on his bike and staring at me.

Good grief, the boy was hot. I couldn't tell how tall he was because he hadn't stood up off his bike yet. His legs appeared long and I could see his muscles bunching underneath the jeans that were hugging him perfectly. The black leather jacket looked as if it would feel like butter on his shoulders and his skin was tanned just enough to make his ice-blue eyes pop. His hair was a warm dark brown, with a few natural highlights spread throughout. It called out for fingers to run through it, which it appeared his did on a regular basis. Each strand appeared as if it had a mind of its own and was going to go whichever way it wanted. The front pieces were long, and I could tell they would get in his eyes, but he obviously pushed them over to the side. His face had just a little bit of scruff to add that rougher look to him. He was definitely no pretty California boy.

When I realized how long I had been checking him out, my eyes snapped up to his and he knowingly grinned at me. Oh, this one was going to be trouble; I needed the ball back in my court. So I tossed my hair over my shoulder, lifted my chest high, and gave him my sexiest wink. Before I turned to sit down in the driver's seat, I saw his jaw drop just a little bit. One point for me. That's right, Motorcycle Boy; I'm the one in control here.

- TWO -

I ran by Quinn's and my apartment to shower and change into different clothes. I slipped on a pair of jean shorts, one of the local campus band T-shirts, and some flip-flops. Quinn had cut a V-slit in my T-shirt, which was meant to show off my cleavage. She said, "We can't have the boys forgetting you're a girl, if you insist on wearing that awful shirt." Like they could forget; I had D's, for goodness' sake. I didn't have time for makeup or curling my hair, though. I never understood waking up extra early to get dressed up for class, but I also wasn't husband-hunting like some of these girls. I barely had time to say hi and bye to Quinn in my rush through the apartment. I gave her a quick kiss on the cheek and made her promise she would be in the cafeteria to meet for lunch.

I made it to journalism before our professor did, so that was always good news. When I dashed into class, I scanned the packed lecture hall for Cole. When I finally spotted him, he had two Chi Omega girls leaning in on each side to talk to him. It was pretty convenient how they leaned in toward him, displaying their breasts perfectly. I'm not judging, though. Can't say I've never pulled that move before; I'm just bitter that they stole my spot. He glanced back at me and instantly mouthed an apology. I rolled my eyes at him and gave him a look that I hoped conveyed how much he would pay for this later.

I walked down the steps of the side row, searching for an open seat, and heard someone call my name. I looked down the aisle I had stopped at and saw Jaxon at the far end, waving me down to the open seat next to him. There was a black backpack in the seat, but when I sidestepped down the aisle, I saw him pick it up and put it underneath his chair.

"Once I saw the 'sorority bimbos' swarming Cole, I saved you a seat," he said, looking up at me and shrugging as if it was no big deal.

"Wow . . . thanks. I'm surprised they aren't swarming you, either; it won't be long until they discover those gorgeous blue eyes," I said, laughing. I can't believe he actually paid attention to what I said earlier. It's like he knew I would be uncomfortable coming in here with nowhere to sit.

"Nah, sorority bimbos really aren't my type," he said in his low southern drawl. I instantly wondered if I was his type. I mean, he did save the seat for me and not someone else.

"They did swarm him, but he scared them off," Tobias Reed interrupted.

Tobias was sitting on the other side of Jaxon. He's pretty much our class know-it-all. He's in everyone's business, but he's smart as hell, so he's helpful to sit by in class.

Jaxon shrugged vaguely. "It's not a big deal. I heard you tell Cole to save you one and figured I could help you out." He started to take off his leather jacket, and I could see he was wearing a dark gray Henley underneath that showed the wide expanse of his chest. I remembered Cole saying that he played football with these guys back home and wondered if he'd be playing for the university.

Before I could ask, Professor Patterson came in through the staff door and placed his briefcase on the desk. Everyone began quieting down as we watched him unpack all of his papers. I've had Professor Patterson every year I've been here, and I've always enjoyed coming to his classes. He's more laid-back than other professors are;

he requires a lot of work, but he's not one of those tight-asses who will call you out and make you uncomfortable in front of all the other students. There's nothing that will have my knees locking and palms sweating like standing in front of a crowd of people to speak. Quinn has been in plays ever since we were in middle school, and she can command an entire theater, but I think I would throw up everywhere if I were to switch places with her.

"Welcome to Journalism 359: Investigative Reporting. I hope you're all in the right class. My assistant is handing out the syllabus; please take one and pass it down. You all know how to read; you wouldn't have made it this far if you couldn't. You don't need me to read over every point on the syllabus; it's your responsibility to read it yourself and do what is required of you." Another reason I like Patterson so much: He gets straight to the point. We don't have to waste an entire hour and a half doing exactly what we'll be doing in all of our other classes the next couple of days.

"With investigative reporting, you're going to be thrown into a situation with people you haven't met, and you're going to be required to come back with the best possible answers you can get from them. You need to learn how to ask questions—good questions—on the spot. We'll just do a small exercise today to practice this," he proposed, while walking back and forth in front of us. "Everyone turn and pick a partner. No crossing the room; just pick someone next to you. Ask them as many questions as you can think of to keep the conversation rolling. You need to be able to keep up a dialogue and get crucial information out of people. I don't need you to write this all down, because I don't have time to read it. I just want you to get comfortable talking to someone you don't know, and asking questions you wouldn't otherwise ask if you weren't working. Go."

Jaxon turned his body to face mine in his seat. "Partner?" he asked and I nodded my head. I wasn't sure if I wanted this gorgeous

guy to ask me a bunch of personal questions; he seemed too observant. On the other hand, I was interested in getting to know more
about him.

"Uh, excuse me, Jaxon, you should be my partner, seeing as I
don't have anyone on the other side of me. Em can be her partner,"
Tobias said, gesturing at the girl on my left, who clearly was already
in a deep conversation with the guy in front of her.

"Nope, sorry, man. I'm definitely going to sit here and enjoy
getting to know Em here." He said my name as if he was unsure of
how to pronounce it. My real name is Emerson, but no one calls
me that. Quinn said that it sounded like a guy's name. I've never
really cared and am just thankful I didn't end up an Ashley or a
Sarah . . . blecch.

Tobias was clearly getting upset that he couldn't get his "assignment" started. "Dude, if you want to get into her pants, it's not
hard. You don't need to sit here and 'get to know' her. She'll give it
up without the twenty questions."

He started to stand up to walk around and find a partner when
Jaxon put his arm around Tobias's shoulders to stop his ascent.
"Tobias, man, chill out. This isn't even a graded assignment."
Jaxon's hand clasped onto his shoulder looked totally innocent
until I noticed Tobias grimacing and realized that maybe Jaxon
was squeezing him a bit hard. Jaxon didn't appear to be angry;
the only thing I could see that would give away his ire at Tobias's
words was the tension in his jaw and the steely gaze he gave him.
"Now, apologize to Em," he ordered calmly.

What? Was he sticking up for me? I should probably stop him
because it's not like Tobias spoke an untruth. To be honest, his
comment didn't even faze me. I learned to block out any irritation
toward the "slut" remarks back in freshman year. The only people
ever to stick up for me were Quinn, Cole, and now, a complete
stranger. It's not as if he knows that I actually am a slut and that his

defense is purely unnecessary. "It's fine, Jaxon. Don't worry about it. Tob, no hard feelings, but go find another partner," I whispered to both of them, trying not to pull any other attention toward us. Jaxon continued glaring at him.

Exasperated, Tobias let out an annoyed sigh before he spoke. "Sorry, Emerson. I shouldn't have said that." Then he turned to face Jaxon and shrugged off the now–white knuckled grip on his bony shoulder. "Chill out, dude. You don't even know who she is," he said under his breath as he walked away quickly. I don't know if he meant for me to hear that, but I did.

Jaxon turned back toward me in his chair and looked me in the eyes for a couple of seconds. I'm not sure what he was looking for, maybe to see if I was upset over what Tob said. "Thanks for defending me, but it really wasn't necessary," I stressed, while he was still staring at me.

"It's not okay for any guy to talk to a girl like that. I don't care if what he said was true or false."

"What he said was true. I'm sure, since you're talking to me, half of these girls will crowd you after class just to let you know my reputation," I said to him.

"I don't care what your reputation is; most of us don't have good ones anyway. That's what makes them reputations," he said, looking at his notebook instead of at me. Then he shook his head slightly as if he were clearing it and turned to look at me again. "So, Emerson, huh?"

"Yeah, but no one calls me that. Tobias only uses it occasionally, and the only reason he knows my name is because we studied for finals together last year and he saw it on my papers. Quinn only calls me that when she's really pissed at me." I leaned forward onto my desk, rolling my pen between my fingers, and laughing at the image in my head of Quinn being mad.

"Be silly, be honest, and be kind," he quoted in a raspy voice.

14

I gasped. My heart sank to the floor and I started to feel the ambush of tears to my eyes. *Emerson, please don't do this here; you will look like a fool.* I quietly calmed myself with a deep breath. I could tell that Jaxon was watching my reaction carefully. "You know Ralph Waldo Emerson?" I asked.

"Yeah, he's a great poet. We had to study one last year in American lit and I chose his name out of the bag. Sorry if that made you upset or anything. I've just always enjoyed that quote. Your name made me think of it," he added.

"It's totally fine. I guess it has just been a really long time since I've heard that. My mom would say it all the time to me when I was a kid. Just nostalgia." I tried to sound light and laugh it off. I wanted to appear as though that one little quote didn't just turn my world upside down.

"You know some people say that he may not have even actually quoted that. That maybe it was just something that was attached to his name along the way," he broke in.

"My mom told me that once; I don't think she cared, though. It's still a nice quote to live by, whoever created it."

My mom majored in literature, fell in love with Ralph Waldo Emerson's simple quote, and always told me to live my life silly, honestly, and kindly. This is obviously my namesake. I'm just thankful she didn't name me Ralph or Waldo instead. She would say his quote to me at bedtime, even up until I was fifteen. I used to roll my eyes because she was being so cheesy, but now I would kill to hear her say those words. If I could, I wouldn't roll my eyes; I would ask to hear the words again.

"So, do you plan on trying out for the football team to play with Cole?" I asked him, hoping he would understand that I didn't like where our conversation was heading.

"Well, since I'm here on a full scholarship for football, something tells me I won't actually have to try out," he said with a sexy half smile.

"Wow, a junior transfer with a full scholarship. I bet Coach Chase wishes he would have found you before freshman year, if you're that good."

"Oh, he found me my junior year of high school along with Jace and Cole. We were the three amigos, on and off the field. Coach Chase wanted all three of us. I messed up in my senior year and Coach Chase pulled my scholarship for two years so I could work some stuff out. So . . . yeah, two years later I finally made it here. Hopefully, I haven't lost too much talent, not being on a team for that long." I wanted to ask what he had done to lose his scholarship, but the way he was fidgeting with his fingers when he said it told me whatever he did made him uncomfortable. I was sure I'd have plenty of time to ask later. This guy just kept getting more interesting to me. It had been a long time since someone had caught my attention and actually held it. He was so easy to talk to. His voice was deep and mesmerizing. I would literally pay money just to hear him talk to me all day. It took me a while to realize that I was leaning toward him with my head in my hand. I slowly pulled myself back so I didn't seem startled to catch myself gawking at him.

"Your voice is a little like cocaine. You could bottle that stuff up and sell it. You would make a killing, especially with the sorority bimbos. Can I pay you just to talk to me all day?" I said with a giggle, so he wouldn't think I was serious. Although I'm pretty sure I was.

He threw his head back in abandon and let out a deep, unrestrained laugh. Thankfully, this place was so packed with talking students we didn't call too much attention to ourselves, just a few confused side glances here and there. From this angle, I admired his smile. His teeth were really white and mostly straight except for one of his front teeth that turned in just a bit to mess up the smooth flow across their surface. I loved that imperfection; it meant this beautiful man wasn't unattainable. I'm almost positive three nights with Jaxon would be incredible.

"Well, the going rate is about twenty bucks an hour," he said, interrupting my thoughts of running my tongue across his teeth and lips, which left me a little bothered.

"Huh?" I blinked at him. *Wow, Emerson, great response, and way to keep up the dialogue.*

He chuckled a bit. "I just got a job at the local radio station as a DJ in the evenings, a couple nights a week. Well, it's actually a paid internship, so I'll mostly be running errands for the lead DJ. I guess I will be paid money to talk, even if they rarely have me on-air."

"That's probably one of the coolest jobs I've heard of a college student having. It certainly comes second to Macy Foster's job of hot-air balloon operator last year," I replied.

"No shit, hot-air balloon operator? They trust a college student to operate those things? That would be a blast," he said, laughing.

"Well, I think they learned their lesson hiring her. I heard they found out she was taking her boyfriend up for a little mile-high-club initiation, if you know what I mean," I said, winking at him.

"Oh, I think I can guess what you mean." He sent an equally sexy wink right back at me that would basically melt the panties off any living, breathing female. Damn, the sexual tension was thick between us. Three times with Jaxon Riley would be phenomenal. Or should I say *will* be phenomenal, because at this point, I was positive it would happen. How could I live right next to this gorgeous person and not have a little fun in the meantime?

"Do you ever watch Cole's games?" He seemed to like to interrupt my dirty thoughts about him and enjoyed catching me off guard.

"Of course, Quinn and I have never missed one, even away games. So far, we've always been able to get off work or away from school. I bartend and my boss doesn't like me too much during the season because I ask off all the time, but I make it up to him later," I answered.

He gave me a confused look. Then I realized my answer sounded sexual and in this instance, it absolutely wasn't. I was never going to go there with Ed. He was a great boss, except for his requiring me to wear a shirt that bordered on sexual harassment. I made good tips, though, and he allowed me to keep them all and take time off when I wanted. But nothing would ever happen between us. It gave me the chills even thinking about it.

"Nice, so I already have my own cheerleaders. Not that it would be hard to gain some after they see me play," he replied cheekily, rubbing his hands together.

"Wow, let me guess: You're a wide receiver, because only those guys are as cocky as you are. By the way, we don't cheer for just anyone; you'll have to earn it," I said, rolling my eyes at him.

"Holy shit, a girl that knows football!" he said, now giving me a full-watt smile. "Yes, ma'am, I was Texas's best wide receiver my junior and senior year. I'll earn it all right. I bet you I'll score at least one touchdown at our first game in a couple of weeks."

"That's a bet I'm willing to take; your ego is out of control. Besides, Dalton Fisher, the quarterback, is a snob. He probably won't even pass to you for at least the first three games."

"Don't you worry about Fisher. I'll get it done. Although it's going to be tough playing without my brother, Jace, being the quarterback," he said, sounding a little disheartened.

"I thought you said Coach Chase wanted all three of you?" I asked him, wanting desperately to cheer him up and get that crooked smile back on his face.

"He did. Jace was never going to take it, though. He doesn't want to play anymore. He's crazy-ass brilliant and in premed here. If there's ever going to be a cure for cancer, Jace will find it. That guy is amazing," he said in almost an awed tone. I loved seeing his adoration for his brother.

"It's awesome that you guys are going to college at the same time. I love that Quinn and I get to do everything together."

"Yeah, we're really close in age," he said, laughing a little bit under his breath, and I felt as if I was missing out on an inside joke. I wonder if Jaxon is the older brother or the younger brother. He really seems to look up to him like a younger brother, and yet he sounds proud of him like an older brother would.

We were interrupted by the sounds of classmates getting up and packing their bags. I guess the class was over; an hour and a half had gone by fast as I talked to Jaxon. "I don't know if Professor Patterson would approve of our dialogue about cocaine-like voices, sex in hot-air balloons, and my awesome knowledge of football," I said while laughing.

He laughed with me while picking up my bag off the floor and handing it to me. "Yeah, maybe we should go ask him if that's what he had in mind. Oh, hey, since we're neighbors and all, probably study partners as well, you should have my number." He grabbed my hand in his and wrote his number into my palm slowly with black ink. Knowing it was going to be short-lived, I enjoyed the feel of my hand in his. The metal tip of the pen tickled as it etched across my skin. I watched each stroke he made. It was only a series of numbers, but I could tell he had nice handwriting. "Don't wash your hand until you save it." He tapped the tip against my palm a couple of times when he was done.

"Thanks. I'll text you later with my number," I spoke while smiling at him.

He stood up to let me follow him out to the aisle so we could leave the classroom, and I realized for the first time how tall he actually was. My eyes followed up his long legs, to his iron-flat stomach, and then to his broad chest to see he was a couple of inches over six feet at least. He was probably an inch taller than Cole, who had always made me feel petite next to him since I barely made it up to his chest. Being five foot five, I thought I was pretty average, but standing next to him, I felt miniature. He definitely had an athletic body with a playground of muscle right underneath those clothes. I realized he was standing there facing me, when he needed to turn around and walk out first. It seemed like he was taking me in as well, with his sexy mouth curling up at the corner.

I straightened my back and pushed out my breasts just a tad, and his eyes widened at the full sight of me. I silently thanked Quinn for cutting up my favorite T-shirts. I reached up to put my hand on his chest and rubbed it up an inch, while watching him inhale. Then I raised my hand and patted twice on his chest. "All right, let's move it along, Motorcycle Boy; exit is this way," I said, gesturing toward the door.

He snapped back to earth at that and quirked up an eyebrow, while starting to walk backward slowly. "Motorcycle Boy?"

"I didn't know who you were outside the frat house, so that's what I called you."

"Hmm, I think I'm going to need a new nickname from you. 'Boy' doesn't work for me," he said while tapping his long fingers on his chin, deep in thought. I could picture him trying to think of what he would like me to call him.

As we were walking out of the classroom into the warm California weather, I was about to tell him *boy* certainly did not work for him and what would. But, Tatum, Sophia, and Ashley, all Alpha Beta girls, assaulted us. By us, I mean Jaxon, because they swooped in front of me to start laying it on thick with him. "Don't say I didn't warn you!" I called out to Jaxon as I started walking away from them. He was laughing and didn't seem to mind the attention. I really didn't want to hear what they had to tell him. I could only guess it was something along the lines of "Stay away from the school slut."

I turned the corner to walk off to environmental biology, my last class of the day. An arm came around my shoulders and I caught a whiff of Tom Ford cologne. Micah. I glanced up to confirm my observation.

"You smell nice, Micah. Are you wearing clean clothes?" I kidded him.

"Aw, come on, Emmy, I'm not that bad. Besides, I hear we have biology together. Come, sit by me, please?" he begged, while gazing down at me with his sweet puppy-dog face.

We continued across the quad to the science building, and he kept his arm around my shoulder. I heard someone calling out my name from behind, so I turned around to see who it was. Jaxon was jogging up to us, and Micah instinctively squeezed me in tighter. Jaxon stopped in front of me but had his eyes on Micah. I've always liked Micah's height, but seeing Jaxon stand next to him was impressive; he was at least two inches taller than Micah. I usually don't mind getting touchy-feely with a guy in public—that's why Micah wouldn't know things were different right now—but I was starting to feel uncomfortable with his arm around me possessively, under Jaxon's scrutiny.

Jaxon pulled his eyes away from Micah toward me, although it seemed to take some effort on his part. He was probably wondering if we were an item. The assumption would've been so outrageous that I didn't even bother clearing it up for him. He would soon learn about me from someone on this campus, I was sure. At some point, after we walked out of class, he had put on a black, worn, and dirty ball cap. Before he spoke, he spun it around backward and I was thankful because I could now see his gorgeous blues.

"Sorry, Emerson, that was rude of me. I didn't mean to just cut you off. I wasn't expecting *that* outside the classroom," he said, pointing his thumb behind him. He had his backpack slung over one shoulder, and his leather jacket was hanging through the strap down by his hip.

"It's really no—" I started to say.

"Emerson? Is that what Em is short for? How the hell did I not know this?" Micah interrupted harshly, looking pissed that this new guy could know more than he did. I shrugged out of his hold so I could face both of them at the same time.

"Guys, it's Em; call me Em. I haven't been Emerson in a long time," I stressed, looking back and forth between them. "By the way, Jaxon, Micah. Micah, Jaxon. He and his brother are moving into the apartment with Cole." They both did the guy nod at each other. Micah seemed to be sizing Jaxon up. Looks like girls weren't the only competitive ones around here; guys were such cavemen sometimes.

I started walking to my class instead of continuing the awkward staring. As expected, both of them followed along. I turned and continued walking the last couple of steps backward. "We don't have another class together, do we, Jax?" That was the first time I'd called him Jax, and he smirked at his nickname. I wondered if Micah would be uncomfortable if I just grabbed Jaxon right now and sucked his lush bottom lip into my mouth.

I stopped walking outside of the biology lab. Jaxon stepped up in front of me and replied, "No, I already took environmental. I'm down the hall in physics. But I wish we did."

"All right. Well, I'll see you around at home then. Thanks for the 'dialogue' today in class," I said, while making air quotes, which earned me a smile.

He started walking past me but stopped and bent his head down to mine. He whispered in my ear as he walked by, "Later, Emerson." As he walked away, I saw him slide his cap back to the front. I turned to walk into class and Jaxon shouted back, "Oh, hey, don't forget that we need to finish talking about our bet. I already know what I'm going to get when I win!"

"Oh yeah, Mr. Confident, what's that?" I tossed back.

"A fucking hot-air balloon ride!" he hollered before stepping into his classroom, not waiting for my reaction. I stood there with my mouth wide open. This guy was ballsy, and he was way too much like me. I needed to think of a wager to leave him speechless as well.

- THREE -

By lunchtime, just thinking about a hot-air balloon ride with Jaxon had me feeling anxious and playful at the same time. Cole had caught up to me right outside of the cafeteria, so we went through the serving line together. Like a gentleman, he carried my tray for me toward our table. Since Cole was in a frat and played on the football team, he had a wide variety of friends that usually came and joined our long table and benches.

When we approached the table, Mason and Garrett simultaneously patted the seats next to them for me to come and sit. I liked to indulge them, but I usually sat next to Quinn and Cole. As I was walking past the guys already seated, I tapped them on the head while singing, "Duck . . . Duck . . . Duck . . ." A few of them started chuckling. Abruptly, I was grabbed by the hips and slung onto Micah's lap. He placed me so I was sitting on him and facing forward toward the table.

"Goose," he whispered in my ear from behind. "I liked you in my bed this morning," he said as he put his hands around my waist just underneath my T-shirt.

"Micah . . ." I warned him. Cole walked past us, snickering, and he set my tray in front of me. "Thanks, Coley, you're always such a gentleman, unlike some people I know," I said, prodding my elbow into Micah's ribs.

He placed his tray next to Quinn, who was laughing at Micah's barbarian tactics. "Oh, God, Em, please stop calling me that," Cole groaned with a wince.

I started eating my pasta salad, while Micah seemed to think that was a go-ahead to explore my body. At least he wasn't conspicuous about it. I don't think anyone even noticed. When he moved my hair away from my neck and started lightly kissing under my ear, I noticed Jaxon come in and sit down in front of Quinn. He took off his ball cap and put it back into his backpack. He was staring right at Micah and me. I was confused by the hard set of his jaw. All of a sudden, the last thing I wanted to be doing was sitting here on Micah's lap with one of his hands drifting dangerously high up on my thigh.

"Micah, it's too hard to eat like this," I said with frustration, scooting down onto the bench next to him. I was looking directly at Jaxon, but he was talking to Cole now about furniture they were having delivered later.

Micah leaned over and whispered in my ear, "Stop staring at him. I hear he's the male version of you; he doesn't settle down. Although I'm hoping I can change that about you." This was exactly why I needed to stop letting Micah touch me, because he thought he could convince me to change my rules for him. No one will convince me of that.

I looked down the table past Cole. "Hey, Quinn, I'm going to go ahead and go home."

I made a face that I hoped would convey to her that I needed to get away from Micah; his behavior was scaring me. I didn't like to be in this territory, where people started thinking you were in a relationship and they expected it from you.

"Emmy, I can't give you the car. I still have class and I promised I would meet up with my study group later," she replied with a regretful look.

Quinn was my stepsister, but we never used the word *step*. That would imply that she was less than what she was; she was my sister and I was hers. My parents got divorced when I was nine and my dad remarried. Thankfully, he married Ellie. She is the most amazing person I have ever met; she saved my life. When they got married, I got a sister, Quinn, who is exactly thirty-four days older than me. We were inseparable from the very beginning. Her dad was never in the picture, so she never had a dad's house she had to go visit because of custody. Most of the time when I had to spend the weekend at my mom's house, Quinn would spend the night with me.

When I was fifteen, I was sitting in my English class when Mr. Smith, our high school principal, walked in and asked if he could speak to me. I walked out into the hallway and saw Ellie and Quinn standing against the wall crying. I immediately ran to them to ask them what was wrong, ready to injure whoever had hurt these two very special people. In a blur I hardly remember, I found out that my mom and dad had been killed in a car wreck. Apparently, a driver in the oncoming traffic had fallen asleep, because she worked a late shift at the hospital. She hit them head-on. She lived, they didn't. At first, I was confused and in denial; I mean, my parents would never be in a car together. They had to have made a mistake. When Ellie told me there was no mistake, I crumpled to the ground. It was the worst day of my life. That day I learned never to get too close to people. It was too late with Ellie and Quinn—we were already bonded—but I swore it would never happen again. There's no point in having a relationship, because if they aren't cheating, they're dying. In my parent's case, they were both.

My family attempted to fight for custody, since my aunt felt it would be best for me to be with a blood relative. It didn't matter to her that I hadn't seen her since I was seven years old. After I very passionately explained to her that I would run away every single day to Ellie's until she let me go, she realized I wasn't worth the fight.

Ellie was beyond happy when I moved in. I'm grateful every day that she didn't hold my dad's affair with my mom against me. She never really spoke about it to Quinn or me.

All three of us moved out of my dad's house and into a new three-bedroom home. The third bedroom was meant to be mine, but I basically moved into Quinn's room. No one argued with me. A year and a half after my parent's death, Ellie was remarried to Charles. He's amazing; he loves Quinn and me and spoils us rotten. Quinn and I do have to have jobs while in school because Ellie and Charles felt it was important for us to know the value of college, but they help us with our bills for the most part. Quinn and I both had our own cars back home, but we decided only to bring one with us to college. It usually works out okay, since we're almost always together, or one of us gets a ride from Cole. I usually give Quinn the car; I would rather be without it than for her to be without.

"Don't stress, Quinn, I'll be okay. I don't mind walking. Besides, if I decide I don't want to walk, the campus added that new bus line that stops right outside the apartment. I just need to go home." She stood up as if she needed to reassure herself that I was okay and to see if I needed someone to talk to. I shook my head and said, "I'll talk to you at home tonight after my shift, 'kay?"

"All right . . ." she said hesitantly, while sitting back down next to Cole. "Text me later." I nodded and waved good-bye to the rest of the table. I tossed my entire pasta salad on my way out the door.

I didn't know if I was going to walk home or ride the bus yet. I still had to walk across the campus, so I guess I would decide when I got there. I didn't get more than twenty feet before I heard someone jogging up behind me. If this was Micah, I would seriously lose my manners and go crazy on him. Mercifully, it wasn't Micah.

"Emerson, wait up," Jaxon said, easily catching up next to me.

"So you're sticking with the full first name thing, huh?" I teased, while continuing toward the other end of campus. The end of August was pretty warm in Southern California, but college kids don't mind. There were girls lying out in the grass, working on their tans, and guys kicking a ball back and forth to one another.

"I was heading home anyway. Need a ride?" he asked while dodging my question. He pulled his backpack around to the front and unzipped it. He reached inside and pulled out that black ball cap. He grabbed the bill and slapped it lazily on top of his head.

"If you don't mind. You should go finish your lunch, though; I saw that pile of food on your tray," I joked with him.

"Yeah, I would have preferred if we both could have finished our lunches. But you seemed upset and since you said you were heading home, and I was going there after lunch, it made sense," he said, eyeing me.

"Thanks. I just needed to get away from Micah."

"So you two aren't together?" he asked, looking confused.

"Never."

"Seemed like you were having a good time with him when I walked up." This guy was observant.

"That's all I want, though . . . a good time. Nothing more. Micah is starting to think I'll change my rules for him."

He stumbled for a fraction of a second and turned to look at me. "You have rules?" He laughed and raised one of those sexy eyebrows at me.

"Only three, but they're pretty important to me," I said, feeling silly talking about this.

He gestured with his hand out in front of him. "Please, do share. I'm intrigued."

He pulled his keys out of his pocket, and I was getting a little excited, because I've never been on a motorcycle before. But he pointed his keys at a massive four-door black truck and clicked the unlock button. He guided me to the passenger side and opened the door for me. I gaped at him and said, "What about the bike? I was excited to ride on it."

"No motorcycle for you, babe. Besides, Jace took it today." *What did he mean by no motorcycle for me?*

"Are you saying I'll never get to ride on it?" He reached down and put both of his hands on each side of my waist. This unexpected contact caught me off guard. There was an exciting charge between us. My mind didn't want to respond to him like this, but my body wasn't listening.

When he leaned in toward my ear, my breath caught. I stared straight ahead so I wouldn't get trapped in those blue eyes. "Motorcycles are dangerous. I would never put you in danger," he whispered. Then he lifted me up onto the bench seat in the truck. His voice returned to its normal deep tone. "Besides, Cole would kill me. He threatened Jace and me if we put you or Quinn on the bike. Jace and I could take him, but I'm not trying to get on his bad side." He winked and I knew he was kidding.

"Oh, I'm going to have to have a talk with Coley."

He burst out laughing while he closed my door. I could see him laughing all the way around the front of the truck to his side. When he opened it to climb in, he said, "Please tell me you call him that in front of his lame-ass frat brothers." He had a huge smile on his face.

"Of course I do. I'm not embarrassed."

"Oh, I'm sure you're not. I mean *he* must love it," he stated sarcastically.

"So, this giant truck—I mean, is it necessary for college in Southern California?" I asked, trying to tease him.

Suddenly his face changed from teasing to a little sad, but he quickly pushed it away with a stiff smile. "It used to be my dad's. But now Jace and I drive it. It was helpful for moving out here with all our stuff, and I could just put the motorcycle in the back." He pulled out of the parking lot and turned toward our apartments. "You're avoiding a serious topic here, though; I need to know these rules of yours." He patted my thigh a couple of times.

"Okay, fine," I said grumpily. "I don't plan on ever actually being with anyone permanently. My parents taught me that it only leads to heartbreak. I like having fun, and I'm not sure I'm strong enough to come back from something like a broken heart. So my rules are: I don't sleep with anyone that I know one of my friends likes, I don't sleep with anyone's boyfriend, and I never sleep with someone more than three times."

After a couple of truly uncomfortable seconds he uttered, "I think you're wrong, you know."

"I don't think it's wrong; I think it protects everyone involved. No one thinks that I'm going to give them more than I have to give. I also don't want to make any enemies by sleeping with someone's boyfriend," I replied softly.

"Not about the rules. About not being strong enough. I can tell you are."

I sat there with really nothing to say back to that. He didn't know me. He didn't know what my parents did to me, to each other, or to Ellie. People break each other's hearts. It's hard to believe I'd only just met Jax this morning. I felt as if we'd already said so much to each other—maybe a little too much.

"Well, all I do know is that I don't require daily phone calls, mushy love notes, bouquets of roses, or cuddles every night."

"A low-maintenance chick. I can dig that," he chuckled.

When we pulled up outside of our building, I unbuckled my seat belt and lunged for the door. I felt naked around this guy; he saw too much or thought too highly of me, and I couldn't figure out which one. I just wanted to get to my apartment, take a shower, and get in a nap before my shift tonight. When I came around the front of the truck to walk up the stairs, Jax met me with our bags. He let me walk up ahead of him and he followed me to my door.

Our apartments are pretty decent. I don't think any other college kids live here. Quinn and I pitch in to help pay for rent and bills, but Ellie and Charles usually cover the majority of it. I don't know anything about Jace and Jaxon's family, but I do know that Cole's dad will basically pay for anything if he stays in the frat and plays football. His dad is a politician, so he likes his son to present a "well-rounded" image. The apartments in this building all have three bedrooms. While the boys will use their third room as something practical and boring like a bedroom, Quinn and I turned ours into a closet. It's mostly for Quinn, though. I don't have much of a wardrobe, although Q and I wear the same size, so I guess all the clothes are as much mine as hers.

When I got to my door, Jax walked past me to his door. "Thanks for the ride; I appreciated not having to walk all the way in the heat," I called down to him.

He stuck the keys in his door and turned to unlock it. "Not a problem. I think we basically have the same schedule on these days. Next time, let's stay for lunch, though." He smiled at me and started to walk into his apartment.

"Hey, do you want to come in here for lunch? I'll cook. I feel bad that you dumped your food as well."

"I never say no to a home-cooked meal," he said, smiling.

"Well, I'm no Food Network chef, but I can make us some lunch."

After I had made chicken wings, he helped me to scrape all the dishes off and put them in the dishwasher. We sat on the couch afterward, watching TV.

"Damn, you can cook. That was delicious. We should just eat here for lunch from now on," he said with a laugh, and I thanked him.

I sat on the couch, leaning up against him. Then he grabbed my hips and pulled me across his lap so I was sitting on the other side of him, but my legs were lying across his. He grabbed the foot I had hurt this morning.

"Are your feet ticklish?" he softly asked.

"No."

Then he tenderly started running his fingers down the sole of my foot and I realized he was searching. He found where the beer bottle cap had cut me and left an indention. He made slow, soft circles around it and then over it. The movement was mesmerizing.

"I noticed you limping on it today, and this morning you were rubbing it," he whispered.

I didn't feel like explaining that I hurt it getting out of Micah's bed. I'm sure he knew exactly what I was doing coming out that frat house this morning anyway.

"That feels wonderful," I sighed lazily. It was really hard to continue watching TV after he started that. I got lost in the soft circles around and over, around and over.

~

Later that week, Jax and I were hanging out in my room comparing notes for journalism class, and I found out we had media law together as well. Studying with him was fun; we usually veered way off topic and just started joking around, pushing our textbooks aside.

"Are you guys doing anything tonight? I don't think Quinn and I have plans."

"I have to work; I'm not sure about Jace and Cole, though," he answered, looking bummed.

"So is the radio station meeting your internship requirement?" I asked him.

"Yeah, it is. At first, I was leaning more toward broadcast journalism, so that's why I took it. All of these classes are kind of opening my eyes to more areas, so now I'm not so sure what area I want to major in," he responded.

"I wish I could get my internship done with over the school year, but I'm excited for it this coming summer."

He set down his pen to look at me. "Where is yours at?"

"I'm majoring in humanitarian journalism, so mine is abroad this summer."

"No shit? Aren't they going to like Prague, Salzburg, or some other amazing European city?"

"Nothing so glamorous. We're going to Africa." I was still really nervous, but I knew it would be a great opportunity.

His mouth gaped open. "Africa? Isn't that dangerous?"

"I think that's kind of the point. Going out there and getting the story that needs to be told about the people that have been forgotten."

He blew out a long breath. "Wow, you're amazing."

Uncomfortable with his compliment, I replied, "No, I'm not. I haven't even done anything."

"You will. You're going to do great things. One day, we'll hear all about the great Emerson Moore: humanitarian journalist."

~

When I came back from work one night, I sat down on the couch and realized Quinn wasn't home. She usually shouts for me when she hears me walk in. Right as I was pulling out my phone to text her, she sent me one.

Quinn: I'm down at the guys' place. Come down when you get here. We're watching movies.

I was exhausted; all I wanted was a shower and my bed. But I thought I should at least go down and say hi to everyone. I slipped off my shoes and walked down the hall barefoot.

When I walked into their place, I saw them all sitting in the pitch dark watching a movie, but I could barely see all their faces. Cole had bought this huge sectional couch that could easily fit ten people. "Hey, Emmy," Quinn and Cole said at the same time. I turned to where I heard their voices and noticed that Quinn was lying with her head on Cole's lap. I walked over to her and gave her a half hug since I couldn't get my arms all the way around her while she was lying down. Jaxon was sitting down past Quinn's feet. I figured if we were cuddling up on the couch together, what I wanted to sit next to was his hunky body.

I sat down next to him and leaned into him to lay my head on his shoulder. "Hey, handsome, long time, no see. Thanks again for helping me with those notes. Oh, and the rides home as well." I patted his rock-hard stomach and took an extra second before lifting it off of him.

"Well, hello to you too, gorgeous. I would love to see you anytime, but trust me, I think I would remember if I gave you a ride and that is something I don't remember doing." His tone was slightly off and extremely flirtatious. I sat up, giving him a puzzled look. What was he talking about?

As I was staring into his gorgeous blue eyes, I heard someone clear his throat from the other side of the couch. "I think you were looking for me?" There's that voice I wish I could cuddle inside of and hear all day. I turned around and looked right at Jaxon with the blue glow of the movie on his face.

I jumped up and ran across the room to flip the light switch on. When I turned around, my mouth hit the floor. It wasn't my most attractive moment. Twins. Identical twins. Identical freaking hot-as-hell twins. Oh, I would kill Cole later for not telling me about this. "What? How? Why didn't you tell me there was a smoking-hot carbon copy of you? How have I been right down the hall and never known there were two of you?" I hollered at Jaxon while looking back and forth to him and Jace. Jace sat there with a smug smile on his face, looking pretty pleased with himself. It was crazy how much they looked alike. Jace even had that imperfection I loved on Jaxon: the slightly turned-in front tooth. The only difference I could notice so far was that Jace didn't get the sex-god voice like Jaxon was blessed with.

Everyone was covering their eyes with their hands and trying to adjust to my assault of sudden brightness. "Emmy, so what if they're twins. It's not a big deal. Turn the lights off; we were watching a movie," Cole said impatiently, and I noticed Quinn had sat up straight.

"My life just got a little more amazing here, Coley. Quinn, a little heads up next time would be awesome. You know, just a little text message saying, 'Oh, by the way, when you get home, there will be two way-too-hot-for-humankind identical freaking twins, living right next door.' Something like that, no big deal," I scolded her while my finger was pointing to my phone.

Quinn had a huge grin on her face. "I would not have missed this reaction for the world. I mean, what a way to introduce yourself to Jace."

"Trust me; my introduction was a thousand times better," Jaxon said to her with a smirk on his face.

Quinn was about to ask what he was talking about when I slapped the lights back off and went to sit between Jaxon and Cole. Quinn laid her head back down on Cole's lap, but I knew she would ask later. I left a gap between myself and the guy on each side of me. "Em, you're more than welcome to come back down here with me. I thought we were getting pretty cozy," Jace loudly whispered over to me.

I started laughing but Jaxon answered for me, "She's good right where she is, dude."

Once everyone settled down and got back into the movie again, I rested my head on the cushion behind me. I felt an arm come around my shoulders and pull me into a hard chest.

"You smell like an ashtray and beer," Jaxon whispered into my ear.

"That happens when you work in a pool hall as a bartender. Sorry," I murmured against his chest.

Unlike me, he smelled delicious—freshly showered and manly. I tried silently to inhale, but the way his hand slightly tightened on my shoulders, I think he knew what I was doing. My head slowly drifted down to his lap as the movie went on. I don't even know what we were watching. When my head hit his legs, he started running his hands through my hair. He grabbed my ponytail holder and gently tugged it out, without pulling any hair. When my hair had been released, his fingers began massaging my scalp. I faded to sleep with his fingers moving around my head.

- FOUR -

The alarm on my phone started going off the next morning, and without opening my eyes, I blindly grabbed for it from my nightstand. I realized I was in my own bed when I felt the glass top of the table, but I don't remember getting up and coming back to our apartment last night. The last thing I can remember was Jaxon's amazing hands on my head. Rubbing those hypnotizing circles. If I could just get him to do that every night, I would never have any sleepless nights again.

I jumped into a quick, hot shower because I had class in two hours. As I was washing up, I noticed a black stain dripping from my hand. I brought it up out of the water before it all washed away.

You're beautiful even when you snore.

I knew this handwriting; I'd seen this handwriting in notes every day. Jaxon had written on my hand last night when I fell asleep. Now I remember dozing off in his lap last night. Oh God, he'd heard me snore? I'm pretty sure I didn't snore, usually people tell you this kind of thing when you sleep with them. I stared at the beautiful handwriting a little bit longer before I let it wash down the drain from my skin.

When I finished running a straightener through my hair to control some of the frizz, I walked down to the kitchen to see Quinn with her wild bed head. No matter how crazy her hair was now, she would soon have her shiny brown locks perfectly sleek and stylish before she stepped out of the apartment. She was setting up the coffeemaker for both of us. I started to get out the pans to make breakfast.

"Man, Quinn, I was wiped last night. I don't even remember walking back down here to go to bed. Thanks for setting my alarm, by the way," I told her.

"That's because you didn't, dummy. Jax carried you down here and put you in bed. He covered you up and everything. He even asked me if you needed to be up at a certain time this morning, so he could set the alarm on your phone. I was pretty impressed. He was so sweet. You didn't seem to mind, either, with your hands wrapped around his neck and your face buried into his shoulder." She smiled mischievously.

"Oh no, did I drool on him? Please say no. You didn't hear me snoring, did you?" I smacked my palm to my forehead. I shouldn't have let myself get so comfortable in his arms last night.

"No, I don't think you did. He seemed to be happy carrying you. He's totally hot, right?" she asked while grabbing two coffee mugs from the cabinet.

"So gorgeous, Quinn! I can't believe there are two of them."

"Did you know he calls you Emerson? How did he even know that was your name?" she questioned me.

"He found out in journalism; we had to keep up a dialogue for the whole class period. How did you know he called me that?" I asked.

"Oh, yeah, I forgot. When he carried you to your bed, he saw your textbook on the side table, and he said he was going to borrow it to study last night. He asked, 'Can you let Emerson know I borrowed it?' I didn't even realize he had called you that till after he left," she confided.

"Crap, I hope I didn't miss something that we were supposed to study," I grumbled.

"Cole's worried about you sleeping with them, you know," she said nonchalantly.

"Why is he worried? He doesn't care who I sleep with. It's not like they would ever move out of the apartment because I slept with one of them."

"He's not worried about them moving out; he's worried about us moving away, if there was ever any bad blood," she said while shrugging her shoulders.

"I'll reassure him we aren't moving anywhere." Cole had never gotten worried when I slept with his friends. I don't get attached to guys and I don't let them get attached to me. I always do well with continuing a friendship after someone's three times are up. He was being silly. "So did you and Cole have this conversation while you were snuggling up in his lap last night, or was this conversation later in the night when everyone else went to bed?" I teased her.

I saw her flush a bit before she turned to grab the French vanilla creamer from the fridge. At some point last year, I noticed Quinn and Cole starting to act differently around each other. She started to care whether she had makeup on before he came over and he started not approving of every guy she dated. I had a strong suspicion they both really liked each other more than friends would. Quinn still dated guys and Cole still slept around, so I didn't really know what to think. I've never deliberately poked fun at Quinn about it before, just tried to subtly bring it up. I just didn't understand: If they liked each other, why didn't they just get together? They're perfectly normal, non-ruined adults, unlike myself.

"Don't say stuff like that, Emmy; we're friends. You lay on Cole all the time," she said defensively while avoiding my eyes.

"The difference is when I sit up, Cole doesn't get frustrated, and he definitely doesn't rub my back like he was doing with you last night." I winked at her.

"You're delusional. I'm going to go get ready. I have to tutor three students today at nine thirty. Hurry and get ready so we can ride together."

Nice deflection, Quinn. "I'm ready now. I'll be down at the guys' place; come get me when you're leaving," I told her as I reached for the door with my coffee.

When I walked into their apartment, Jaxon—or was it Jace?— was sitting on the couch in just his dark green boxers, eating a bowl of cereal. Holy crap, he had the hottest tattoo wrapping around one of his shoulders. The intricate black lines started near his collarbone and went all the way down to hug his enormous bicep. I wanted to trace it with my fingers or tongue, whichever got there first.

"Well, good morning, Beautiful. Come on in, and don't even bother knocking." Jaxon. If I could get them to talk, I could easily figure out who was who. He was teasing me about not knocking, but I guess since Jaxon and Jace live here now, I should consider doing that before just barging in.

"Sorry, I'm used to just walking in when it was only Cole," I apologized. "Besides, it looks like you were expecting me anyway. Thanks for wearing my favorite outfit of yours; I'll expect you to be in this whenever I come over." I winked at him. His abs went on for days and all I wanted to do was smooth my hands against his wide, hard chest.

I was so focused on his abs, I became mesmerized when they starting shifting with his laugh. He interrupted my ogling and said, "I'm guessing this goes two ways? I can just walk in anytime I please to your place?" He gestured with his finger between the two of us.

"Of course. I'm usually naked between two and three, so come on over—the more the merrier," I provoked him.

Just then, Jace walked in the room, "Hell, yeah, Em, you are the hottest girl I've met so far in California. I'll be over around two thirty; I expect you to be ready." He gave me a sexy smirk. He kept walking to the kitchen and began pouring himself some cereal.

"You're not so bad yourself, Jace." I went and sat down on the couch with Jaxon, but I noticed he was glaring at his brother. Jace started cracking up when he saw his brother's face.

I reached over and poked Jaxon in the side. "By the way, I do *not* snore!" I lifted up my now-blank hand to show him I'd seen his little note. He didn't confirm nor deny; he just chuckled and continued eating his breakfast.

I sat in the living room, talking to Jaxon and Cole about our schedules this semester, while waiting for Quinn. Jaxon never went and got dressed, which I didn't mind. He said he didn't have classes until right before lunch. Quinn finally made it down the hall ready to go. She was wearing a coral jersey dress with a small cut-out in the back and brown strappy wedges. Her long, tan legs looked amazing and I watched as Cole openly gawked.

"Why are you all dressed up today?" he frowned and asked brusquely.

"I'm not dressed up. Just figured there's no need to slum it," she said while picking up the hem of her dress and letting it fall back against her thighs. Quinn dresses nicely every day; she could never understand my need to wear shorts and a T-shirt to school. Typically, I wouldn't have looked twice at her outfit, but she did look like she'd put more effort into her appearance than normal. Her curls were a little tighter and her mascara was a little thicker outlining her bright green eyes. Our eyes were the only part of our appearance that we had in common. While her hair was a warm brunette, mine was more a dirty-blond. She had long legs that I would kill for, although I had been more gifted in the chest department than she had.

"Is this because you're tutoring that asshole Bryce today?" Cole asked from behind the kitchen counter. How did he even know whom she was tutoring this semester?

"He could be a small incentive to look nicer." She giggled and smiled at me.

I couldn't help rolling my eyes at the both of them. They were so oblivious to each other.

"Q, he's a douchebag. Last week he took one of the Chi Omega girls out to the movies, saw Rachel Morgan in the hallway, and just left his date sitting in the theater all alone so he could take Rachel back to his room at the frat house." He grimaced at Quinn.

Jaxon and I just sat there watching the two of them, getting a little uncomfortable. I finished up my coffee and placed it on the table in front of me. Jaxon leaned forward and set his bowl down next to my cup.

"Well, it's a good thing I'm not trying to be his girlfriend, Cole." She smiled coyly.

Cole's jaw got tight and he pounded the countertop with his fist lightly, almost silently, and started to walk toward the hallway to his room. "I'll see y'all later. Ems, I think I'll come to the bar tonight to shoot pool with Jace and Jax. You working?"

"Sure am!" I said as I swung my backpack onto my shoulder, happy to get away from the tension in this room. "Bye, guys." I waved, walking for the door with Quinn in tow. "See you later, Jace!" I yelled down the hallway, and then winked at Jaxon. He squinted his eyes and glared at me. It was fun messing with him; he obviously wasn't crazy about his brother's flirtatious behavior with me, but I enjoyed it.

That night while I was mixing drinks at the bar, I noticed Jace and Cole walking in the front door. I waved at our bouncer, Mark, to go ahead and let them in. I loved being able to work in a bar, even though I really wasn't allowed to. I was still only twenty, but Ed, my boss, wasn't running the most legitimate establishment, so he hired me on as a bartender, knowing I'd turn twenty-one soon. I was damn good at it, so that was another reason I usually got my way around here. I think he just wanted a female bartender that would bring in regular customers, and I was an expert at leading them on.

"Hey, boys, I saved table number twelve for you." I pointed to the pool table closest to the bar. "Quinn didn't come with you?"

Cole tapped the bar with his fist, which I was coming to realize was a sign of frustration toward Quinn that he was trying to tamp down. "She's tutoring."

"Where's Jaxon?" I asked while pouring Cole's favorite whiskey into his glass. I didn't want to upset him anymore with talk of what Quinn was most likely up to tonight with Bryce.

"Right here, Beautiful." He grinned from behind me. "I was just outside talking on the phone with my mom. By the way, Jace, she said you couldn't use studying as an excuse not to call her, jackass."

I smiled at the fact that he enjoyed calling his mom and he wasn't ashamed of it. I had heard him on the phone with her a couple of times already. I still had my back turned toward him. When I finished with Cole's drink, I turned around to ask him what he wanted and his eyes bugged out at the sight of my shirt. It was just a tight black T-shirt that said NICE RACK across my chest, which is the pool hall's name. But Ed had thought it would be a fantastic idea for me to wear a deep V-neck T-shirt. My boobs were on display nightly at the bar. I learned quickly to get a tight-fitting bra, one that wouldn't expose anything when I bent down a hundred times a night. I tried to get the rest of the employees of the bar to have to wear V-necks as well, but since they're all male, they weren't having it.

"I agree with the shirt," he said while beaming.

Jace came up beside him with a devilish grin and said, "Me too, Emmy."

Jaxon slapped him upside the head and pushed him toward the pool table. It was fun to watch these three playing pool together; they really were the three amigos. Cole looked so happy to have his two best friends finally back with him, and I was pretty happy they decided to join our little group as well. Cole was decent at playing, but that was because he came in here a lot to play with Quinn when she wanted to hang out with me while I worked. Jace and Jaxon knew how to work a table, though, and they were extremely competitive with each other. There were lots of cuss words and playful punches thrown.

∾

Jaxon: We have that test today in media law. Come over to crash study with me? Pleeease.

Me: I'll be over in 5. But it's nice to hear you beg. ;-)

Jaxon: Bring breakfast. I'm hungry ;-)

Me: What do I look like . . . a maid?

Jaxon: Do you have one of those little outfits? If so, I'll come over there right now.

∾

The next couple of weeks of school and work went by pretty fast. I picked up a lot of shifts since tomorrow was the first game of the season and I knew I'd be taking off all Fridays and some Saturdays until the season was over. Ed complained that he would fire me, but I was the only female bartender, and I pulled in a lot of customers, so I knew he wouldn't. I usually just picked up extra weekday shifts to appease him and the other bartenders that had to cover for me.

A couple of times I met up with everyone at some of the frat parties after work. Jace usually didn't go to those; Cole said he was pretty bogged down with premed. Every once in a while I would see him on campus, and he always had a new entourage of girls on each side of him. I couldn't blame them, though. The Riley boys were hot.

I heard rumors every now and then about some girl saying she hooked up with Jaxon, but I never asked him if they were true. Micah had said that he was a lot like the male version of me. I did notice Rachel Morgan always sitting next to him in the cafeteria, but I knew they weren't dating or anything. Not yet, at least. Some girls took it upon themselves every once in a while to come and sit in his lap. He usually let them for a couple of seconds and I always laughed into my hand, as he would try politely to move them off.

We continued flirting with each other, but nothing more ever happened between us. Mr. Patterson assigned us a huge midterm project that we had to have partners on, so Jaxon and I would meet in one or the other's apartment to work on it. As we were walking out to his truck after lunch one day, I asked him if he was nervous about the game tomorrow, since he hadn't played on a team in a couple years.

"No, I don't think so. I've been doing well during practice. I worked my butt off the two years after high school so I could stay fit. I woke up every morning at five a.m. to practice before classes and then I would hit the gyms in the afternoons and evenings. I used to drag Jace with me every morning. He would bitch my head off for making him get up and throw me the ball so early in the morning," he said while walking over to my side of the truck.

He opened my door and dipped down to grab my waist. This was always my favorite part. I told him once that I was completely capable of getting into a truck on my own, but he just ignored me and did it anyway. He lifted me up into the seat, looking right into my eyes. I swear, every time we did this his face got closer to mine, and I almost leaned in to kiss him today. By the time I realized

I should, he was already backing out to close my door. He came around to the driver's side and slid in. His dark jeans made a slight scratching noise across the leather seat.

I realized I hadn't replied to him yet. "You have a pretty awesome brother to get up every day at five in the morning for two years to throw a ball."

"I didn't say he liked doing it," he returned.

"If he didn't like doing it, he wouldn't have been there, Jaxon. He loves you. Besides, you said he stayed behind to go to community college with you when he obviously had a university fully ready to pay four years for him in premed."

"Hmm . . . yeah, I guess you're right." He said this like he'd never considered that his own brother loved him before. "After a while I guess he became used to waking up so early because there were a couple of times that I just didn't feel like getting up. I mean, we did it every single morning, even on the weekends. Jace would be there, slapping me upside the head to get me to wake up." He laughed at the memory and I let him think about it the rest of the drive home.

As we were walking up to our apartment doors, I looked back at him and said, "Hey, you should really think about doing something nice, thanking Jace for helping you."

"I was just thinking about that. I have no idea what, but I'll think of something. I'll catch ya later, Beautiful," he said while smacking my ass on his way to their door.

He got inside before I even got my keys out. I knelt down with my bag in front of me so I could dig around for my keys. I'm pretty sure this violates Self-Defense 101: Be prepared and always have your keys ready. Oh well, I guess if anyone were to try to attack me, I could shout loud enough for either the guys or the seventy-year-old lady down the hall to hear. Surely she would help out. I kept digging around but I wasn't feeling the familiar cold metal. I turned my backpack upside down and dumped all of the contents out. No keys. I checked every tiny pocket this backpack had, but still no luck. Damn—I must have forgotten to grab them this morning when I left with Quinn.

Lately, since I've been working so much, I've been taking a nap before I go in. I didn't have to work tonight, but I was really looking forward to a nap before the party that we were going to hit tonight. I figured I could go take a nap in Cole's bed. When he lived in the frat house, Quinn and I used to sleep in his bed all of the time, when we drank too much at their parties. He would sleep on the floor instead of the couch downstairs, because he didn't want any of the drunken guys to come in and mess with us while we were asleep.

I walked down to their apartment and knocked on the door. It took a while but Jaxon finally answered, wearing only a navy blue towel wrapped around his waist. *Well, hot damn.* He quirked an eyebrow at me as he raised his right arm, resting his hand on the top of the doorframe. It wasn't a long reach with his height, but the way it stretched him out made my legs tingle.

Guys shouldn't be allowed to look like this, especially ones that live next door to me; it really wasn't fair to all the other more average-looking guys. I looked up from his muscular calves, over the ridges of his abs to his broad chest. I had to pause for a couple of heated beats when I roamed over the V-shaped indentions at his hipbones disappearing under the towel.

"I see you've upgraded your home attire. I approve," I said softly. My voice sounded raspy. "I don't have my keys. I was just going to come down here and nap on Cole's bed till Quinn gets home to let me in."

He nodded his head but didn't say anything and didn't move from his position, so I stepped up closer to him. Something in his eyes was different. They were smoldering and oozed sex. I'm not sure what had changed between now and when I saw him two minutes ago, but I wasn't going to question it.

If I looked straight ahead, all that was in my line of vision was a hard muscled stomach. I reached out and put my palm against his abs. My hand seemed to have a mind of its own as it slowly climbed up his chest. He was looking down at me with a heated stare. When I rose up on my tiptoes, I could trace my hand up past his collarbone, over that sexy shoulder tattoo, to the back of his neck. His lips were slightly parted and I heard the slight hitch in his breath. The tips of my fingers met the ends of his hair on the back of his neck.

He still had one hand up on the top of the doorframe. He lightly brushed the tips of his fingers along my arm on the way down. I reached up with my opposite hand to join the other behind his neck. Then I grasped his hair in my hands.

His voice was barely a whisper, "Emerson . . ."

Once I heard my favorite voice laced in sexual desire, my control was gone. Still up on my toes, I quickly pulled his head down to me and crushed my lips into his. His hands were staying at his side, though. I pushed my body up against his and I could feel how he was reacting to me, so I couldn't understand why he wasn't moving beyond kissing me. I wanted to beg him to touch me. I slid one hand back down and grabbed hold of him through the cotton towel, hoping to get my message across. He groaned into my mouth through my lips.

"Emerson, if you keep this up, I swear I won't be able to stop," he said almost painfully.

"Don't you dare ask me to stop," I quickly said as I came back off my toes and kissed a line down his chest.

Before I could even finish saying, "stop," he grabbed me by the waist and lifted me effortlessly up to his mouth again. My legs instinctively wrapped around him and I dug my fingers through his hair roughly. *Finally.* This was finally happening.

He walked us down the hall toward his bedroom, which was directly across from Jace's. Thankfully, neither of the other guys was home yet. I feel as if I've been in his room to study a thousand times already, but it felt different today. Today there wouldn't be any textbooks involved. He always kept it perfectly tidy. I also noticed when I would sit on his bed to study that his sheets always had a clean scent to them. He climbed onto his bed, still holding me from behind with one arm. When we reached the middle of the mattress, he laid me down on top of the comforter. His hands came down on either side of my head. Our lips never parted. I felt as if he was devouring me, as if he couldn't get enough. I prayed that was the case, because I knew I couldn't; I'd been waiting for this for too long.

I kept my legs wrapped around his waist and he dipped down to rub up against me. The longest moan ever escaped from my mouth before I could catch it. He made me feel as if I'd never done this before; it was almost embarrassing. I reached down to pull open his towel and I tossed it off the bed. *Holy shit, he's gorgeous.* I couldn't help running my tongue down his neck and sucking on his pulse point.

Without moving his neck away from my mouth, he whispered in my ear, "You have me at a disadvantage here; it's not fair."

Throughout my perusing of his body, I forgot that I was still fully clothed. He didn't let that last long, though. He took the hem of my shirt and pulled it over my head, tossing it behind him. In one swoop, he grabbed my shorts and panties and slipped them down my legs. I sat up and reached behind my back to unhook my bra. He was right there sliding the straps down my shoulders, leaving a trail with his lips after them.

"Fuck, your body is amazing," he growled.

He ducked his head down to kiss the swell of my breasts, and I fell back onto the bed. He went down with me, and I ran my hands down his back to get him closer. He reached down with one hand to see if I was ready, and I heard his muffled groan on my skin. The vibrations rocked all the way down my body. I had never been more ready in my life. My breath was coming in small gasps now in anticipation of him.

Suddenly, he sat up on his knees, leaving me cold. I followed his movements with my eyes as he reached into his nightstand to grab a foil packet. When he came back to kneel between my thighs, I took the packet from him. Without letting my eyes leave his, I tore the package open and I watched his eyes close as I slid the condom on him, slowly. When I finally felt every inch of him inside me, I couldn't keep my eyes open any longer, either. His name passed through my lips.

"Emerson, you're so beautiful. I need to see your eyes." He continued rocking into me as I peeled my eyes open and looked up at him. The view from down here couldn't get any better. "I've wanted to be this close to you since the moment I first saw you."

I gripped his back tighter to pull him even closer. "I was basically naked; of course you did." I tried to laugh but a moan escaped instead.

"I'm not going to lie; you were fucking hot sneaking out of that house. This has nothing to do with your gorgeous body, though. It was the way you squared your shoulders when you knew you'd been caught and decided not to be embarrassed. Oh, and the way you were limping on your foot . . . so damn adorable. " He grinned down at me.

I'd never met a guy who could carry on a conversation so well during sex. No one had ever said anything like that to me before, either. I didn't want to like it, but I usually got bumbling idiots that were either way too excited about the size of my boobs or were done by now. Jaxon's words were refreshing to hear but deeply terrifying at the same time.

"Shut up," I said as I pushed up against him to meet his strokes and smashed my lips against his. He pushed my legs up closer to my head as I shouted his name again.

His movements came quicker and shorter, and he buried his face in my neck. I loved the sound of his groan as he pushed into me one more time. Then I felt the full weight of his body on top of me. When he rolled off, he pulled me with him so that I was laying my head on his shoulder and our legs were tangled.

"I'm going to have to get up; I have practice in like fifteen minutes. But I want you to nap in my bed anytime you want. Seriously. Just don't go getting in Cole's bed, please, or Jace's, for that matter. That's *my* rule." He winked at me.

"You do understand we're not dating, right?" I sounded like such a bitch saying that right now, but his possessive tone was scaring me. I didn't need another Micah.

"Oh, I understand. Crystal clear."

He scooted out from under me and came down to brush his lips across mine. I closed my eyes to inhale his scent. I loved that his scent was mixed with mine in this bed. He finally pressed his lips down on mine and pushed his tongue inside. The kiss became more eager and I wanted him all over again. I couldn't stop my fingers from sliding into his hair and holding his mouth to mine.

I heard him groan and say, "You're revving me back up again. I wish I could, but Coach will bench me tomorrow if I'm late, and I have a bet to win." He leaned down to kiss me again and then got up to grab clothes out of his dresser. "Are you and Quinn going to go to that house party with us tonight?"

"Yeah, Cole said we could all ride together after you guys get out of practice," I replied while smiling at him.

I watched him pull on some running shorts as I moved underneath his comforter. He smiled over at me getting comfortable in his bed. He pulled a university football T-shirt over his rippling muscles, and then said, "Nice, I'll catch ya later then, Beautiful." He pulled the door closed behind him and I was already halfway asleep before he got out of the apartment.

After spending the next couple of hours lounging in Jaxon's bed, I finally got up when I knew Quinn would be home. As I was walking out of Jaxon's bedroom in one of his long T-shirts, Jace came out of his bedroom across the hall at the same time.

I froze and pointed behind me at the bedroom, "Jaxon . . . was here . . . earlier. But he had . . . to leave." I sounded like a child getting caught with my hand in the cookie jar. Why was I nervous about Jace seeing me leave his brother's room? It's not like I'd run into his mom.

He burst out laughing at my appearance. "You're so cute, Em. Don't worry; I've been waiting for this to happen. Maybe now he'll shut up about you."

"All right, well, thanks . . . I'll see you tonight?" When he nodded his head, I said, "Tell him I'll give him his shirt back later."

When we walked into the house party that night we heard chanting coming from the kitchen in the back. The house was already packed bodies-to-bodies and they were all heavily intoxicated. The music was so loud that I could feel the beat in my chest to the rhythm of the music. Jaxon and Jace made a barrier to help us squeeze through the crowd while Cole stayed in the back to make sure no one pushed us from behind. I never hold hands with anybody; it's just an unspoken rule of mine. But when Jaxon grabbed my hand as we walked into the house and wouldn't let me go, it didn't take long for me to stop fighting him. For some reason, it felt nice to have his big, strong hand wrapped around mine. These guys were way too protective of us, though. Quinn and I had gone to plenty of parties on our own and survived.

When we walked in, there were guys lining up shots in front of Garrett. Apparently it was his birthday and he needed to finish off his celebratory birthday shots. When he was done, I reached in between the guys and grabbed five shot glasses and the bottle of tequila.

"Come on, Garrett, do another birthday shot with us!" I shouted.

Quinn and I were both leaning up against the bar while the guys stood behind us. I felt Jaxon's fingertips touch the skin under my shirt around my waist. I moved just an inch backward to lean into him a little bit more. When he didn't move forward any, I leaned over the counter so my backside would move up against his groin. The instant I touched him, he shot forward over me and groaned. Quinn shot him a dirty look, thinking that he had just crashed into me.

"Someone shoved me," he said, pointing behind him.

He sat up a little straighter, not moving away from touching me, though. I tried holding it in, but I couldn't stop laughing at the scared expression he gave Quinn, and he pinched me in the side. It only made me laugh harder. By this point, Garrett had lined up a row of shots for everyone around him.

"I'm only doing this for you, Em, because I'm already fucking hammered! Also because I owe you one for throwing your clothes in a tree, although I heard some guys got a pretty good wake-up call that morning." He winked and my mouth dropped open.

"You did that?" I yelled.

When he nodded his head, Jaxon reached past me and high-fived Garrett in the air. "Thanks, man; that was the best damn morning of my life!" he boomed over the crowd.

Everyone around us started laughing and I elbowed Jaxon in the ribs behind me. With an "oomph" he leaned forward and said into my ear, "What? I can't help but thank the guy."

"Okay, get ready, boys!" Micah interrupted by yelling. "And ladies." He smiled at Quinn and me.

"Hold up! I think Jax needs to do the toast; he was always good at those in high school," Cole shouted above the noise. Jace started laughing as if he knew exactly what Cole was talking about.

"All right, hold 'em up high!" Jaxon shouted in a heavier southern accent than he normally had. I melted against him further when I heard that. Suddenly, I felt him lean forward across me. His solid chest smashed up against my back. For a second, I remembered what it felt like to run my hands across that wide bare chest and I lost my breath. He was damn sexy, and now that I knew what he was capable of, I was seconds away from pulling him across this bar top and making a scene for everyone around us. I felt his mouth next to my ear.

"Don't get offended at me for this," he whispered, and then his warmth disappeared and I whimpered at the loss. The hand not holding the shot glass came around my hips and squeezed me in close to let me know he heard that.

"Here's to honor. Get on her. Stay on her. If you fall off, get back on her. If you can't cum in her, cum on her! Happy birthday, man!" Jaxon shouted in his deep voice.

Everyone was laughing so hard they couldn't take their shots at first. When they finally calmed down enough, I watched as all of their heads rocked backward and they poured the tequila down. Cole pulled Quinn to the dance floor immediately afterward, and Jace found a small, pretty brunette that he could dance with.

"You didn't take yours. You didn't like the toast?"

I spun around to face Jaxon. He was still right up against me so that we were almost touching when I turned. He had a sexy smirk at the corner of lips. How is it fair to all the other men in the world for Jaxon to have so many sexy qualities? I didn't even want to start thinking about the fact that he had an identical version of him twenty feet away from us.

"The toast was great. I just wanted to take mine with you," I replied, smiling.

The seduction in his eyes was inebriating—I could get drunk on that look alone; forget the tequila. I lifted my glass to him and he grabbed my waist roughly. I kept my eyes on him the entire time. When I got an idea, I lowered the shot and he gave me a confused expression. I rotated slightly, not letting his hands slip from around me.

"Hey, Gar, do you have lime and salt?" He nodded as he slid it across the counter.

Jaxon raised an inquiring eyebrow at me. "I shoot cheap tequila with lime and salt," I replied to his unspoken question.

I reached up and tugged the collar of his shirt over, and his mouth opened slightly. I grabbed the lime and slowly dabbed it on his collarbone. Still looking into his eyes, I sprinkled salt across the wet area on his skin. I heard his breath suck in past his teeth when I moved my mouth to hover over him. He was so much taller than I was that I had to stand on my toes while he leaned down some for my mouth to reach. My tongue slowly swiped across his skin and I could taste the mixture of the salt and him together. I let my lips glide across his collarbone in a leisurely kiss. When I pulled back, his eyes were closed. When they finally opened again, they were clouded with desire. I lifted my glass back up and slowly brought it to my mouth. I raised my eyebrow at him. He pulled my hips sharply up against him and I could feel his sexual need growing. The feeling made me moan.

"Bottoms up, Beautiful." His whisper sounded raspy and thick.

Our faces were so close to each other now that I could barely fit the shot glass between us. I leaned my head back and let the liquid slowly flow into my mouth. When the glass was empty, I opened my throat and let it course and burn on its way down. I brought my face back to his and bit into the lime.

"You're hot as hell, babe. I'd kill to have you in my bed every night." He leaned down to trail kisses and his tongue down the curve of my neck.

I leaned in and let his delicious torture continue. "Sorry, that can't happen; but I'll unquestionably enjoy a couple more times with you."

He grabbed my hand and pulled me out to the dance floor with the rest of our friends. He made me laugh all night long and he didn't try to push the topic of a relationship anymore.

- FIVE -

I hadn't seen Jaxon since we got home from the party last night. They were all gone when I woke up the next morning. I don't know why, but I hadn't told Quinn yet that Jaxon and I had slept together. I was pretty sure that I didn't want Cole to know yet, and Quinn seriously couldn't keep her mouth shut around him. I knew that he was worried about any future mishaps between Jaxon and me. I just wanted to reassure him myself that that wouldn't happen, before everyone else told him.

I didn't have classes on Fridays, so I usually tried to pick up an early shift at the bar, especially during football season. Ed didn't need me to come and fill in today, so I stayed home and cleaned up the apartment. I did both Quinn's and my laundry. Being the awesome sister that I am, I even folded and put it all away. I scrubbed down the countertops and mopped up the kitchen. By lunchtime, I was incredibly bored. It had been a long time since I'd had nothing to do. Even Quinn was gone, tutoring until later in the afternoon.

I was going stir-crazy staying in this place alone. I decided to get out and jog. My dad was a runner; I can remember when he used to wake up early before work every morning to go for a run. If for some reason he wasn't able to get a run in the morning, he would come home and run before dinner. I didn't like to wake up early, but if I could, I would run with him in the afternoons. Quinn and Ellie used to look at me like I was crazy to want to go running in the afternoon heat. For me, running was relaxing. There's a point where you don't notice the heat (or the cold) and you just hit this runner's high. Besides, I hated the gym, so I needed to get my exercise somewhere.

It took me a long time to start running again after he died. Ellie noticed that I had stopped, and she tried numerous times to get me out. She even attempted to go with me. I adored her for it, but I just hadn't been ready. Recently I've been able to get out a couple of times a week again.

After my second time getting back out, Quinn went and bought me all new, name-brand running gear to celebrate. She got me tons of running boy shorts and matching sports bras. I told her it was unnecessary, but once again, she hated when I "slummed" it and she wanted me to look good, even while profusely sweating, apparently. I don't try to argue with her—there's no point. Once she bought all this for me, she went and threw away all my old sweats while I was in class.

I left the apartment and ran past the university and toward the beach. Running across sand was a lot harder than concrete. For me, dry sand is the hardest because my feet sink down into it with each stride, but it's a good workout. By the time I ran all the way down to the water, I had gotten about four miles under my belt. I was way too tired to turn around and run back already, so I decided to lie down in the sand and soak in some vitamin D.

I lay back and closed my eyes. I'm not sure how long I dozed there until I realized the sun wasn't on me anymore and I'd lost my warmth. I slowly opened my eyes to adjust to the light and saw Cole standing over me looking down and blocking the rays.

"Hey, Ems, you should have told me you were running; we could have gone together," he said while sitting down. He sat right down next to me and threw his sweaty arm around my shoulder.

Good thing I was already sweaty myself or I would have been thoroughly grossed out.

"You know I don't like running with you, Cole; you push too hard for me." I nudged him while smiling. I think I'd gone running with Cole twice, and both times he left me panting and heaving for air in the dust. We continued to stare out into the water, just sitting there together.

Eventually he sighed and said, "Why'd you sleep with him, Em?" He spoke in a whisper, almost like he didn't want me to hear his question.

"He told you?" I gasped. I knew it wasn't going to be a secret but I didn't think he would go off telling the guys so soon. I shouldn't have been surprised, though; guys were all the same.

"No, don't worry; he didn't. He's not the kiss-and-tell type. But he didn't have to. I know him, Em; I've known him my whole life. I knew something was up with y'all last night when we were at the party. I didn't ask him about it, but you just confirmed it for me." He ran his fingers through his sweaty brown hair, frustrated. "Fuck, Em, you're going to ruin everything. If y'all fight or he upsets you, Quinn will take your side, and she'll leave if it upsets you too much. I know she will."

I turned around and moved to kneel in between his outstretched legs, facing him. He had a sad look on his face. I was absolutely sure this had more to do with Quinn possibly not living next door to him and less to do with Jaxon and me potentially fighting. As one of his best friends, all I wanted to do was make him happy again.

"Jaxon and I are adults. He knows about me, and knows about my rules. He knew all of this, weeks before. He knows I don't plan on being his or anyone else's wife or girlfriend, for that matter. This is all for fun," I said, raising my hands in the air.

"Ems, do you truly believe that? Do you really think you're never going to marry anybody?" he asked.

"Absolutely."

He sighed. "You really should let someone in someday."

I needed to stop where this was going. I grabbed his face and looked into his hazel eyes. "The point is, Jaxon and I are fine. We aren't fighting and no one's moving away. Are you kidding me? We begged you for two years to move in next to us. We aren't going anywhere now that we've finally got you." I laughed and smiled, happy when he laughed along with me.

We were interrupted by a familiar voice. "Dude, what the hell, I thought we were meeting up at the lifeguard stand?" Jaxon was standing above us, looking down at me but talking to Cole. He frowned at my position in front of Cole and I slowly moved my hands down from his face. I hated that I felt awkward about my close friendship with Cole in front of him. I moved back to sit next to Cole's side again.

"Chill out, asshole. I came across Sleeping Beauty here and stopped to talk," Cole responded while swatting at Jaxon's legs.

I shoved at him and said, "I wasn't sleeping. I was just enjoying the sun."

Jaxon gave me an angry, confused look. "Sleeping? Emerson, you can't sleep on the beach out here alone." His voice was hard as he sat down next to me with his legs stretching out in front of him.

"Don't worry. Next time I feel the urge to sleep on the beach, I'll invite you along," I replied while winking at him. He looked shocked that I would say this in front of Cole. "He knows, Jaxon. Apparently you were pretty obvious last night." I punched him in the arm. He grabbed the hand that punched him and pulled me into a scorching kiss.

"Ugh, okay, guys, gross. Seriously, I don't need to see your friends-with-benefits action live. I'll see y'all at the game tonight." He got up and started jogging back down the beach.

I was barely paying attention to Cole, because Jaxon's lips hadn't left mine yet. Eventually, I broke the kiss and pulled back. "You can't just kiss me whenever! I have rules," I said nervously.

"I know your rules, and kissing was nowhere in there. Kissing doesn't mean we're dating; don't stress," he teased nonchalantly. "Besides, you didn't seem to mind when I did this to you last night." He proceeded to run his tongue along my neck beneath my jaw.

I'd never thought about someone kissing me outside of sex. In fact, that had never come up. I mean, some of the guys would kiss my neck occasionally, but I'd never actually let them kiss my lips unless we were in the bedroom. I'd never had an opportunity to make a rule for that. "You're okay with this, even knowing that I will at some point sleep with someone else?" I felt like kissing on occasion would lead to his having feelings for me, and then I would have to cut him off. I didn't want to. I enjoyed Jaxon far too much to cut him off, but I couldn't risk breaking his heart in the process. So that's what I would have to do if I felt as if that's where it was leading.

"As long as that someone else isn't my best friend or my twin brother, I can try and deal," he finally said, although I felt as if there was a lot more he wasn't saying.

"Damn, and here I thought when my time was up with you I could still have my fun with another smoking-hot Riley brother," I badgered him.

Instantly, he had me lying on the beach with his mouth above mine. "Not funny." I laughed at his seriousness until he kissed my smile away. I combed my fingers through his hair, the way I always saw him doing. He pulled back and stared in my eyes.

"When you say you'll try to be okay with it, what do you mean?" I don't know why I ask questions I don't want to know the answer to.

He let me go and lay down on the sand with his palms over his eyes and his fingers in his hair. "I think you know the answer to that."

I sat there waiting to see if he would elaborate further.

Suddenly he removed his hands and rolled to his side to look right at me. "You like me, don't you?" he asked, and I froze with no way to respond to his candid query. "It's a safe question; just answer it truthfully. I promise I won't ask to date you. You like me, don't you?" he repeated. I nodded my head and he smiled back at me.

I'd never admitted to liking anyone before. I don't think I'd really ever liked anyone enough even to think about admitting it to him. I felt as if everything was going to be ruined now; we were having so much fun I wasn't ready for us to stop yet. How could we possibly keep this casual bond and someone not get hurt now?

Noticing my grim expression and panic, he quickly pulled me into his lap with my legs wrapped around his hips. "Hey, hey, stop thinking about what you're thinking right now. All we're doing is having fun. I just needed you to know that I like you too. I like hanging out with you and I certainly like kissing you. There's nothing more going on here." I nodded my head and laid it against his shoulder. I felt him lean down and kiss the top of my head.

"You do understand that you're going to be with other people and I will be as well, right?"

With a heavy sigh, he replied, "Emerson, I think you've made that known loud and clear. I can handle it, okay? I'm a big boy." I could tell he was getting annoyed with me, but I had to make sure he knew what was involved here. Just because we liked each other, that didn't mean I was just going to be kissing only him. I'm such a bitch; I wish I weren't this way.

"I'm sorry; I just can't hurt you. I've never cared about that before with anyone; I just never wanted them getting attached to me. With you, it can't happen; I can't be responsible for that. But I also just can't do relationships." Without realizing it, I was tracing my finger around his lips, outlining the plump bottom one and running my finger directly over the top one. I really didn't want to hurt him, but I think I will enjoy having the freedom to touch him.

"I hope one day you'll tell me why that is," he probed. I just continued my exploration of his lips, not wanting to give him an answer.

His hands started rubbing circles on my back. Since I was only wearing a sports bra and running shorts, he was caressing a whole lot of skin.

"I'm still fuming that you were sleeping out here alone, practically naked." He pulled me back to glare at me.

"Please, this is more coverage than a bikini, and like I said before, I wasn't sleeping."

"You should never be set loose alone in a bikini, either; I can only imagine." He shook his head.

I laid my head back down on his shoulder, enjoying the sound of his voice.

"Are you and Cole just friends, or am I missing something there?" He was still wondering about what he saw when he came upon us sitting so closely together on the beach. With my reputation, I couldn't blame him for thinking that about me.

"We're just close friends, nothing more. There's never been anything more between us and there never will be. I was just reassuring him that nothing would change since you and I have slept together. I'm almost positive he's worried Quinn will leave. Those two . . . are frustrating . . ."

"He's in love with her, you know. He hasn't said anything about that to me, but I can tell." I don't know if I should be shocked to hear it or relieved that someone else could see it too.

"I'm positive the feelings are mutual, but they won't act on it for some reason."

"When he came home over the summers he would talk about the two of y'all all the time. Jace and I swore he was banging one of you, if not both. He always said he would never do that, that y'all were different and he couldn't risk ruining everything. But the way he talked about Quinn was different," he added.

"Yeah, I don't even know how to talk about it with Quinn. She's just as stubborn as Cole." I reached out and touched the sides of his face. "Speaking of stubborn, so when can I ride with you on your motorcycle?"

"That would be never," he clipped out.

"I don't understand why. I've seen Jace ride around with girls more than a couple of times," I countered.

"I don't care; it's not you on the back. I could never handle the idea of you getting hurt."

I lifted up so I could kiss him on the neck and he groaned. He slid his hand in between us and started running his fingers across my most intimate area. The spandex shorts didn't allow much of a barrier from his quick strokes. I leaned back with my eyes closed and placed my hands on his legs to brace myself. Right as he had begun working me up to a fever pitch, he seemed to realize where we were and pulled his hand back. My eyes snapped open with my frustration.

"Okay, I seriously have to get you out of my lap. If you don't, we're going to get in trouble for public indecency and then some." I moved off with a groan to sit next to him and my hand trailed down past his hand that had just been stroking me.

"If you want me to hold your hand, all you have to do is ask." He winked at me.

"Uh . . . no, I don't hold hands." I brought mine back to my lap.

He reached over and squeezed my hand into his. "Let's head back."

"Good, I'm starving." I stood up and started stretching out my legs and dusting the sand off of me. "Do you want to race back?"

"Sure, I'll smoke you and it won't be fair, but I'm a guy, so I love competition." He grinned while trying to reach behind himself and get the sand off his back.

"Always so cocky. I think you should at least give me a couple of seconds' head start, seeing as I'm not an all-star athlete." I beamed at him.

He grabbed me into his chest and bent my head back so I was looking directly up at him. My chin was against his chest and he ran his hands over my hair. "For you, Beautiful, I'll give you a whole minute."

"Okay, first one home wins?" I asked and he nodded his head, looking down at me. I turned around, moved out of his arms, and started jogging. I looked back at him and yelled, "Loser can't have sex for two weeks!" I saw his mouth drop open.

"Game on!" he hollered back with an arrogant smirk.

I was pretty positive I knew how Jaxon would run home. Our apartment was basically a straight shot to the east and then you had to cut north a bit from the beach with the university in between. So it would be a given that he'd take that route. But I knew of an alley that runs at an angle, which shaves off time. I knew without a doubt he was faster than I was, but if I had less of a distance, then hopefully I could win.

As I was running, I could see down the sides of each house onto the main street, and so far, no sign of Jaxon. I reached the apartments and took the stairs two at a time. Once I turned down our hallway, I darted for our doors. Quinn was coming down the opposite way, and she leaned up against the wall, looking at me with confusion.

"What is up with you guys? Why are you two barreling down the hallway?"

"What? Why do you say 'you guys' like that?" I asked her quickly and out of breath.

"Jax just came down the hallway like a bat out of hell."

"Shit! How did he do it?" I yelled.

Right then I heard his deep laugh coming out of his doorway. I turned around with my arms folded over my chest, glaring at him. I walked toward him and stood in front of him. He was drinking cold water out of a glass, with sweat rolling down his head.

"How did you do it? I even took a shortcut . . . did you take a cab?" I reproached him.

He handed me the last half of his water and I gratefully chugged it down. Then he bent down and picked me up, my legs automatically wrapping around his waist.

He laughed at my accusation. "No, I'm just faster." He shrugged. Our sweaty bodies were mixing together. He was a bit intoxicating when he smelled like this. "You need a shower. Wanna join me?" He smirked at me, turning to go inside his apartment.

I leaned in toward his mouth and almost said yes, but then I heard Quinn gasp in the background. *Crap, how did I forget she was back there?* I was in trouble now, because I hadn't talked to her about Jaxon at all yet. I groaned as I slid down Jaxon's body to the floor. He inhaled sharply at the touch of our bodies skimming together. I downed the rest of the water and handed the glass back to him.

"I'll see you ladies at the game tonight?" he asked us, backing inside his apartment.

"I'll see Cole there, but I don't think I want to see you!" Quinn glared at him. I knew she was only half kidding.

Cole stuck his head out of the doorway, laughing. "Aw, thanks, babe."

She glared at all three of us and pointed to me. "You, follow me."

"Gee thanks, Jax, you got me in trouble with Mom," I teased.

"Hey, Beautiful, don't forget . . . no sex for two weeks!" he reminded me.

I grumbled at him as I followed Quinn into our apartment and then the bathroom. She turned on the shower and checked the temperature.

"Get in there and make it fast; you have a lot of explaining." She pointed to the shower.

I stepped out of my clothes and got into the steaming-hot shower. "I'm sorry, Quinny, it all happened so fast. But at the same time, it's nothing at all."

"Nothing at all! Em, he picked you up and almost kissed you in front of everyone. You seemed totally fine with it. That's not nothing at all," she yelled back.

"Okay, well, yesterday we had sex . . ."

I heard her gasp.

"Why does that surprise you? You knew it was coming! I've only been talking about how gorgeous he is for weeks now."

"You never told me. You always tell me, and sometimes you even tell me before it happens."

"I had no idea it was going to happen. Then we were at the party all night, and you were gone before I got up this morning. I'm sorry, I should have texted. Next time I'll send a pic."

"Promise?"

"Absolutely, except I lost a bet, so now nothing will be happening with anyone for two weeks." Never mind the fact that he was free to go off with someone else. But that didn't bother me. Not one bit. I finished rinsing and grabbed the towel to dry off. When I stepped out, Quinn was standing in front of the mirror straightening her hair. I pulled on a robe and walked out to the "closet." We always got ready together in here.

Quinn brought her straightener and my curling iron and plugged them in. We sat on the floor together in front of the mirror and finished our hair.

"Why would you agree to that bet, Em?"

I groaned. "Because it was my idea. I thought I had a surefire way of winning. Apparently I'm an idiot, though, because I tried to race a football star."

I could feel the wheels spinning in her head as she thought about everything I had just told her. Then out of nowhere she looked at me through the mirror and said, "I feel like he's different."

I sighed. "He is different, but the outcome will be the same."

"It doesn't have to be. Not everyone cheats."

"Quinn, it's not just about the fact that he could do that. I just can't hurt him, and I will if I pretend I can handle a relationship," I said.

"Just the fact that you care enough not to hurt him shows me that maybe you can handle one." She got up to go get our makeup.

"I don't want to handle one. If we're talking about relationships here, what about you and Cole?" I watched her flinch in the reflection of the mirror. When she came back, sat down, and still didn't respond, I continued, "It's okay to like him, Quinn; he's a great guy."

"It's not okay to like him. If he doesn't feel the same way, I'll ruin everything. It'll hurt too much to be rejected by him." She said barely above a whisper.

"If that's what you're worried about, then just stop. I see the way he looks at you, the way he worries about you and what you think of every situation. Trust me, there's no problem there."

She gave a little nod but didn't say anymore on that topic. I decided to give her a break because she let me distract her from my interrogation about Jax. We finished getting ready quickly so we could make it to the stadium in time to get good seats.

- SIX -

When we arrived at the stadium, we picked up our tickets at will-call. Cole always made sure there were tickets there for Quinn and me at every single game. Usually our tickets came together because they were both from Cole. Today she handed one to Quinn and then kept searching for mine. Finally, she found it and handed it to me with a note attached. She stared at me like she was scoping me out. I bet she was wondering if I was with the drop-dead gorgeous guy who had left this for me.

Enjoy my touchdown, Beautiful.
Scream my name nice and loud, just like yesterday. — J

"What does that mean?" Quinn asked, reading the note over my shoulder. When she read the second half she burst out laughing. Now I understand why the attendant was staring so much.

"It means this guy is in serious need of a blow to his ego," I replied while laughing.

"It's sweet he left you a ticket." Quinn has been begging me to date someone for years; she's always wanted to double date.

"We made a bet that first day we met. He said he knew he would score a touchdown at the first game. Well, we all know what a snob Dalton is; he never throws to the new guys at first. This will be fun," I said while walking up to our seats.

"What did you wager this time?"

"He wants a hot-air balloon ride." I giggled.

"That's . . . a strange request. What do you get if you win?" She was looking at me like I was crazy.

"I never decided on anything. I'm hoping he scores, but he does need his ego deflated as soon as possible." I smiled.

Since we always get here early enough, we're able to sit in the same spot directly in front of the team bench. Today there were two girls already sitting in our usual seats. We had to sit in a whole other section farther over because we wanted the front row, but we were still close to where the guys would be sitting. The stadium filled up fast and everyone was excited for the new season to begin. This whole half of the stadium was decked out in our school colors. Jace found us and came to sit next to me. It didn't take long for the seat on his opposite side to fill with another girl who leaned over toward him, blatantly showing her breasts. Jace appeared to enjoy the show.

With the cheer of the crowd, the teams came running out and lined up in front of their field-side benches. First we spotted Cole, who was already looking into the stands for us; he knew where we always sat. When he looked in our usual spots, he made a disgusted face. Quinn and I both started giggling at his expression. The girls in our spot noticed him looking at them, so they started waving and smiling at him. He quickly started walking down the line, scanning the stadium seats. Quinn finally put him out of his misery and whistled at him. The second he heard it, he whipped his head toward us and I swear I saw the relief flash across his face. Yeah, there was no denying that boy's feelings for my sister.

"You're only torturing him the longer you guys don't get together."

"Emmy, it's not just me; he hasn't done anything, either," she said, frustrated.

Jace interrupted us. "The feelings are mutual, Quinn. He's just afraid of messing up your friendship."

I saw her jaw hit the floor as she stared at Jace. I beamed, reached up, grabbed his face, and gave him a big kiss on the cheek. This was exactly what she needed to hear. I could never convince her when it was only coming from me. All of a sudden, I heard a loud bang that made me jump back. I looked right at Jace, who was shaking his head back and forth with a little smirk on his face.

I looked toward the field and Jaxon was right on the other side of the barrier separating the stands from the sidelines. "Hey!" he shouted. "You do realize you're doing that to the wrong twin, right?" He turned and glared at Jace, who only started laughing. Oh my God, he looked so damn sexy in his uniform. It was tight in all the amazingly right places. I was almost jealous that every other girl here could see how well defined his muscles were, but I don't get jealous.

"Oh, I knew exactly which twin I had between my hands," I cracked.

"Emerson, I'll pull you over these railings and make you sit down here with me." He still looked a little angry. I realized that maybe this whole him-not-wanting-me-to-like-his-brother-or-best-friend thing was more serious than I had thought. I got up, walked to the railing, and crouched down so I could be face-to-face with him through the bars.

"I only kissed his cheek, and I only did that because he just helped me out with Quinn in a big way." I felt like I needed to sweet-talk him.

"I'm being an asshole, I know. I'm trying real hard to not be possessive over you, but please, just not my brother, okay?"

"You're right, you are being an asshole. You're also not allowed to be possessive over me, but I promised no brother or best friend." I leaned in and gave him a loud smack on the lips.

A megawatt smile was plastered across his face as he backed up toward his team looking at me. He turned around and listened to what the coach was telling the rest of them. He stood right next to Cole, who had a big grin on his face. They both smiled and then punched each other on the arms. I could tell they were thrilled to be playing together again; it was amusing to watch their interactions.

I turned to Jace to see his reaction to his brother and best friend in uniform together again. "Do you miss it?" I asked him.

"Not really. It was fun to play with those two, but I never took it as seriously as they did." He looked happy to be watching them as well.

"You're a great brother, you know that? I wish I had a brother like you. Jaxon told me how you helped him stay in shape to come back and play again."

He shrugged, like I predicted he would. "He's my brother; that's what brothers do."

We watched the guys take the field and they huddled around each other. Jace put his arm around my shoulders and squeezed.

"You're playing with fire," I mumbled to him, trying to extricate myself.

Jax popped his head out of the huddle, pointed his finger directly at Jace, and glared harshly. Jace raised his hands in surrender, laughing, and someone smacked Jaxon in the head to get him to focus. The crowd laughed at the drama of the Riley twins.

By halftime, the other team was up fourteen points. The guys walked off the field to head to the locker rooms. Cole looked frustrated and Jaxon just looked pissed. As I had suspected, Dalton wasn't throwing to Jaxon at all and Cole was constantly being outnumbered, so it was hard for him to connect with the ball. Jace had stopped paying attention to the girls around him and had leaned forward in his seat the majority of the game. Even though he claimed he didn't miss it, I could see the wheels spinning in his head. His hand would move every once in a while to indicate a throw or fight off a block.

"I'm guessing if you were out there as quarterback, you would have handled that differently?" I asked.

"Absolutely. Either Dalton is blind or he's just an asshole," he ground out.

"It's the latter."

Quinn stood up in her seat and straightened her shorts. "Come on guys; let's go get something to drink."

We both got up and followed her out. As we walked underneath the stands, we could hear the coaches yelling all the way in the locker rooms. You couldn't pay me to be those guys right now. Jace bought Quinn and me a soda and himself water. We hung out under the stands, talking to other classmates. Quinn and I had found Sophia and some of the other girls that Quinn works out with. Some people were talking about where the parties were after the game. All the frat and sorority houses were on a three-week party ban. The school wanted them to prove that they could study and maintain decent GPAs. I didn't understand the point. So what—they would behave for a couple weeks then go right back to having parties every other night?

Quinn started saying that maybe we could have people over to our place. I just shrugged. Every once in a while, we'd have people over; it always got overcrowded and someone was always trying to get into our rooms to have sex.

"I don't care, but I'm locking my door."

"You can lock the door with you and me inside it, babe," Micah said, putting his arm around my shoulders, and I watched as Sophia's eyes locked on his arm.

"Not a chance, unless you want to watch that new Channing Tatum movie with me," I said, laughing.

He leaned in to whisper in my ear, "Come on, Em, I could do that thing that makes you scream real loud." I knew I looked flustered; I couldn't help it. Micah was good, but it wasn't happening. I started shaking my head.

Jace slipped his hands, followed by the rest of his body, in between the two of us, forcing Micah to take a wide step back away from him. "Come on, Em and Q; let's get back to our seats." He looped my arm through his elbow and walked off with Quinn following on the other side of him.

"Real smooth. I don't need someone intervening for Jaxon; he does that enough. You know we aren't together, right? I can talk to whoever I want about whatever I want." Although I was glad he rescued me away from Micah, I didn't want him to think that I was Jaxon's. I don't need someone trying to maneuver me away from guys when Jaxon wasn't around to do it himself.

"I know that Jax cares about you a lot."

"It doesn't matter. We'll never be together, like that."

He gave me a confused look. "Why wouldn't you?" he asked. "You're perfect for each other." Quinn stepped up next to us with a beaming smile, looking victorious.

"I don't date. Anybody. Period."

His look told me that he hadn't heard about my rules. "You're a strange girl, Em."

"He knows all of this about me. I told him basically my life story the first day we met," I countered.

"Just don't hurt him; he doesn't need that again." He looked right at me when he said that and my heart started beating through my chest. What did he mean by 'again'? Wasn't that what I was trying to prevent here? How come no one understood me, and more importantly, how come I was starting to not understand myself?

"That's exactly what I'm trying to avoid!" I snapped in return. I took a deep breath and stepped back from the two of them, "I'm going to the restroom, and I'll meet you at the seats later." Jace gave me an apologetic face.

Quinn tried to follow, but I shook my head at her and told her I'd be right back. Instead of going to the restroom, I walked all the way out to our car. Lying down in the back seat, I stared up at the fabric on the ceiling. What the hell was I doing with Jaxon anyway? Why did I bother getting close like this with someone? Without breaking my rules, I was somehow breaking them. Every time Jax was near me, it was like everything I had tried to push away in the past was rushing at me full speed. The problem was that I was enjoying every second I spent with him. We'd talked about this; we'd talked about what my needs were. He seemed to understand, and he was continually telling me he could handle it. I just needed to stop listening to everyone else around us.

By the time I made it back into the stadium, they were already ten minutes into the third quarter. The concessions and the walkway under the stands were completely vacant, besides the few stragglers trying to finish off their cigarettes before they went back to their seats. From under here, you could feel the rumble of the crowd above. Some were bouncing their feet, most were cheering loudly. I walked up the stadium stairs to where Quinn and Jace were sitting. I heard Jaxon immediately, even before I could see him.

"Well, where the fuck is she? What if something happened to her?" He sounded panicky and irritated with whomever he was talking to. "You said she went to the restroom fifteen minutes ago." *Had I really been gone that long?*

Jace responded, "Dude, chill out. She'll be back." When I walked toward our seats, I saw Jax leaning up on the railing barriers talking to them. He had his helmet on as if he needed to be on the field at a moment's notice. His last name was called and with a frustrated breath, he turned around and hustled for the field before he could see that I'd made it back.

"Where the hell have you been? I just tried to call you!" Quinn yelled at me as I sat down between her and Jace.

"I needed a breather; I must have left my phone in the car."

"The car? You were supposed to be in the bathroom!" Quinn screeched at me.

"Jax was freaking," Jace began. "I didn't mean to make you mad. I'm sorry."

"Everything's fine, Jace. You didn't do anything wrong. Protecting your brother is what family does."

"But I shouldn't have even opened my mouth about the two of you. He'll kick my ass for meddling."

"Let's just forget about it, okay?" I begged. He nodded his head and patted my leg.

"Man, I wish he would have seen you before he headed back out there. Now he's going to be distracted," Jace complained.

At that, I stood up with my hands above my head clapping and yelled, "Wooo! Go Jaxon!" He was all the way on the opposite side of the field, but his head instantly stood up from his ready stance and looked directly at me. From all the way over here, I could see his piercing blue eyes. He gave me the "okay" signal with his fingers, gesturing to confirm that everything was all right with me. I gave him the signal right back and he nodded his head and smiled, then returned to his ready position. "I think he'll focus now," I said to both of the wide-eyed busybodies on either side of me.

Ten minutes later, Cole scored a much-needed touchdown. Quinn and I jumped up and down. Jace clapped but also gave a determined look to Jax. I watched as he nodded back to his brother. This twin communication was bizarre to watch. When our team got the ball back, all of the offense, including Cole and Jax, lined back up on the field. The ball was snapped back to Dalton and he launched it toward Cole almost instantly. Cole caught it between his hands and tucked it in protectively. He started shuffling, trying to get down the line. He didn't see it coming, but one of the defenders came barreling for him from his right side. I heard Quinn's intake of breath right before the crash. When the guy smashed into Cole's side, the ball flew high in the air and Cole hit the ground hard, straight on his back.

All of a sudden Jaxon was in the air, and he snatched the ball so fast almost none of the defenders noticed. By the time they realized the ball hadn't come down with Cole, Jaxon was halfway down the field. Everyone in the stands stood, yelling for him to run faster. Jaxon passed the end zone effortlessly without even being touched. He let the ball slip through his fingers and pointed right at me with a huge grin on his face. I pointed back to him and clapped. I've got to hand it to this sexy man—he was good. He didn't stand down in the end zone and celebrate, either.

When I looked over at Quinn, my smile dropped. She was still staring out into the field. When I followed her line of sight, I noticed Cole was still lying down flat on the ground. During his fall, his helmet must have been knocked off. Jace, Quinn, and I immediately moved up against the railing. Jaxon was sprinting back to Cole's side. In his haste, he slid on the ground on his knees to stoop right next to Cole and pulled his helmet off as well. We all watched as Jaxon cupped Cole's face and practically yelled at him in obvious frustration. Quinn took a stuttering breath in. I think Jace was about to jump over the side and take off running; his knuckles were pale white as he gripped the railing. The coach and the team medics were already jogging across the field.

Then Jaxon reached out his palm and Cole grabbed it. When Jaxon pulled him to a standing position and we all watched him walk normally back to our side of the field, everyone jumped up and cheered. Quinn let out a long, relieved breath. I looked at her and noticed a tear slip down her face, but she quickly batted it away before anyone else could see. When Cole reached the bench, he sat down and chugged water from a squeezable plastic bottle. Jaxon walked by, patted him on the back, and sat next to him. Jace obviously couldn't take it anymore; he swung his legs over the railing and went to sit on Cole's opposite side. We watched as they all talked to each other. Cole shook his head at something Jace said, and both he and Jaxon burst out laughing. It was a relief to watch; laughing meant Cole was okay.

Quinn and I both sat back in our seats to continue watching the remainder of the game that had resumed while we were glued to watching Cole recover from his knockout. I was a little disappointed none of the guys had come over to talk to us about what had happened. They hadn't even looked back our way. They really were each other's best friends, sitting there in their own little world, talking and joking around.

The score was tied and the other team had the ball. Their quarterback was almost immediately sacked and the ball was returned to us. I was surprised to see Cole suiting up and going back out there.

"It must not have been that bad, Quinny," I told her while pointing at him.

"I still don't think he should be going back out."

For the next two plays, Dalton threw straight to Jaxon as he ran it down the field, getting closer and closer to the end zone. He must have deemed him fit to catch his precious golden-boy throws after that last touchdown. I don't know why I was extremely uncomfortable watching Jaxon get tackled. I'd seen Cole get tackled numerous times. This was football and it was expected. Each time I watched him go down, my stomach dropped a little bit more, and without realizing it, I grabbed Quinn's hand on a particularly hard hit.

"It's not so easy when you care about them, is it?" Quinn squeezed my hand back.

"I don't know what you're talking about," I said, avoiding her eyes.

"Whatever. Your heart knows what I'm talking about, and one day your brain will catch up."

"My heart is for pumping blood, not for caring about a guy and whether he gets hurt or not." I realized how unconvincing I must sound when Quinn just rolled her eyes at my response.

In a trick-play, we watched as Dalton handed off the ball to Jaxon. He took off in a dead sprint right into the end zone for his second touchdown of the game. I hope he didn't think he was getting more than a hot-air balloon ride for the additional touchdown. One of the defenders chasing Jaxon couldn't stop his momentum and barreled right over, knocking him to the ground.

I stood up and impulsively yelled, "Hey!" It just popped out of my mouth. Jace turned from his spot on the bench and smiled perceptively up at me. I rolled my eyes at him while Quinn covered her laugh with her hands. These two were getting on my nerves.

Jaxon was the first one to stand back up. He surprised us all when he reached his hand out and helped the other guy to his feet. So many of these guys would have yelled or even started a fight with that guy for knocking them over. Not Jaxon, though—he helped them up and laughed along with them.

The game ended shortly after that, and we had won thanks to Jaxon's last touchdown. For obvious reasons, I loved when we won games, but mostly I loved it because the guys were in such a better mood afterward. Last year, we lost two games, and Quinn and I avoided Cole like the plague for the rest of the weekend. Usually by Monday, he had cooled off. We learned the hard way freshman year, though, when he used to snap at us over absolutely nothing. It took us a while to realize that his attitude was related to football.

The team was walking along the field after the game, shaking hands with the opposing players. Quinn and I found the stairs and went down to meet up with them. She was walking at a much quicker pace than I was, and I had to take longer strides to keep up with her. I smiled as I watched her dodge and dart between the other players to get to Cole. When we reached him, she stepped right up to him and put her hands on each side of his face. I didn't hear what she asked, because I was still a couple of paces behind. His face became instantly serious and he nodded his head, looking directly into her eyes. They stared at each other for a bit until, surprisingly, Quinn took the initiative and crushed her lips to his. I froze in my steps.

Taking advantage of the opportunity, Cole extended his arm behind him and handed his helmet off to whoever would take it. Jace grabbed it from his hand. He brought both hands to Quinn's waist and walked her backward, never breaking the kiss. When the back of her legs knocked the bench, he sat her down while he kneeled on the ground in front of her, his knees in the dirt. He separated from her mouth and we all watched as he talked to her in a low voice. He looked like he was asking her questions while she would nod her head for a yes or shake it for a no.

I started to step forward so I could hear what they were talking about. These were my two best friends in the whole world, taking this monumental leap, and I just wanted to be there to see everything happen. Jaxon grabbed the hem of my shirt from behind and pulled me backward until I collided with his chest.

"Let them do it, Beautiful." I remained quiet and nodded, while I kept my eyes glued to the two of them.

From behind, I heard Jaxon ask his brother if he had a pen; then he reached around me, grabbed my hand, and started writing on it. I pulled my eyes away from my two friends on the bench who were deep in conversation, and watched Jaxon etching letters into my skin. His hands were sweaty and warm from playing, but I didn't mind. When he was done, he smiled at me and let my hand fall from his. I brought it up to read.

You're my favorite cheerleader.

I giggled at his message and playfully elbowed him. I knew I hadn't hurt him because my elbow hit his padding, but that didn't stop him from making a grunting noise.

When I finally heard Cole excitedly shout, "Really?" I turned away from Jaxon's.

Quinn nodded her head up and down, and then they both grabbed at each other and started kissing passionately. A couple of minutes later, they finally came up for air, but continued staring at each other and smiling. I couldn't hold it in any longer. I ran over to them and wrapped my arms around the both of them. Cole chuckled and wrapped his arms around the both of us and we all three sat there in a mixed-up hug.

When I was ready to give them their space again, I turned to Cole. "Are you okay, from earlier?" I asked, pointing out to the field where I could still picture him lying on the ground not moving.

"I'm good, Emmy, I just got my lights knocked out. When I came to, Jax was screaming in my damn face that he would kill me all over again if I didn't wake up." He laughed. I turned to look at Jaxon, who shrugged sheepishly.

I looked at Cole again and made a serious face. "If you hurt her, I'll castrate you, Cole West."

"Are you kidding me? I've been dreaming about this since orientation freshman year, when she let everyone in a five-yard vicinity know that I was a sex god!" he replied with a cocky tone, and I watched as Quinn blushed a deep scarlet.

We all waited outside of the locker room for the boys to go inside and change out of their uniforms. Quinn just leaned up against the wall with her fingers on her lips, smiling and looking off into the distance. I could take a guess as to where her mind was.

"This doesn't mean you get to move out, away from me," I said, while glaring at her with my arms crossed.

"No way. I'm not the let's-get-married-in-college type."

"Thank God." I hugged her tightly, hoping that wouldn't change anytime soon.

The guys came out, freshly showered with wet hair dripping down onto their clean shirts. Cole walked right past us, grabbed Quinn's hand, and kept walking.

"Hey, guys, wait a second. Quinn, you're totally not ditching me tonight to go get your love show on. You invited everyone over—you get an hour and a half, and then you better be back at our place! I mean it! This wasn't my idea."

Quinn frowned, forgetting she had suggested our place for the party. "Fine, we'll be there." Then they were gone, off into their own little world.

We got out to the truck with the motorcycle parked right next to it.

"Dude, I'll take the truck," Jaxon said to his brother as they exchanged keys.

"Hey, Jace, can I ride with you on that?" I tried to say it softly so only he could hear.

He gave me a strange look and said, "If you want to. I'm sure you'd have more fun riding with Jax, though."

"Shut up, Jace. Get in the truck, Emerson." Jaxon stepped in between us and opened the passenger door for me.

I leaned over to see Jace around Jaxon's body and said, "He won't ever take me on the motorcycle, but I've seen you ride around with girls. Please." I knew I was begging, but I really wanted to know what it felt like to be on one.

"What? Jax takes girls on this thing all the time," Jace said, shocked.

"Shut the hell up, man!" Jaxon yelled. "I haven't taken any girls on this bike since we've been in California." I watched as Jace shrugged his shoulders, got onto the bike, and started it up.

I turned around and stepped up into the truck. Jaxon tried to help me up, but I got into it before he could even touch me.

"Emerson, I don't take you on the bike because the idea of you getting hurt makes me physically sick to my stomach. I need you here." He patted the leather bench seat. "Safe, not on the back of a motorcycle where one mistake can end you. You're so small. It worries me even to think about you back there." He turned my body to face him and his hands were on my thighs.

"I don't need a protector, okay?" I breathed.

"I'm trying my fucking hardest here, Beautiful."

He stepped up into the cab and leaned in over me. His lips were hovering lightly over mine. I couldn't resist him when he was this close. I wrapped my arms around his neck and pulled him down on top of me as I lay back onto the leather. I knew anybody walking by would see our legs sticking out the open door, but I really didn't care right now. He kissed me hard and fast. I ran my hands down his back and dug my nails into him through his T-shirt. He groaned against my mouth, while I could feel how ready he was for me through his jeans.

He placed his hands down on the bench on either side of my head and started pushing away from me. "Emerson, no." I looked up at him, speechless. "You're not allowed to have sex for two weeks; if you keep this up, I'm not going to be able to say no soon."

Well, that was easy enough. I grabbed hold of his shirt and pulled him back down to me. He shook his head before our lips could meet and climbed off of me and out of the truck. He came around to the driver's side, scaled in, and started up the truck.

"Seriously?" I asked him. "This has never happened to me before." I actually couldn't believe this was happening; what guy denies sex? Especially with a girl he was obviously attracted to.

"Oh, trust me; I'm calling myself an idiot in about ten different languages at the moment." He avoided my gaze.

The drive back to the apartment was long and quiet. He had country music turned up loud while very softly he sang along. I loved listening to his voice and could melt into a puddle in his lap hearing him sing for the first time. I wanted him so badly. I needed to think of a way to change his mind. I knew how to seduce guys; I'd been doing it for years. There's no reason why I shouldn't be able to seduce Jaxon Riley. We pulled up to the apartment and he parked the truck in their designated garage. When he turned off the ignition, I quickly pulled my shirt over my head. I knew he would appreciate my lacy black bra.

"Fuck . . ." He instantly put his palms over his eyes.

I climbed over into his lap and straddled him. He still had his elbows in the air, with his palms pushing into his eyes.

"Emerson, you're cheating," he spoke in a breathy voice.

I leaned in very close to his lips and whispered, "No, I'm not." He let out a long, frustrated groan.

The cab of the truck was silent as he waited for my next move, or for me to get off. I reached behind and unclasped my bra. I grabbed his hands from his eyes. When I removed them from his face, his eyes slammed shut. I pulled his hands down to my chest and cupped each hand to me. He gently squeezed and moved his hands around slowly. I smiled when I saw his eyes open and look right at me. He brought a moan out of me with how good it felt to have him touching me again. The second he heard my moan, though, he lifted his hands away from me and put them behind his head.

With a cocky grin he said, "Uh-uh, you're not getting me like this. I'm going to make you wait two weeks, and then you'll be dying for me."

Just then, we heard the roar of a motorcycle pull into the garage next to the truck. Jace parked on the passenger side. When I realized

Jaxon wasn't kidding, I reached out and pulled the door lever. Before he could stop me, I slipped off his lap onto the ground.

I walked down the side while Jace was on the opposite side of the truck bed. Only my shoulders and head were visible to him. He looked at me and cocked an eyebrow.

"Um, Em, are you missing something?" he asked.

At the same time, Jaxon was jumping from his seat, standing right behind me, covering up my breasts with his hands. I tried my hardest to not close my eyes in that moment and make Jace uncomfortable. "Not funny, Emerson," he growled in my ear. "Keep walking, Jace."

"I took my shirt off to try to seduce your brother, but he refuses to have sex with me," I blatantly told Jace, pouting.

Jace bent over, laughing hysterically. "Oh, buddy; there is something wrong with you, Jax. I'd take care of you in a heartbeat, Emmy." Even though I knew he was kidding, I still smiled back at him.

When I perked up, Jaxon yelled, "Fucking leave, Jace!"

Jace walked up the stairs to the apartments, laughing. I turned around to face Jaxon. Still standing in front of me, he leaned over and grabbed my shirt from the truck. He slipped it over my head and pulled my arms through the holes as if I were a toddler.

"You're no fun." I stuck out my bottom lip to him.

He leaned down and bit it between his teeth, "I think you're enough fun for the both of us."

We walked up the stairs to our apartments. When I reached my door, he leaned over and kissed my cheek before continuing down to his.

Before he stepped inside, he said, "Jace and I are going to do a beer run to bring over tonight. Any requests?"

"Sex on the beach? Slippery nipple? Screaming orgasm?"

His eyes got dark as he looked at me. "Do you serve these often, Miss Bartender?"

Very slowly, I replied, "Every. Single. Night." His eyes widened as I walked in and closed my door before he could add anything else. Let him stew on that for a bit!

Great, now I was sexually frustrated and there was no way I could fix it. Well, technically, I know that I could go out and fix it and Jaxon would never know. For some reason, though, I knew I couldn't go back on our bet, especially since it was my idea. I don't doubt that he would have held up his end of the bargain if he had lost. That was two bets I had lost to him in a row. I needed either to step up my game, or to stop betting with the hot country boy.

SEVEN

By ten o'clock, people started arriving at our place, all on a high from the team's win. Quinn still hadn't come back down to our place. I had been texting her for the last thirty minutes with no reply. Jaxon was still out doing a beer run. Jace, who I guess decided not to go, had come over to help me rearrange furniture and move all the breakable things to a locked closet. We pushed chairs and tables against the wall to allow for more room. I put trash cans on the patio for the smokers and beer cans that will undoubtedly pile up. I walked down the hall to the guys' apartment. Just as I expected, Cole's door was closed.

"Quinn! I'm counting to three and then I'm dragging your butt out of there. You promised!" I heard shuffling around and laughing. "One . . . two . . . th—" I was interrupted by Cole opening the door in front of me with a huge grin on his face.

"Emmy, give us a break." He laughed. He only had a pair of navy blue boxers on.

I pushed past him and found Quinn buttoning up her shirt. I walked over and grabbed her arm as she reached the last button. "You've had your fun; you'll have plenty of time later for this business. There are five of us and Jace is the only one that's helped me so far. This wasn't even my idea." I walked her down the hallway to go out the door. She wasn't saying anything, just had a satisfied smile on her face. While it frustrated me that I was left to take care of her party, I was still really happy for her and Cole. I loved seeing her this peaceful and happy.

"Hey, I resent that," I heard Jaxon's voice saying from the doorway. "I just supplied your whole party with booze." He pointed down the hall. I lightly shoved Quinn toward the door to make sure she wasn't going to turn around for more lovin' from Mr. Cole West.

"Thanks, Jax, that was nice of you," Quinn said while walking past. Jaxon was still staring at me.

Before I could make a smart-ass comment to him, some random guy knocked on the open front door.

"Do you guys know the people next door? I have a delivery and they aren't home." He was wearing a shirt displaying a local florist shop's logo but was holding a giant box of chocolates.

"We live next door," I told him, gesturing to Quinn and me.

"Sweet. Then this is for Quinn Montgomery." She walked up to him with a confused look and took the box.

"I'm sorry, but I don't have any cash for a tip," she told him.

"No worries, I was paid a lot for this late-night delivery. He said you wouldn't be home till about now. You guys have a great night." He closed the door behind himself.

"What the hell, Quinn?" Cole stepped forward, now fully dressed.

"Don't 'what the hell' me; I have no idea." She slipped the little card out from the tiny envelope and read it. "It's just from one of the students I tutor. Here, Ems, go ahead and take out the one piece that you only ever eat." She handed me the monstrosity of chocolate.

"You're so weird about that, Em," Cole mentioned while he was trying to peek at the card Quinn was holding.

"Who needs this much chocolate?" I asked while sorting through for the lone piece of my favorite that's in every box.

"What does she mean 'the one piece you only eat'?" Jaxon stepped up behind me to ask.

"They usually only put one chocolate raspberry truffle in these things, and it's the only one I care about. Why they would have this giant box and only one raspberry is beyond me."

I finally found it and pulled it up to my lips. When I took a bite, my eyes rolled back in my head. I never buy candy, but every once in a while, someone will give Quinn or me a box, and waiting for just this one piece is worth it. When I opened my eyes, Jaxon was watching me intently with his hands gripping the countertop.

"Fuck, you can't keep doing that in front of me. At least not for the next two weeks," he said with a sigh. I darted my tongue out to taste the last half in my fingers, and I heard him groan while leaning forward closer to me.

Cole's deep voice shook me out of my Jaxon-seduction. "Bryce! This is from that asshole Bryce, Quinn?"

"Babe, we literally got together like two hours ago. No one knows yet. Give me a break!" she said while hugging him around the waist.

He started dragging her toward the front door. "You better damn well believe everyone will know on Monday," he grumbled and she patted his chest.

"Thanks again, Jax, for the alcohol," she sang while continuing down the hall to our place.

He looked right at me after she said that. "Don't look at me; I'm not thanking you. There was something I needed you to take care of earlier and I was embarrassingly denied," I said, walking past him.

He grabbed my arm before I could make it down the hall. "Wait, I embarrassed you?" he asked honestly with concern in his eyes. He backed me up and placed his hands on the wall on either side of my head.

"No, not really, but I was rejected while I had my breasts in your hands. I can definitely say that has never happened."

"Ask me again in two weeks and I fucking swear, I'll never say no again."

"I haven't gone two weeks since freshman year," I divulged nervously.

"Wow, really? Well, this will be good for you, then."

"You don't have to judge so loudly," I grumbled, trying to squeeze out from underneath his arms, and I heard him groan.

I should have known I wouldn't make it far. He scooped me up into his arms and carried me back into his apartment. He walked us to his room and kicked the door closed behind him. We sat back against his headboard on the bed with me in his lap.

"Emerson, I would never judge you. I, of all people, have no place to judge. I don't care what you've done," he said, looking into my eyes.

"It's okay; everyone does. I understand what people think of me."

"If they think you are beautiful, feisty, and brilliant, then I would agree with them. Anything else, I don't care about."

I should be pushing him away right now; that would be the smart thing to do. The more I let him get close to me like this, the more I know I'll only let him down. He just kept sneaking underneath more of my obstacles and I was standing on the sidelines watching it happen. I told him up front that I couldn't do relationships; I hope he understood that was still the case. I'm not sure if he has an ulterior motive by being this way with me.

He interrupted my fears by running his fingers through my hair and pulling my head toward him so our lips could meet. His kiss was aggressive and his tongue found mine quickly.

"Holy shit, you taste good." I could tell he tasted the chocolate from earlier, so I giggled.

I wasn't even thinking about my fears right now. The way he was kissing me was so overwhelming that I could think of nothing else. I pulled his shirt over his head and he didn't fight me. To my surprise, he pulled mine off as well. We were grabbing at each other like we needed to be inside of each other, as if each of us needed the other one to breathe.

My bra was still in his truck, so when he bent down and started kissing the swell of my breasts, I was surprised by the instant contact. Abruptly we heard a hard pounding on the other side of his door. All of a sudden, Cole burst through, startling me. Jaxon pulled me to his chest and laid his T-shirt across my naked back.

"Fuck, why are we always caught with your shirt off?" Jaxon grumbled.

"Oh, hell no, you guys get your asses up. There's no way you're going to interrupt Quinn's and my first day together, so y'all can turn around and do the same thing," Cole shouted.

"Okay, point made. Leave," Jaxon said in a hard voice.

"I'll wait; make sure you don't get lost along the way," Cole responded cheekily.

"Turn the hell around so she can get her shirt on, jackass."

He rolled his eyes and turned around. "Trust me; I've seen all of Em."

I felt Jaxon tense at that, and he dropped his hands from my back. It didn't matter how nice he tried to be, how understanding he wanted to be: It was always going to bother him that I sleep around. Even though I had reassured him I had never been with Cole, he still seemed perturbed by the fact that Cole had seen my body before. Cole has walked in on me many times; it's a hazard of my ways. His eyes wouldn't meet mine and he didn't move.

"Hey, nothing has happened between him and me. You know that, right?" I asked while grabbing at his face. He still didn't budge and his mind was still in some faraway place, so I helped him out. I got off his lap and threw my T-shirt back on. When he still hadn't moved, I walked out of the room. On my way out the door, I heard

Jaxon talking to Cole, but I didn't stick around to see what they were saying about me.

When I went back to the apartment, it was packed with football players, cheerleaders, frat guys, and everybody in between. I ran down to the closet and changed into one of Quinn's one-shoulder mini-dresses. This one was a deep red, and since it was Quinn's, it was a little tight in the chest . . . perfect. As I was pulling my hair up, I noticed Jaxon's message still on my hand. I doubt I'm his favorite right now.

An hour later, I was three margaritas into my night and there was no sign of Jaxon. I was in the kitchen playing bartender, as usual, with a hot guy I had never met before named Gage. He was pretty hands-on and I didn't mind, since he was helping me not to think about the fact that Jaxon couldn't even look at me. There were a bunch of guys at the dining table playing a drinking game. Every once in a while, someone from the table would shout for more beer or liquor from me.

After about the third shout, Gage hollered back, "Shut the hell up and get your own damn beer, you idiots!" He smirked at me.

"Thanks. I always get suckered into being the bartender." I smiled back. I noticed he took a final chug from his beer, so I popped open a new one for him. Old habits die hard. I also decided to switch to beer, because the tequila was going straight to my head. "Do you go to our school, Gage? I've never seen you around." I was pretty sure I would remember him, although he did look vaguely familiar.

"No, I go to Columbia University. I'm just out here visiting the little brother."

"Wow, Columbia. What a way to empty the parents' bank account."

He shrugged like it was no big deal. I understand that going to college in Southern California wasn't close to being cheap, but I tried to work as much as I could to offset those expenses.

"So who's your brother? I probably know him."

"Micah Woods. He's a Sig Alpha." Of course he was.

A couple of guys at the table started laughing and Garrett opened his big, fat mouth. "Oh yeah, she knows Micah, all right," he teased.

"Oh, Garrett, let's not talk about the time we 'got to know' each other. I know forty-five seconds was probably an all-time high for you, but trust me; most girls would prefer at least a minute," I scolded.

Everyone at the table, including Gage, started hooting with laughter. They all had their heads thrown back and were slamming their bottles on the table. There was a chorus of cuss words and slaps on Garrett's back.

"Yeah, yeah, Em, that was freshman year. Try me out again," Garrett laughed, taking the ribbing well.

I turned around and pulled more bottles and cans out of their boxes to put into the fridge for later. When I turned back around, Gage was right up against me.

"Let's go dance," he whispered into my ear. I thought he was hot, but I really didn't want to do anything with him. Honestly, I wanted to know why Jaxon never came. I was almost tempted to go down the hall and ask him myself. Almost. I hated that I was missing him. That thinking is exactly why I grabbed Gage's hand and pulled him out to the makeshift dance floor in our living room. I can't allow thoughts like that. This is who I am, right here on this dance floor with Gage.

When we got to the middle of all the other dancing bodies, I turned toward Gage and lifted my hands above my head. I started dancing in his wandering hands to the fast beat of the song. When I turned to my left, I noticed that Quinn and Cole were right next to us. I leaned over and bumped her with my hip. When she turned to look at me, she had a happy, glazed-over look in her eyes. Cole didn't even look in my direction; his face was stuck in the side of Quinn's neck. They were already disgustingly cute.

When Quinn finally noticed who I was dancing with, she gave me a confused look. "Where's Jax?"

I shrugged my shoulders at her. "Not here," I said and turned back toward Gage.

He leaned down and asked, "Who's Jax?"

The last person I wanted to talk with about Jaxon was this guy. I turned around in his arms to grind up against him. I heard him groan when he grabbed my hips to pull me in closer. I knew the question was lost with each move of my hips. This was what I was good at. This was what I did. Not wondering about some guy with a sexy southern accent. He turned me around and dipped down to trail his lips up the line of my jaw to just behind my ear.

He straightened up and said, "Wanna get out of here? My car's outside." I stared into his eyes for a long moment trying to figure out what I wanted to do.

"Yeah, that's not going to happen."

Startled, I turned to see Jaxon standing right next to us, glaring down. He was a good three inches taller than Gage and had about forty more pounds of muscle. The contrast between them was staggering; I hadn't realized how big Jaxon was. I always saw him next to his identical twin brother and Cole, who was equally built. I was so shocked at my comparison that I forgot to respond to Jaxon's statement.

Gage raised his hands from around my waist, "Sorry, man, didn't realize she was taken."

I should've been angry at the fact that he thought I could so easily cheat on my boyfriend, if that's what Jaxon actually had been. But he wasn't. I waited for Jaxon to correct him—to say something—because not saying anything at all was pissing me off. I wasn't anyone's.

"*She* is not taken, thank you very much!" I yelled over the music at both of them. When I started pushing my way through the writhing bodies, Jaxon caught my arm. I spun around to glare at him. Gage had already pulled one of the sorority bimbos into his arms. Typical.

"I'm sorry, Emerson." He pulled me up against his chest. "I shouldn't have left that open like that." I enjoyed the feel of his chest against my face; his warm scent assaulted me every time. When he bent down and pulled me into a fervent kiss, I noticed the room got a little bit quieter. I pushed away from him when I realized that it was quiet because they were all gawking at us.

"No! Just back off, Jaxon!" I yelled.

I was scared. I didn't want people thinking that I belonged to someone. That can never happen. I was also mad at him for shutting down on me earlier. The instant the words left my mouth, I realized how much of a bitch I had just been to him. I watched as his face dropped and his hands moved away from me. It took him a second to compose himself, but then his face hardened and he nodded his head as he backed away. I walked over to the kitchen to open another beer.

When I leaned against the counter looking out into the living room, I noticed Jaxon was still on the "dance floor" in the middle. He walked up to Rachel Morgan, who was sitting in one of the chairs that was pushed up against the wall. She looked up at him with seduction in her eyes. I wondered what kind of look he was giving her—if it was the same look that made my knees weak, the same look he had just given me in his bed before we had this freaking party. I watched as he pushed her hair away from her ear and he slowly bent down to whisper something in it. Her face lit up and she nodded her head up and down. She stood up and he held out his hand for hers. When she grabbed his hand and he led her to the door, it was then I realized he was leaving with her, and my stomach dropped.

Jace walked over and caught them at the front door. "Don't do this, man."

"Do what? Leave with a girl who actually wants to be with me?" he questioned rhetorically, as he walked out the door with Rachel in tow.

I slumped a little bit against the counter. Jace, Cole, and Quinn all walked over to me in the kitchen.

"Em, go stop him. Apologize!" Quinn begged me.

"Apologize for what? For being completely honest? It's better that I upset him now than destroy him later, if it even made it that far. I can't be with anyone. It doesn't work. Even Jace warned me not to hurt him." I turned to the liquor bottles on the counter and started searching through them. When I didn't find what I wanted, I turned to look in the cabinet above the fridge. Even standing on my tiptoes, I was still inches away from reaching into the cabinet.

"What are you looking for, Em? I'll get it," Jace said from beside me.

"No, I need to find it." I went to the counter to get on top of it, but Jace lifted me up by the waist so I could reach. I dug past all the other bottles, the glass clinking together loudly, until I found the tequila I wanted. Jace set me back down on my feet.

"No way! Put that stuff back," Quinn said, pointing to the expensive tequila, like it might jump out and bite her. It was an old bottle that used to belong to my dad; I'm pretty sure it was a gift because he rarely ever drank any of it.

Ignoring her, I grabbed a clean shot glass from the cabinet below. I knew better than to shoot expensive tequila, but I needed this in me via the quickest route I could get. I wanted to forget about where Jaxon may have taken Rachel and forget about what they could be doing right now, possibly right next door. Hadn't I been the one telling him we would still be sleeping with other people? I should be happy he was holding up his end. I needed to wash away Emerson and be Em again. I lifted the old bottle and poured the golden liquid into the shot glass with CANCUN, MEXICO imprinted on the side. I remember getting this glass on a trip I took with my dad, Ellie, and Quinn when I was fourteen years old, the summer before he died. I guess it was fitting I was pouring his drink into this glass.

"Anyone joining me?" I looked around at the three sullen faces staring back at me. I couldn't tell if they felt bad for me that Jaxon left with Rachel, or if they were disappointed in me for being the reason he left in the first place. No one stepped up to join. "Suit yourselves."

"I'll join you, Emmy!" Micah boomed as he came toward the entrance of the kitchen. Instantly, Jace and Cole held out their arms to bar him from coming in. "Fine, assholes. You know I'm getting really tired of you and your cock-blocking brother," he said, pointing to Jace while he turned to go out onto the patio.

I shrugged my shoulders, not having the energy to get upset with yet another person for making decisions for me again.

"Here's to losing Emerson, and finding Em again!" I raised the shot glass in the air.

I carried it back down to my lips and poured the liquid into my mouth. To compensate for shooting expensive tequila, I held it on my tongue for a couple seconds to savor the taste. The smooth burn down my throat made me slam the glass on the granite countertop.

"I was enjoying Emerson," Quinn stated with a sad look on her face.

"Okay, are you done now?" Cole asked me with a worried expression.

"Cole, I know all you want to do right now is take Quinn back to your place. I don't need a babysitter. You guys can go," I snapped, while pouring another round.

He stepped up and grabbed the bottle from my hand while moving the shot back with the other. "Right now, all I care about is making sure that one of my best friends isn't going to drink herself into the hospital tonight. You're upset and that's okay; just please don't be stupid."

I reached around him and downed the second shot. I stepped past the three of them and moved to the middle of the dance floor. I lost myself in the thumping of the music, the smell of sweat rolling off of bodies around me, and the feel of my body dancing to the music. I needed to get off this treacherous path that I was finding myself on. I'm not sure how much time went by, but I know that when I stumbled into the kitchen later that night, I was a couple of shots drunker. I'm pretty sure the word for me wasn't *drunk* anymore, it was *wasted*. Quinn, Cole, and Jace had stayed in the kitchen to keep an eye on me, even though I had told them to leave; I was a big girl.

When I came in and saw Jace, I knew it was Jace, but he just looked so much like Jaxon. I wondered what kind of look I was giving him because he looked a little worried. I couldn't stop myself from going up to him and putting my hands around his neck. The only thing that stopped me from trying to kiss him right then was the fact that he didn't smell the same as Jaxon. I don't know what kind of cologne Jaxon wore, but it lingered in all of his clothes and I smelled it in my dreams. I loved when he would come over to study, because when he sat on my bed, I swear I could smell his cologne for days.

"Why do you have to look so much like him?" I slurred into his chest.

He rubbed my back. "Are you kidding me? I'm the good-looking one." I tried to laugh at his attempt at a joke.

"I like him a lot. I like him so much it hurts," I drunkenly admitted.

He leaned down to whisper in my ear, so he could give our conversation some privacy. "I know he feels the same way about you. You have to let him in."

"I wish I could. I wish I were that type of girl." A tear slipped down my cheek and Jace wiped it away with his thumb. "I'm sorry, I'm drunk and I'm rambling. Now I'm crying in front of his twin brother like some idiotic girl."

"Hey, don't say that. I would rather you ramble to me than to anyone else. Unless it was Jaxon himself." I leaned more of my weight into his body as I began to get tired from all the alcohol in my system.

"Em, let's get you into your bed before you pass out," Quinn came over to say to me.

"Please don't. Jaxon and I share a bedroom wall and right now, I just can't handle that. When everyone leaves, I'll crash on the couch," I said, incoherently, I'm sure.

"Shit, I forgot about that," Cole said. "Well, it's too loud over here anyway. You and Quinn can take my bed."

"I don't want to hear anything, Cole. I can't go over there."

"You have to sleep somewhere, and it's not going to be alone. Come," he spoke, kindly.

"I'll shut this place down," Jace said while transferring me over to Cole.

Cole and Quinn helped me get down the hallway to the guys' apartment. I was dreading the idea of running into Jax or Rachel. When we got to the apartment, it was blissfully quiet and dark. I didn't want to think about where they would have gone instead. We walked into Cole's room and he handed Quinn and me both some big T-shirts we could wear to bed. Quinn helped me out of her dress and tossed it on the ground.

"Fuck, I'm living every guy's dream right now. Two girls in my bedroom helping each other out of their clothes," Cole said with a laugh.

"Yeah, except there's no way you're getting laid tonight." Quinn winked at him.

"And . . . my bubble gets popped," he groaned sarcastically.

I grumbled. "Guys, I'm ruining your first night together. Please just let me sleep on the couch. I can't do this to you. I love that you're finally together."

Cole came over and wrapped me in a bear hug. "Quinn's not just a fling for me; I'm in it for the long run with her. Which means we have a million more nights. Right now, we need to make sure our best friend, who is drunk off her ass, is safe."

Quinn grabbed my hand and pulled me into Cole's large king-size bed. She pushed me down and lay next to me. Cole came in and lay down next to Quinn. I remember mumbling a "thank you" to my best friends before passing out.

I don't know how long I was sleeping before I was jostled awake by warm hands and angry whispers.

"Dude, leave her here, and go back to bed. You can talk to her tomorrow. It was a rough night for her."

"I know. Jace told me and that's exactly why I'm taking her back to my room."

"Jax, I'm being completely serious, don't fuck with her."

"I need her next to me right now."

"She's going to be so pissed."

"She'll forgive me."

"She's so drunk; please just make sure and watch her."

I was being lifted up off the bed into a warm, bare chest. I snuggled in closer, smelling my favorite scent. I locked my hands around his neck and sighed. Shortly after I was picked up, I felt a soft mattress underneath me again. Strong hands came up from behind me and pulled me back into a hard body. A comforter was pulled up and over me.

"I'm so sorry, Beautiful," the angel voice whispered before I passed out again in an alcohol-induced haze.

- EIGHT -

When I woke up the next morning, my face was smashed up against hot skin and my body was overheating. I started feeling around and realized it was Jaxon's solid body lying curled around me, with my face in his chest. He had his chin resting on the top of my head and one leg draped over my hip. His slow breaths coming in and out were blowing wisps of my hair back and forth. When I fell asleep last night, I'm pretty sure I was in Cole's bed with him and Quinn. I started remembering the angry whispered conversation and Jaxon picking me up and bringing me to his bed.

Last night wasn't a good night for me. I was a bitch to him because he made people think that we were together. I hurt him and he left with Rachel. I drank way too much beer and tequila. Thank God, I wasn't the type to ever get drunk enough to throw up, because if I had, it would have been an even worse story. I remembered babbling to Jace about his brother. I'm pretty sure I cried in front of him. Then it hit me—Jaxon had left to be with Rachel last night, and when he finally came back, he pulled me into bed with him? That was wrong on so many levels. I'm the queen of sleeping around, but I would never sleep with one guy and go get in bed with another on the same night. That was tacky. I needed to get away from him. I was too close to his delicious-smelling skin, but I know that Rachel was all over him last night. Who could blame her?

I slowly lifted his arm off of me, moved it down to his side, and then gradually rolled over to the edge of the bed. I felt Jaxon reach out for me in his sleep, so I darted away from his searching hand. He mumbled something about "beautiful" and rolled onto his stomach. Thank goodness, he was a heavy sleeper. I didn't want to have the conversation I'm sure he was anticipating we would have this morning. I only had on Cole's T-shirt and a pair of panties, and I'm thankful for Cole's height because this shirt went all the way past my knees.

When I stepped out into the hallway, I grimaced because I could hear Quinn and Cole making up for lost time last night. I was happy for my best friends, but I absolutely did *not* want to hear this. I hurried to the bathroom and when I finished, I washed my hands and used the mouthwash that was on the counter. It didn't help. I needed to get down to my apartment to brush out the aftertaste of tequila, beer, and sleep. I walked past the kitchen, heading for the front door, when I noticed that the clock in the living room said it was only seven in the morning.

"Sneaking out?"

I jumped at the sound of a voice. "Holy Crap, Jace. Why are you awake?"

He was pulling earbuds from his iPod out of his ears and gestured at the four textbooks lying open in front of him. "Damn, those two are still going at it?" He pointed toward Cole's room and scowled at the noise.

"Yeah, that's why I need to get out of here." I was only half-lying.

"Right . . . it doesn't have anything to do with a certain guy that might resemble me, does it?" He smirked.

"I'm not sneaking out. Thanks for telling him about last night, by the way."

"Em, he came back here in a pissed-off mood last night and all I said was that it wasn't a picnic for you here, either. I swear." I nodded at him. "Oh, and if you actually do happen to be sneaking out, I'd hurry it up. He never sleeps in."

With that, I slipped out the door quietly and walked down to our apartment. I decided I needed to go for a run before I had to go to work. I made a quick breakfast for my empty stomach and changed into a running bra and shorts. As I was tying my sneakers, I heard the beeping tone of a text message on my phone.

Jaxon: You snuck out. Can I come over?

I decided I didn't have time to text back. I needed air immediately. I stepped out of the apartment and jogged down the hallway. When I made it outside and down the stairs, I almost got to the street before I heard my name called from across the parking lot. I pretended that I didn't hear it and turned for the road.

I usually ran toward the beach; it was a good marker for me to know how far I had run. The beach was also a good spot to stop midway and rest. Today I decided to run in the opposite direction for a change of pace.

I wasn't sure what I should do about Jaxon. I liked being around him, and it wasn't just the sex that I enjoyed with him. I liked the way he made me feel that I didn't need to sleep with anyone else. Hell, I didn't want to, for that matter. I thought two weeks without sex would be difficult, but the only reason they would be hard is because I couldn't sleep with *him* for two weeks. I loved the way he made me feel so safe when I was around him, as though he would protect me no matter what, even if I didn't need it. Why couldn't I just let him protect my heart as well? Why couldn't I just live in the moment, relationship-wise, like everyone else in college? Quinn and Cole were finally doing it. I was worried about the future, about deaths and cheating. I couldn't handle being left behind again the way my parents left me, hurting a trail of people in their departure.

I just needed some distance from him to gain some perspective. Once I wasn't around him all the time, I'd remember the reasons I originally had for not getting into a relationship. I was too easily distracted by a deep, sexy voice, miles of muscles on a tall body, and blue eyes that could read your soul.

Running toward the east, I encountered more hills than I was used to running. It felt good to push myself harder. Today I needed to be pushed. I ached for that runner's high and that little bit of euphoria that I could only get from pounding my feet into the pavement. I didn't know how long I had been running until I passed a bank and the sign read almost 9:45.

Crap! I had been running for over an hour and a half. I needed to hustle back if I was going to get home to shower and get ready for work on time. As I started to spin back around, my feet hit some loose gravel on the sidewalk and I went down face-first. Luckily, I only scraped my lip across the gravel before my hands finally caught the rest of my face from smashing. Great, now my lip was bleeding and my palms were all scratched up.

It took me just as long to get back to the apartment, if not longer, because I had to keep wiping blood from my face. When I walked in my front door, I was drenched in sweat. Quinn was sitting on the couch with her phone in her hand. When she saw me, she jumped up and ran toward me. She crashed right into me and held me so hard I could barely breathe.

"Quinn, stop. I'm sweaty, bloody, and I can't breathe," I gasped.

"*You idiot*, where have you been?" she yelled.

"I was running, and besides, I left you a note on the fridge."

"Jaxon said he saw you leaving three hours ago, and you *never* run for more than an hour."

"I'm sorry, I had a lot on my mind and I went farther than I thought. Besides, you and Cole were occupied this morning anyway."

"What the hell happened to you?" She gestured toward my fat lip.

"I fell in some loose gravel. I'm sure it'll look better after I wash off."

"Shit! Cole and Jax went to look for you. I need to call them," she said while dialing her phone.

"You guys are so ridiculous." I walked to the bathroom for a shower and heard her saying that I had made it home.

I washed my hair and shaved my legs. I mostly just stood under the spray of the water with it turned on as hot as I could stand it. There were still tiny pieces of gravel embedded in my palms, which I gently removed. When I got out, I brushed out my hair and scrubbed my teeth until they felt clean again. My bottom lip was so swollen it looked like I had been punched. When I walked out of the bathroom, Cole looked down the hallway and saw me walking toward my door. He met me halfway.

"Em, why are you scaring the hell out of me lately?"

"I'm fine. I didn't mean to scare anyone."

"Jax is going to freak when he sees your lips."

"Just don't tell him about it. I'm sure the swelling will go down soon," I responded.

I walked into my room and closed the door behind me. Sitting down on the edge of my bed with a towel wrapped around me, I thought about everything that had been going on lately. I felt like a mess. I was usually so in control, but now I felt as if I didn't have an ounce of it. I wasn't surprised when my door flung open and Jaxon walked in. I fell backward onto my bed, looking up at the ceiling.

"Jaxon, I can't do this right now," I said, frustrated.

He climbed up onto my bed and looked down at me. He ran the pad of his thumb over my swollen lip. "Emerson, what happened?"

"I fell. I'm fine, but I'm going to be late for work if I don't hurry up." Although my argument was a little weak, considering I wasn't attempting to move from my position on the bed. Having his gorgeous body leaning over me again had me frozen with desire.

"Please stop running from me," he whispered.

"Please stop trying to catch me," I said, getting up to leave.

He grabbed my hand and squeezed. "I didn't sleep with her. All I did was take her home. She was pissed, but that's all that happened."

"There's no reason to tell me this—"

"Damn it, Emerson, just stop!" he yelled. "Stop pretending you don't care. Why won't you let me in? Why won't you let me care about you? Because for some maddening reason, I do!"

"I warned you from the beginning. Don't make me out to be the bad person here."

"Emerson, I know we would be great together. You're scared, and I get that. I swear I won't get all crazy-serious. Just give us a shot."

He was starting to break me down the longer I stood here. I needed to leave. "We're just having fun, Jaxon, and that's it."

He lowered his head to his hand and pinched the bridge of his nose. I heard him inhale and exhale slowly while silently warring with himself. When he lifted his head to look me in the eyes for a couple of seconds, I didn't say anything, so he turned around and left my room. I heard Quinn and Cole talking to him before the front door opened and slammed shut. How come every time I wanted to avoid hurting him, all I did was hurt him more?

When I was finished getting dressed, I came back out to the living room to grab my purse and keys. Cole and Quinn were lying on the couch together and Jaxon was gone.

"Don't look at me like that, you two. I'm super happy you finally opened your eyes and now you have each other, but that doesn't mean it's the same for everyone else."

Quinn gave me a sympathetic glance and Cole looked as if he was dying to say something. "Spit it out, Coley."

"You could at least explain to him why you are the way you are. He's crazy about you and I know you are about him." When I rolled my eyes, he retorted, "Don't give me that look, because you're lying to yourself if you think that's not true. We're all here waiting for *you* to open your eyes now, love." Usually his term of endearment was like a lovable big brother; now it just sounded patronizing.

"I was honest from the very beginning. I don't do relationships! It's not something that's going to change just because some gorgeous guy walks into my life."

When I turned the doorknob to leave, Quinn sat up and said, "I love you, Emmy."

~

It was a rough night at work for me. I wasn't as flirty and nice to the customers as I typically would be. Even Ed came out and asked me what was wrong, and when I told him I was fine, he shrugged his shoulders and went back to his office.

One of the regulars, Joe, came up to the bar to talk to me. "Hey, Em, did your boyfriend knock you around or something? What's up with the fat lip?"

"No, this was my own stupid fault. I fell," I said, motioning to my lip.

"All right, well if you ever need me to kick some jerk's ass, you just let me know," he said while holding his fist up like he was in a boxing ring.

Joe was about seventy-five years old and skinnier than my twelve-year-old cousin. But he always kept me company on slow nights at the bar. One time, he told me how his wife had died of cancer about a year ago. They had been together over fifty years. I'm not sure how he could be so happy when his other half just left him here all alone.

"Hey, Joe, can I ask you a personal question?"

"No question is a personal question for me. Shoot," he answered back, while I poured him a Sprite, his drink of choice.

"How are you so happy after your wife, your best friend, died? I just don't think I could come back from something like that. I know I couldn't be as happy as you are."

"Didn't you tell me once that you lost your mom and dad a couple of years ago, kiddo?" he asked.

"Yes, sir, I did," I replied solemnly.

"And yet, here you are functioning perfectly fine. I've seen you with those three boys and that beautiful girl Quinn in here; you're always so happy when they're around. Just because someone you loved dies, it doesn't mean that your world ends as well." When he noticed his reply didn't seem to help, he took a long sigh and continued, "The first year after Violet died, I felt paralyzed, as if she had frozen time around me when she left. Then I realized I'm still here and I can keep going, or stay in the same spot forever and be unhappy. I decided to keep going and live my life fully, because I would want Violet to do the same thing if the roles had been reversed."

"It sounds so easy when you say it like that." I sighed.

"Once you think about it, it is that easy." He smiled at me.

He patted my hand and walked back to his pool table with his drink in hand. I felt like such a chicken. Here I was afraid just to date someone because the idea of losing him in the future was so painful. I wasn't completely delusional. I knew that if I allowed it, Jaxon and I could have something great. I'd been shown glimpses of that already. I also knew how easily I could screw it up and he'd be gone, leaving me shattered. Yet Joe can still be happy after actually losing his wife of fifty-plus years. At times like these I craved advice from my mom. Ellie has always made it known that I could come to her for anything, and over the years she has become my mom, in a way. I took out my phone and texted her.

Me: Can I come home for a couple days?

Ellie: Come home tonight. I'll have chocolate ready.

No one has a better stepmom than I do. Ellie has never tried to force me to talk about any of my issues. She was always just there whenever I needed her, any time of the day or night. Before I left, I asked Ed if it would be all right if I took off the remainder of the week. He took one look at my fat lip and nodded. I almost told him my lip had nothing to do with it, but I decided not to push my luck.

I didn't even go back to the apartment. I still had a ton of clothes at home that I could change into when I got there.

> Me: Quinny, I'm going home for a couple days, probably all week. Enjoy the apartment alone with Cole. xoxo
>
> Quinn: Come get me. I'll come too.
>
> Me: No, I know you have a test this week. You already told me about it.
>
> Quinn: If you need to go home, I need to be with you.
>
> Me: Ellie will take care of me. It's nothing serious. I just need a refresh.
>
> Quinn: I love you.
>
> Me: xoxo

I got home late that night. Ellie and Charles lived about an hour away from campus. She told me that Charles was away on a business meeting, so she was excited that I decided to come back home and keep her company. Ellie didn't have to work anymore because Charles made more than enough to support us all. She did have to attend a bunch of fund-raisers and special dinners with her husband, so that was almost a full-time job in itself.

It was dark when I walked into the house. I tiptoed up the stairs and peeked into the master bedroom. She was lying in bed and when she saw me peek in, she lifted the covers gesturing for me to climb in. I instantly scooted in next to her while simultaneously kicking off my shoes. I loved coming back here because it was home to me. Ellie had always made me feel completely comfortable.

"It's good to see you, little girl," she said in a tired voice.

"It's nice to be back." I yawned. She tucked me in and I passed out quickly after.

~

The first couple of days I was there, we lay out by the pool, went shopping, and ate delicious meals downtown. She loved to spoil Quinn and me when we came home. At one point, Jace had started texting me to ask if I was okay. I always smiled at his concerned messages. Quinn would call me every day to ask when I was coming back, and even Cole would get on the phone to ask if he could come get me yet. I never heard from Jaxon, but who could blame him? I wouldn't want to talk to me either after how I'd acted toward him.

By Saturday, I knew I would have to go back to the apartment and school soon. I had skipped classes all week, and if I didn't want to be dropped by my professors, I needed to make all of my classes for the rest of the semester. I also had a lot of studying to do to make up for this past week. Cole was upset that I had missed their game yesterday, but he called last night to give me the play-by-play. I didn't have the heart to tell him that I didn't want to hear about Jaxon scoring the winning touchdown again.

"Okay, little girl, it's time to fess up. It's not that I don't love the alone time with you, but I know you had classes this past week. Spill the beans," Ellie said to me out by the pool.

"I'm just a really messed-up person. I don't know how to handle life like every other normal college student out there." I sighed.

"I highly doubt that, Emerson." Ellie had never really gotten on the Em train, either.

"Yeah, I am. I made all these rules for myself to keep people at bay. I just wanted to have fun with guys. I didn't want any of them to actually stick around and become anything serious. I can't be left behind again like I was with Mom and Dad. Not only did they both go and die at the same time, but even worse, they were cheating as well." I'd never, ever come out and said the word *cheating* when talking about my parents to Ellie.

She sighed. "I wish I would have known all of this, Emerson. I'm supposed to be able to help you go on with your life. Maybe by not forcing you to talk to me more, I enabled you to hold back like this. First of all, we can't do anything about the fact that they died. Second of all, of course I have always wondered why they were in that car together, but we can't just assume they were having an affair."

I started to insert my opinion and tell her there could be no other reason. She interrupted me. "So what if they were. Life can hurt sometimes, but you know what? I wouldn't have traded a single second I had with your dad. I was happy and he gave me a bigger family than I had before I met him. Don't hold back your life because of the choices someone else made. Now, quit stalling and tell me about the boy." She smiled.

"Cole had his friends from Texas move into his apartment with him. They're twin brothers, Ellie, and they are so hot!" She giggled at my excitement.

"Well, which one caught your eye, and please don't say both . . . I can't handle that," she asked.

"Of course they both caught my eye! Did I mention that they're identical twin brothers?"

She shook her head and smiled at me. "Which one has you running back home, though?"

"Okay, okay. So Jaxon is the one that seems to be turning my world upside down. I've never cared if I hurt someone. With him, I feel like I'm doing everything to avoid hurting him, but then that's all I end up doing."

"Well, that's easy. Just stop hurting him," she laughed.

I lay back down with my palms on my eyes and groaned, "I've already done too much damage now. He hasn't said anything to me all week, and even his brother, Jace, has texted me daily to check up. I wouldn't want to talk to me either after how I treated him, though."

"Honey, have you ever thought that his brother is checking up on you for Jaxon's benefit?"

I thought about that for a second. "It's possible, but Jace is also just a really nice guy."

"You just need to go back there and let him know you're truly sorry, and you want to give him a shot."

"I can't do a relationship, though. I don't know how to act or what to do. I know I'll end up ruining it somehow."

"If this guy knows you, then I'm sure he'll be willing to grade you on a curve," she said while winking at me.

"A relationship scares me to death."

"I know, but it'll be worth it. I promise," she replied, sliding her sunglasses back down over her eyes and laying back on the lounger.

I pulled out my phone to text Quinn.

Me: I'm coming back tonight. I need to make things right with Jaxon.

Quinn: Err . . . Call me before you do anything Jaxon-related.

Me: Ok? I'll just talk to you when I get home.

Quinn: Drive safe. xoxo

- NINE -

I pulled up to the apartments and parked the car. I'd decided to bring back a couple of outfits I had previously forgotten from home, and some more that Ellie had bought while we were out shopping. As I was hauling my bag out of the trunk, I saw Jace jogging down the steps toward me.

"Hey, stranger, I missed you." He smiled and pulled me into a bear hug.

"I think I kind of missed you too," I confessed. He grabbed my bag and slung it over his shoulder. "Is Jaxon here?"

"Uh . . . yeah, but I think he's busy right now," he replied awkwardly and walked up the stairs with me to my apartment.

"Why is everyone being so weird when I mention Jaxon?"

When we got down the hallway, a tall brunette in cute little pajamas walked out of Cole's apartment and I heard Jace sigh under his breath.

"Is she here for you?" I asked him in a whisper.

"Hell, no," he replied irritably.

"Oh," was all I could say.

That could only mean one thing, because I knew she sure as hell wasn't here for Cole. My stomach hit the floor along with my heart. It figures, though, that right when I decide maybe I can try this relationship thing on for size, the person I wanted has already moved on to someone else. It serves me right for being such a bitch to Jaxon in the first place. He finally went off and found someone that actually wanted him.

"You must be the golden girl, Em, that all of my boys are talking about," she said to me icily when we approached her.

"Audrey, we aren't your boys, so turn around and walk back inside," Jace said to her, seething.

Before either of us could say anything else, Quinn whipped our door open and pulled me inside. Jace squeezed in behind me before she could slam him out.

"Ugh! I was hoping you wouldn't come across the she-devil," Quinn said.

"Who is she?" I asked softly, not sure I wanted to know the answer.

"Audrey," Quinn said in her high-pitched, singsongy voice that I knew meant she didn't like someone.

"Well I got that much, but what's going on?" I asked.

Jace put my bag down on the dining room table and went to join Cole on the couch. Both of them looked at me apologetically; that's when I knew this wasn't good.

"These guys won't help out. Trust me, I've been drilling them all week."

"It's not for us to tell. It's Jaxon's business, baby," Cole claimed, looking defeated.

She ignored them and dragged me down the hallway to my room. I placed my bag on the bed and opened it up to unpack. Going home was so relaxing, and I'm thankful I was able to get Ellie all to myself. I'd only been back here for two minutes, and I feel like all that relaxation and reassurance was flying out the window faster than I could catch it. Quinn sat down in a blue wing chair that I had at my desk while I sat on the edge of my bed.

"She's the worst, Emmy. I refuse to even step foot into their apartment as long as she's there."

"I'm so confused. I have no idea what is going on. You have to remember when I left, Jaxon was asking me out!" I responded.

"I don't know who she is, just that she showed up here earlier this week. Cole said that she went to high school with all of them and she has history with Jaxon. Their stupid bro-code is stopping them from saying anything. I can't hold Jaxon down long enough to ask him. It's so frustrating. I've barely talked to Cole all week."

"Okay, first of all, Quinn, you were supposed to enjoy this week of having the apartment all alone with Cole!" I hollered at her. "I don't care what kind of drama Jaxon has; you need to make up with Cole."

I jumped off the bed and shouted for Cole down the hallway. I heard Quinn groan from behind me, but knew this was for the better. Cole made his way down and into my room; he looked really overwhelmed. Quinn had not gone easy on him.

Jace poked his head in. "Mind if I join, or am I interrupting something private?"

"Get over here, gorgeous." I patted the spot next to me on the bed and he hopped on right beside me. I appreciated when he slid his shoes off so they weren't on my white comforter.

Cole stood leaning against the doorframe. "Ems, I've already said this to Quinn a thousand times. It's not my place to tell you all of Jaxon's business, and I have no idea why she's here now."

"Let's get this straight. I may have had a different assumption of what would happen when I came back here and could finally talk to Jaxon. But, right now, I just can't worry over any of that. You and Quinn are being silly. Quinn, don't get upset over what's going on with Jaxon and respect that Cole's not going to gossip," I begged her.

"Fine . . ." she said quietly.

Cole beamed as though I had just lifted a huge weight from his shoulders. He came over to Quinn and picked her up to place her in his lap in the chair. I fell backward onto my bed and sighed. Jace scooted back, lying down on his side and looking over at me with his hand propping his head up.

Cole had started roaming Quinn's body with his hands. Clearly, he hadn't gotten much this week with a stressed-out Quinn. I snapped my fingers to get them to stop.

"No way, that's not happening right in front of me." I pointed to my door.

"Sorry, Emmy, we'll talk more later." She smiled at me and I nodded.

"I freaking love you, Ems! I knew I should have gone and brought you back," Cole said, walking out the door with Quinn in tow.

"Hey! Shouldn't you be saying that to your girlfriend instead of my best friend?" She fake-pouted. He continued to push her out the door and we heard him sweet-talking her all the way into her room.

"Oh God, did you have to listen to *that* all week?" I looked over at Jace, giving him my best sympathetic look.

"No, it was worse. I had to listen to them fight and get all sexually frustrated with each other. It was better than hanging out next door, though," he groaned.

I didn't know how to respond to that last part. What was going on next door? Have those two been alone in that apartment all week? If this was someone from Jaxon's past and he was letting her stay with him all week, I couldn't compete with a past love.

The way Jace was lounging on my bed, I could see down his shirt through the open collar. I noticed familiar black intricate lines touching his collarbone. I slipped my finger onto the collar of his shirt and tugged it across his shoulder.

"You have the same tattoo as Jaxon? Is that a requirement, if one twin gets a tattoo the other must as well, so they can remain identical?" I asked, shocked.

He laughed at my stunned face. "No, I don't think it's a requirement. We just got them together after our dad died. If you look closely, they aren't the exact same, but from afar, they appear that way."

"I had no idea that your dad passed away." This was difficult territory for me.

"I suppose you didn't. Jaxon never talks about it."

"When did it happen?"

"When we were seventeen, he went on a business trip to Colorado and his plane had engine failure and went down. Jaxon went a little wild after that; our mom kind of let him get away with murder because she knew he was grieving. He's gotten a lot better, though. He seemed really happy when we got here, a lot happier than I've ever seen him. I can't help but wonder if it had anything to do with a certain frustrating blonde, though." He laughed and nudged me.

"My parents died when I was fifteen. I can understand going wild after something like that," I replied morosely.

He ran his hand through his hair like I'd seen Jaxon do a million times. "Shit, Em, I had no idea. I'm sorry."

"Don't be sorry, it wasn't your fault."

"Have you told Jax?"

I shook my head and continued to stare at the ceiling.

"You guys really need to talk more," he replied.

"Has she been staying there?" I knew that I didn't need to clarify whom I was talking about. It wasn't any of my business, but I was hoping Jace could help me out.

"Em, earlier you said you had some assumptions of what would happen when you got back here, and those obviously didn't pan out," he said, ignoring my question. "Did you come back to make up with Jaxon?" His voice had taken on a serious tone, but his face didn't look upset at that prospect.

I rolled over onto my stomach to hide my face in the crook of my elbow. I just wanted to forget that this whole Jaxon thing ever happened. I wish that I could ignore the fact that I had developed all these feelings for him, that I had decided to let down my guard, and now the door was being slammed in my face. I knew Jace wasn't going to let it go.

"It's okay if you did," he said, interrupting my thoughts. "I think you need to talk to him; he really needs to hear what you have to say."

"Like you said earlier, he's busy," I replied in a clipped tone.

"Call him, text him, meet up with him somewhere. Please just tell him. I don't know why Audrey's here, but she's bad news, and he doesn't need her in his life again."

"We live right next to each other and we have classes together. I'm sure I'll run into him at some point. In the meantime, will you promise me you won't tell him I'm back? That's if he even noticed I was gone in the first place."

"Oh, he noticed." He collapsed onto his back and his arms shot up in the air. "I don't understand girls. I thought I did, but California girls are on a whole other level, it seems," he grumbled.

"I don't think we understand ourselves, either. I sure as hell don't know what to do about myself." I patted his chest and sat up.

"He asked about you every day."

I nodded my head. "I figured that's why you texted me."

"I texted you because you're my friend, Em, but he also needed some peace of mind."

I patted his leg. "It's fine, Jace."

"Mind if I hang out over here for a little longer? I need to study and Audrey's voice is like nails on a chalkboard for me."

"Of course, we don't mind. Sleep on the couch if you want to." I didn't like the idea of Jaxon having the whole apartment alone with her, but I couldn't throw Jace to the wolves.

"Sweet, thanks, Em," he said with a smile.

- TEN -

Somehow I managed to avoid Jaxon for three more days. I didn't know if I just knew how to evade well, or if he was busy with Audrey; I hoped it was the first one. I showed up late to our classes and managed to snag a seat in the back. I always had my bag packed and ready to leave before the class was over so I could sneak out without his seeing me. I had no idea if he knew I was back or not. Jace never told me if he asked.

As I was walking across the courtyard toward the cafeteria on Wednesday after biology, I noticed Jaxon sitting alone under a giant oak tree. Seeing him reaffirmed how much I'd missed him the last week and a half. He was so striking lounging in the shade of the tree. He had on blue jeans with a long-sleeved red shirt that made his skin look bronzed. His dark hair was poking out from under his black ball cap, which was placed haphazardly on top of his head. He hadn't noticed me yet because he was reading one of his textbooks.

I walked up next to him under the shade. I saw that he finally noticed me when his hand just slightly slid off the page of the book. His eyes trailed up my legs to my denim skirt, and I swear they left a trail of goose bumps as they roamed upward to my face.

The sexy smirk on his face was almost my undoing. "I was wondering if you would ever come talk to me again, Em," he finally said.

Ouch. "Don't do that. Don't call me Em like everyone else; you've never called me that before," I said quietly.

"Aren't I just like everyone else to you?"

He was not going to let me off the hook easily. I had hurt him with my rejection and I needed to make it right. He deserved to know that he had been right all along, that I was just scared. When he called me out on running away from him and us, he was accurate, and I didn't like that. I knelt down in the grass as gracefully as I could with a skirt on. I wanted to be able to see into his blue eyes and apologize.

"Jax—"

"There you are!" I heard a girl interrupt from across the courtyard.

I turned to see that it was Audrey with her curly brown hair pinned to the top of her head. Jaxon cursed under his breath and slammed his text shut. *Shit, does she go to school here now or something?* I turned back around to face Jaxon, giving him a questioning look. He was too busy looking at her, though.

"I've been looking all over for you, Jaxy." Ew, I hated that nickname instantly. I don't know if it was because it was coming out of her mouth, or if it was just horrible in general, but I did not want to hear this. I stood up and grabbed my bag off the ground from beside me.

"What are you doing here, Audrey? I said I would come back to meet you at the apartment after my classes." He sounded frustrated. I noticed that he had spun his ball cap to the back, and he was standing up as well. I guess his quiet solace was entirely interrupted now.

"What, I can't come hang out with my hubby? Besides, it doesn't look like you're in class anyway," she said while looking directly at me.

What the hell did she just call him? "Hubby?" I gasped, looking at Jaxon. Was he married? Had he been married when we slept together? I started backing away from both of them.

"Audrey, shut the hell up!" Jaxon hollered. He pinched the bridge of his nose and when he brought his hand out toward me, I shook my head and continued walking away. "Emerson, please!"

I didn't look back or respond, but I could hear him in the distance talking to Audrey in harsh, clipped tones. I couldn't believe this was happening. Who the hell gets married in college, or did it happen before college? Why would Jaxon chase after other girls while he was married?

I ran all the way out to the parking lot, intending to run straight home or catch the bus if there was one waiting. Here I was once again running from Jaxon. When I got out to the lot, Jace was sitting on the tailgate of the truck reading from about four different textbooks again. When he looked up and saw my face, his dropped and he hopped off the back of the truck and came running up to me. He grabbed my shoulders and bent down to look in my eyes.

"He's married?" I shouted at him.

His hands dropped and he backed away. "Shit . . ."

"I don't care what kind of bro-code you guys have, but don't you think that kind of thing should be made known?" I started walking again. My body was feeling antsy, like I couldn't control this painful current flowing through me.

He reached out and stopped my movement. "Em, it's not what you think."

"I don't care what it is anymore. This whole 'relationship' situation is already too painful and it never even began. This is exactly why I never wanted to go down this road in the first place, why I made rules. I give up!" I shouted.

"Just stop for a second, Em. Let me at least take you home; we can talk this over," he pleaded.

"Forget it, Jace. I'll see you later. I'd rather walk right now anyway." I continued walking away from the parking lot and he didn't follow after me.

On my walk back, I decided to call Quinn, hoping that she was available to take a call. She answered on the third ring and I could tell I had interrupted her, because she told me to "hold on" in a whisper.

"What's up, Emmy?"

"Audrey called Jaxon her hubby."

"What?" she shrieked, "Emmy, she's a crazy bitch. Just talk to Jaxon."

"Quinn, what if he's married?"

"I'm going to kill Cole. I've got to go, but I'll see you at home later."

"Later."

I should feel bad for Cole, but this time I didn't. He was supposed to be my best friend; shouldn't he be looking out for my best interests? The mile walk back to the apartment took longer than it should have taken me. I just wanted to lie down in my bed and mope for a couple of hours. Then I would dry my eyes and move on. This wasn't me; I didn't get upset over anybody. But for now, I just needed a couple of hours to feel sorry for myself.

It's nice having such close friends. I love it, really I do, but you get absolutely no privacy or solitude. People feel comfortable just walking in on me all the time. Especially Jaxon. I was lying on my bed with my headphones on and eyes closed, listening to angry rock music, because that always gets me out of my funk, when I literally felt my door slamming. My eyes popped open to see Jaxon standing there in front of my closed door, looking extremely livid.

The whole right side of his face was flaming red and he had a large gash right above his eyebrow that was dripping blood down his face. It had already streamed down his cheek onto his shirt. I also noticed his hands were balled up into tight fists. I jumped up to look for a towel to put on his face.

"Oh my God, what happened to your face?" I cried, ripping the headphones out of my ears.

I snatched a washcloth out of my closet and came back to help him clean up. He grabbed me and slammed his mouth onto mine. For a moment, I forgot about my rejection, his "wife," and even his bleeding face. There was only he and I, with nothing between us. I missed him so much. I missed the feel of his body under my hands.

Before I was ready, he pulled back and ended the kiss. "Are you ready to listen to me now?" he asked in a husky voice and I could tell that kiss had the same effect on him as it did on me.

"Let me grab some supplies to help clean up you first." I left my room before my face turned as red as his. I grabbed all of the first-aid supplies Quinn and I had from the bathroom.

When I got back to my room, he was sitting in the chair at my desk, and I gestured at his shirt. "Take it off."

His uninjured eyebrow cocked up at me in question, although he was smiling at my request.

"Your shirt is getting ruined by your stupid face bleeding all over it," I replied to his cocky look.

"It's already red; who cares?" he asked, but he reached behind his neck to take it off anyway. I loved the way he dragged his shirts over his head.

It took every ounce in me to stop myself from sliding my hands up his abs and around his neck. I wanted to put my lips on that tattoo hugging his right shoulder.

"Are you going to tell me why half your face is busted?"

"Are you going to talk to me without running away?"

"Touché. I'll talk," I replied, leaning in quietly and inspecting his eyebrow. "You should probably get stitches."

"Hell no, I don't need stitches, just slap a bandage on it." He grabbed my hips and placed me in his lap with my legs wrapped around him. I instinctively grabbed his bare shoulders to steady myself.

When I gave him a questioning look, he shrugged. "Just so you can get a closer look, Nurse Emerson." I watched as a smile broke out across his face. Playful Jaxon was hard to resist.

I tapped his forehead above his gash as if to remind him he had some explaining to do first.

"I was in the parking lot coming to find you when that idiot Cole came blazing down the lot yelling at me. He fucking just started wailing on my face. He was pissed." He let out a small laugh. "I knew he had a right to be, so I didn't stop him. Jace jumped in there after a few good ones, though. I'm almost fucking positive he could have stopped him sooner, but I think he's pissed at me too."

"Cole did this?" I hollered at him.

This cut was really deep; I had no doubt that he needed stitches. One time I had opened the kitchen cabinet and a glass cup came flying down at my face from the top shelf. It sliced a cut across my cheek right under my eye. The ER doctor didn't want to place stitches so close to my eye, so he sent me home with a box of butterfly stitch bandages. I still had a couple left over that I could use on his eyebrow to hold the cut closed; hopefully it would heal without a scar or infection.

"Yeah, I guess he was finally tired of me ruining things with Quinn for him, because she got pissed at him for not telling you about Audrey. Man, don't get in the way of that guy and his girl."

I groaned. "They just got started and we keep spoiling it for them. I'm an awful friend." I continued wiping up all the blood and trying gently to scrub off the areas that had already dried to his skin. When it was all clean, I smoothed some ointment across it. He continued to sit there quietly, watching my face while I worked. Every once in a while, we would make eye contact and I had to force myself to break it before I started something up with him I wouldn't be able to stop. I needed to know who Audrey was and what he hadn't told me yet.

He was still staring into my eyes as I pushed his cut together and applied the bandage so it would hold the skin firmly in place. When I was done, I dropped my hands into my lap.

"I'm not married, Emerson." I slowly let out a breath I didn't realize I had been holding. "I used to be, though."

The breath I had just released was sucked right back in. He laid his forehead down onto my shoulder, probably so that he didn't have to look at my shocked face.

"I told you I had no room to judge anyone. I was a moron." He lifted his head back up to look at me. His face appeared sad and guilt-stricken. I gently tried to smooth away the lines across his face, carefully avoiding his cut. "I went a little crazy in high school and I started dating Audrey. My senior year, right after I turned eighteen, she got pregnant. She was so pissed at me and pressured me to do something to make it right. I couldn't tell anyone; I was disappointed in myself. I didn't tell my Mom or even Jace. I snuck off with her to get married since we both were eighteen. I thought that was the right thing to do if she was going to have my kid." He laid his forehead back down on my shoulder.

"Wow, a kid?" I whispered. I couldn't even imagine having a kid at thirty, let alone eighteen. "If you aren't married anymore, what happened?" I asked.

"Well, after we came back from getting married, I told my mom. She blew a gasket, called me an idiot in as many different ways as she could think of. Then she calmed down and asked me if I knew for sure that the baby was mine. I'd never thought of that before. I'd never even fathomed the idea that Audrey would cheat. Holy shit, was I a cocky idiot."

This whole story was messed up. I hated Audrey even more for where I was assuming this was going. I wanted to go find her right now and give her a gash or two on the side of her face. Or twelve.

Who in their right mind would cheat on this beautiful, caring man sitting in front of me?

He lifted his head. "After much reluctance on Audrey's part, we finally got her to agree to a paternity test, and it turns out it was her married physics teacher's kid, not mine. She got everyone into a whole mess of trouble. Not that our teacher wasn't equally guilty, or me, for that matter. My mom ended up finding a lawyer to annul the marriage on account of my idiocy and Audrey's fraud. Before the annulment, Coach Chase caught wind of everything and that's when he pulled my scholarship and spot on the team for two years. He said if I cleaned up everything before my junior year, I could come out here. My mom's the best; she had it all taken care of before I walked the stage at graduation, but Coach wouldn't reinstate my scholarship for the freshman or sophomore year."

He let out a relieved breath and his shoulders relaxed, like it felt good to finally get all of that out. Cole should be a little happier now with him as well.

"I'm glad you're not actually married." I gave him a small smile.

He leaned in and whispered underneath my ear, "And why is that?"

"Because the idea that I slept with a married guy freaks me out," I responded breathlessly.

"Well, it's a damn good thing I'm not married then, huh?" He started kissing from behind my ear, down the edge of my neck.

My thighs impulsively clinched tighter around his hips. I felt his hands come up the sides of my legs, moving my skirt upward until it was bunched up around my waist, and he squeezed me from behind. He finally moved his mouth in front of mine and I reached out and nipped his bottom lip between my teeth. The space between my thighs tingled when I heard him moan. Suddenly, he was squeezing my backside harder and he stroked his tongue across mine, leaving me breathless.

As we started speeding up, I pulled back. "Wait. Stop," I gasped.
He tucked his face into the nook of my neck and groaned.

"You're just going to leave here and go get into bed with Audrey after this; it kind of kills it for me."

"What the hell? No, I would never. I would never do that to you nor would I ever touch her again." His eyebrows shot up and he looked disgusted. His expression made me giggle.

"Why else is she living in your apartment then?" I asked, even more confused now.

Frustrated, he said, "Ugh . . . it's been three years and that girl is still messing everything up. She showed up here hoping that I would take her back. I'm supposed to forget the fact that she has a kid with some other guy, that she cheated on me, and that I think she's disgusting. I tried all week to get her to go back. She finally bought a plane ticket, but it's not till tomorrow morning."

With that, my fingers danced along the waistband of his pants. I could feel him through the denim of his jeans and I was instantly tired of talking about that girl. He leaned in to capture my mouth.

"Mmm . . . Emerson, I missed you," he said on a moan.

He raised my shirt over my head. "I missed you too," I said between our lips.

He lifted me with one hand while he unbuckled his belt and shoved his pants and boxers down with the other. The second I felt his warmth between my legs, I let out a ragged breath. When I leaned back to open the drawer of my desk, he clinched his fingers into my sides hard enough to keep me in place. I continued to reach for the drawer and when I pulled it open, I grabbed a small packet. He quickly took it from me and ripped it open. He reached down and ripped my panties into two pieces of tattered silk and tossed them to the ground.

"I know all you want is to be friends. I'd rather have that than have you running away from me all the time," he whispered in my ear, while sliding inside of me.

Damn. That is not where I was hoping this was going. I had spent all my time trying to make sure we were going to stay only friends; how would he know any differently now? I knew I couldn't have that kind of conversation right now, or if I knew how to have it, period. I'd never been anyone's girlfriend, let alone get asked to be one. How could I yell at him to leave me alone multiple times and then expect him to turn around and do the opposite?

I felt a warm hand pulling my chin up to look in his eyes. "Hey, did anyone ever tell you how damaging it can be to a guy's ego when the girl looks off into space during sex?"

I came up on my knees to stroke him again. Then I leaned up to kiss him and said, "I'm here."

Thirty minutes later, I was sweating and collapsed on Jaxon's chest, laying my head on his shoulder, panting. He had his head back on the headrest of the chair, equally spent and breathless. He was running his fingertips lightly across my bare back.

"Hey, so why did you come up to me in the courtyard this afternoon anyway?"

"Um . . . I just needed to get my journalism textbook back from you. I'm really far behind," I said, chickening out.

"I'll grab that for you," he said, leaning into me, and then he looked over my shoulder. "Damn, at some point we should have moved this over to the bed; it probably would have been easier on your legs." He sucked in a heaving breath.

"Anytime you're game," I said, snuggling into his chest.

He suddenly lifted me up, moved us over to the bed, and shoved all my covers back. He fell back on the bed with me on top and he rolled me over to my back. When he positioned himself on top of me, I giggled. I hadn't meant right now, but the way he was looking at me had me ready to go all over again. He pulled on my bunched-up skirt until it was sliding down my legs, then he tossed it behind him, dove down, and started kissing my neck.

- ELEVEN -

The next month and a half went by annoyingly normally. I was being a huge chicken. I just didn't have the guts to fess up to Jaxon that I had real feelings for him, and that I wanted to give a relationship a shot. So, we just continued being friends, no matter how maddening it was to me. I had run a ton of sexually frustrated miles this past month. I was hoping that my runner's high would compensate for the lack of other highs. But I couldn't even reach that moment lately while pounding the pavement. I ran farther and faster, doing anything to get that feeling, but I guess my runner's high and my sexual fulfillment were connected in some way.

I found enjoyment in the nights when I wasn't working and Jaxon was. I always stayed home to listen to him on the radio. He didn't get a lot of chances to talk because the main radio DJ did most of the chatting while he ran around the office doing errands. But when he did, I would snuggle in closer, listening to that magnificent voice. It was comforting, even though he wasn't actually talking to me.

Jaxon and I still hung out before and after our classes, and he would come over to study a couple of times a week. I would make him lunch on our short day together, and sometimes I would even make dinner for all five of us if I wasn't working. We would often fool around at times in the afternoon when everyone else was at school, but we hadn't had sex again. I wasn't sure why that was; we just never took it that far.

I ended up having to miss another game to make it up to Ed for skipping out for a week unexpectedly. I had been able to make all of the ones after that. Currently we were undefeated, and it was amusing to see how Dalton thought that Jaxon was his best friend now. I'm sure it had nothing to do with how good Jaxon made him look. Every party that we went to, Dalton would pull him in to be some kind of wingman for him.

Quinn and I had gone back home for the short, four-day Thanksgiving break. It was nice to have that time with Ellie and Charles. I was really looking forward to spending time alone with Quinn, but she sulked around the whole time, depressed about missing Cole. He had gone home with Jace and Jaxon to see their families. I don't know why either of them bothered going home, because they spent the majority of their time on the phone together. I called Jaxon occasionally while they were gone and he seemed busy when he answered, so I let him go shortly after. He texted me a few times, but overall, nothing was going anywhere between us.

We had been to a bunch of fraternity parties over the last month. Cole and Quinn would usually dance together the whole time they were there. Jaxon would wind through the crowds, dancing and talking to everyone. Jace would pop in and out, but he wasn't a big partier.

It was second nature for me to go find some frat boy and go upstairs with him to have a good time. A part of me wanted back that old me that could just hook up with some hot random guy and then go back to enjoying my night. Ever since Jaxon, I just couldn't follow through with it, and it was beyond frustrating. I would go upstairs with them and start making out. But for some reason, I just couldn't get my body to go any further. Usually after about ten minutes of trying to make advances on me that I wasn't reciprocating, or when they got tired of my rejections, they would get up and leave me there.

The first couple of times it happened, I tried sneaking back down the stairs without people seeing me do my walk of shame. Even though I hadn't actually done anything, everyone here knew my reputation. I was mainly trying to avoid Jaxon; it felt wrong for him to know about me being with someone else. After I had finally made it back down, he would ultimately always come seek me out to make sure I was okay. Eventually, I stopped caring if he saw me come down or not. His eyes would always find me coming down the stairs and he would give me the "okay" signal with his fingers. I always gave it back, gesturing that I was. I'm such a liar.

After Thanksgiving break, I was beyond frustrated; it had been way too long since I had had sex. I was determined that if I wasn't going to "woman up" and talk to Jaxon, I needed to get laid by someone. We were all at the Sig Alpha "Welcome Back from Thanksgiving, Let's Have a Party" party. Seriously, if there was any reason to drink, dance, and have sex, these guys would come up with a party for it. I had gone upstairs with Easton, one of the football/frat guys, and he took his shirt off the instant we walked in the room. I'm not sure what I was thinking; Easton and I have hooked up before. I don't remember him having a tattoo on his bicep, but maybe I had been too drunk to notice last time, or maybe it was new. I was determined to follow through, but the second I caught a glimpse of that tattoo I couldn't take my eyes off of it. It reminded me too much of Jaxon's, only Jaxon's was ten times hotter. Then I just started thinking about everything Easton was lacking compared to Jaxon.

I was sitting on the edge of the bed and he came down with his arms on either side of me, trapping me while kissing my neck. I let him go for a while, hoping that my sex drive would kick in. Please just feel normal again, Emerson. After what felt like five hours, although it was probably only five minutes of the most awkward advances, I finally heaved him off of me with a frustrated blow of air.

"Fuck, Em. What is wrong with you?" Easton growled.

"I don't have any idea."

He sat up, pulling his shirt back on over his head. "It used to be so damn easy with you. You weren't one of those chicks that needed sweetening up."

I don't know why he sounded so frustrated. He wasn't the one that could have sex with only one person all of a sudden. I knew he would end up grabbing some other girl before the night was over. Me? I was going yet another night unsatisfied. I shoved past him and slammed the bedroom door on my way out. Out in the hallway, Jace had his back against the wall with a blonde leaning into him, kissing his neck.

When he saw my face, he stood up straighter and balanced whoever was attached to his neck with his hands on her shoulders. "Is everything alright, Emmy?" he asked, concerned.

"I'm fine, Jace; don't stop on my account." I gestured to his date.

When I bounded down the stairs, there was no Jaxon in sight. That was probably for the best because if he gave me the "okay" signal, I might have given him the middle-finger signal right back for cursing me.

I went into the kitchen to find the tequila and a shot glass. When you sleep with a frat guy, they usually end up showing you where they keep the good stuff, or maybe I just knew to ask. The Sig Alphas keep theirs hidden in the dishwasher because who the hell needs one of those when you only eat out of pizza boxes and drink from red plastic cups. I was throwing back my first shot when Easton came pounding through the kitchen past me to go straight out to the patio.

I looked out the kitchen window and noticed a group of guys sitting out there drinking, smoking, and talking. I spotted Cole and

Jaxon in the mix with beer bottles in their hands. Easton hadn't closed the door all the way when he came through, so I could hear them all laughing at some joke Garrett had just made.

Right as Easton came out, I heard Jaxon's voice. "What the hell's wrong with you? Did you fucking do something to Emerson?" He stood up from his seat.

"Chill the hell out, Riley, your precious Emerson is fine and fucking untouched. You don't need to run in there and make sure she's okay." He was definitely frustrated.

All of them laughed and ribbed at Jaxon for always checking on me.

"You do realize we used to fuck her just fine before you got here. She was always okay afterward; she doesn't need you to check on her," Easton prodded him.

I heard a scuffle and then a loud pop followed by the sound of Easton groaning.

"What the fuck is wrong with you, Jax?" Easton yelled.

"Shut up, East, you deserve about twenty more blows for saying that shit. Keep your mouth shut or I'll kick your ass alongside him," I heard Cole growl.

I felt small hands on my back. "What are we listening to?" Quinn whispered over my shoulder.

"Nothing," I snapped and pulled back from the window.

She walked up to glance out and smiled at me knowingly. I heaved a sigh at being caught eavesdropping on the guys.

"I'm almost positive Jaxon just punched Easton."

"Did he do something to you?" she demanded in an angry voice.

"Nothing besides speak the truth. I guess Jaxon doesn't like that side of me."

"He's protective of you, Em."

"Just what I need, another protective *friend*," I grumbled.

She was about to comment on that, when we heard the guys start talking loudly again.

"Man, Em's no fun anymore anyway," Easton complained.

"Yeah, I swear I've taken her to my room four times this semester and she just zones out while we're making out, and then pushes me away. Last year, she was much cooler," I heard Blake say.

"Maybe it's your moves, dude. I wouldn't want to get with your ugly ass, either," Cole joked.

"I reached that fucking three-time limit, so I wouldn't know how she's been lately," Micah griped.

The other guys chimed in with the same complaint as Blake. Traitors, all of them. Guys aren't supposed to get together and chat about this stuff. It was also kind of embarrassing to hear about how many people I had gone upstairs with lately. If this were last year, I would have slept with all of them. Jaxon thought that's what I'd been doing.

"Hold up, what are y'all saying? None of you have slept with her this entire semester?" A familiar southern accent chimed in.

Crap. He was putting the pieces together.

When I heard a round of no's, I downed another shot and scrambled out of the kitchen toward the front door. I knew he was going to want to know why, and I was still frightened to tell him that he was the only person I wanted to be with. That I had never felt so close and safe with someone before I met him. I was also terrified to explain to him that even though I wanted him, I knew I would be terrible at a relationship. I would mess it up and I would piss him off. At the same time, he seemed to have moved on, so maybe all this worry was for nothing.

Just as I was hitting the front door, I heard the back door open and Jaxon hollered, "Emerson!"

I kept going and knew he hadn't seen me because, right before I slipped out, I overheard him ask Quinn if she knew where I was.

Here's hoping my best friend and sister has some sense of solidarity. When I reached the driveway, I realized I couldn't drive home. I didn't have the car keys and I was far too intoxicated. I reached Jaxon's truck, which was parked a couple of houses down the street, and I laid the tailgate down to sit on it.

Since it was November, it was a little chilly out. Southern California doesn't have much of a winter, but the breeze blowing off the ocean was giving me chills on my bare legs. Another reason I would never make it in the north; I loved wearing shorts and flip-flops year-round. When you have to hunt down gloves, hats, scarves, and boots at any time of the year, that's when I call it quits. I have a grandma that lives in upstate New York who we visited once for Christmas. I was miserable in the cold; I stayed indoors the entire week we were there.

Suddenly, I heard boots hitting the sidewalk at a quick pace. I knew it had to be Jaxon because he doesn't like to let anything go. He was still pretty far away and I realized he wouldn't be able to see me, since the truck was facing him and I was sitting on the tailgate.

"Emerson!" he barked, sounding a bit panicked.

He continued running down the street and I watched as he passed right by me. His body froze and he whipped around to face me. I made eye contact with him as he stalked toward me with a determined look on his face. The air around me grew warmer and there was a current charging between us. He came right up to my legs and placed his hands on my knees. I gasped as he shoved my legs apart so he could come even closer to me while his hands rested on my thighs.

With his intoxicating voice at a low tone he asked, "You reckless, frustratingly beautiful girl, why are you out here all alone? Don't you know it's not safe to be on this street alone with all these drunken, idiotic frat assholes?"

"I was hiding," I admitted meekly.

"Why have you been torturing me by making me think that you were sleeping with all those guys?" He pointed back to the house.

"Because I wanted to sleep with all those guys." I watched him wince, and knew I needed to clarify. "I mean I wanted to *want* to sleep with them. I don't like Emerson; she's too confusing and complicated. I just wanted to be Em again. But every time I went upstairs with one them, I always chickened out." I said the last part barely above a whisper.

I felt his hands flex on my thighs. I imagined what it felt like for those hands to lift me up as he always does. How it felt to wrap my legs around his waist. I scooted forward even closer to him so he would be farther between my thighs. He brought his face down to the side of mine, and with his nose he moved my hair to the side so he could bury it in my neck. I panted at his proximity. Once again, a month and a half had been a long time for me.

On a groan he said, "You're driving me fucking insane. The only reason I can stand coming to every single one of these parties is because some crazy-ass masochistic side of me needs to know, when you come out of those bedrooms, that you're still okay. But every time I watch you walk up those stairs with some new douchebag, I beg Cole to stop me from going up there, pounding that guy into the ground and throwing you over my shoulder because I know you would be pissed at me," he exhaled on a long breath. "Emerson, tell me what you want." Each word was said in a short, clipped tone.

I clutched the waistband of his jeans as tightly as I could manage and spoke directly to his chest. "I don't know how." I turned my head up to run my lips across the edge of his jaw. He seemed to be unconsciously squeezing my thighs now, and I'm sure I'll have bruises there tomorrow. I'll welcome them if it means I can be with him tonight.

"Tell me that you want me," he whispered.

"I want you." Always.

"Only me?"

"Only you." Had there ever been anyone else?

He shuffled around, feeling at his pockets. When he found what he wanted, he reached in and pulled out a pen. The second I saw it I knew what he wanted, so I stretched out my hand toward him with my palm facing up. He grinned at my forwardness and grabbed my wrist so he could turn it. I closed my eyes and let the tickle of the ballpoint consume me. At this point, I didn't care what he wrote as long as he continued stroking it across my skin. He finished quickly, closed my fingers into my palm, and kissed them. I slowly uncurled them to read his message, which was written boldly across the expanse of my palm. One word that screamed a whole lot more.

Mine

I lifted my eyes up to his and nodded. Quickly, he slid his hands underneath me and lifted me up around his waist. He slammed the tailgate shut and walked around to the driver's side. I don't know who leaned in first, but our lips were crushed together and I felt safe again in his arms. Safe from myself.

"Do you have the keys?" I asked through his lips.

"No, I don't need them." I watched as he pressed a series of numbers on the keyless entry system just above the door handle. I was confused how we would drive home without keys, but at this moment I couldn't find a reason to care, either.

He didn't open the front door, but instead opened the door to the backseat and slid inside with me still in one arm. He closed the door behind us, and the heavily tinted windows, along with the night sky, provided us with complete privacy.

When I gave him a confused look, he said, "I can't drive—I've had too much to drink—but I can't wait until everyone else is ready to go home, either." He smashed his lips back to mine. I pulled back and looked into his gorgeous eyes. He had a faint scar above his eyebrow where Cole had punched him, so I lifted up and kissed it softly and his eyes fell closed.

I pushed off of his chest and knelt down on the floorboard between his legs. He looked down at me from under his long eyelashes, and the look he gave me spurred me on. I reached up, released his button, and unzipped his pants.

"No underwear?" I smiled at him as I pulled him out.

He moaned when I wrapped my hands around him. When I bent my head down, I heard his head hit the glass window behind him. I continued to look up at him the entire time my mouth worked up and down because the emotions running across his face were enough of a turn-on for me. His blue eyes looked impossibly silver in the light of the moon.

"Fuck, baby, that feels so damn incredible." I loved his term of endearment coming out of his mouth. "But you don't have to do this; come back up here." He tugged on my arms.

"Do you have a condom?"

"Shit . . ." He closed his eyes in frustration.

"Let me do this. I want to." It was true: I did want to. If I couldn't tell him how I felt, I wanted to at least try and show him.

After I had tucked him back in his pants, I came back up to sit in his lap and nuzzle into his neck. He was so warm and had a light gleam of sweat on his body from his exertion. The smell of his cologne mixed with his perspiration was an intoxicating mixture. We just sat there for who knows how long, his fingers running through my hair while I listened to the thump of his heart slow to a normal, steady pace.

"What the hell's wrong with my truck?" We instantly sat up when we heard Jace's voice outside. "The windows are all fogged up!"

I heard Cole's irritating laugh break out immediately afterward. "Fifty bucks says Jax went to make sure Em was okay." I heard the mocking tone in his voice when he said the word *okay*.

"Guys, we should go back. Wait until . . . they're . . . done . . . you know." I heard Quinn say uncomfortably.

I shoved Jaxon a bit to bring to his attention that we should tell them we were decent and we absolutely wanted to get home. I didn't need to say anything because I knew he felt the same way.

He propped open the back door. "Get in here, assholes."

"Hey! Don't call my girl an asshole," Cole shouted and wrapped his arm around Quinn's shoulders. I watched as he gave her a kiss on the temple.

"What? No! Quinn, I swear I wasn't saying that toward you." He gave her an apologetic look. His puppy-dog eyes were so sweet. If he ever directed them at me, I would give him anything he wanted.

"Don't worry, Jax, I know you weren't talking about me," Quinn responded as she bumped Cole in the chest. "Give him a break, Coley." Cole grimaced that his girlfriend was using my favorite nickname for him.

Sarcastically, he looked back at me. "Ems, have I ever thanked you for that nickname? Because seriously, it's the best . . ." We could all hear the satire dripping from his voice, which made everyone besides Cole fall over laughing.

Jace drove us all home; I never saw him drink, ever. If he actually came out to a party with us, he was nice enough to be our designated driver. I was so happy in this moment with all four of these people, and it was amazing how close we had all become in only a few short months. I felt as though I could share almost anything with them. As though I could be at my worst around them and they would still be there for me. I know I would do it for any of them. Apparently, when you start opening the emotional gates, they all come flooding out.

"Your smile is breathtaking right now. What are you thinking about, and please tell me how I can keep it there?" Jax whispered in my ear.

I shook my head because I didn't know how to describe to him what I was feeling. I leaned in and laid my head on his shoulder. He laid his head on top of mine and kissed my hair.

When we got back to our apartments, we all just stood in the hallway staring at each other—I guess trying to figure out who was going with whom and into which apartment. Jace shoved past all four of us.

"You guys are nauseating," he said before going into their apartment.

"Emerson will be in my bed," Jaxon said while dragging me behind him. I laughed at his caveman attitude.

"Love you, Emmy!" Quinn shouted before going inside our apartment with Cole.

- TWELVE -

The next morning, I woke up immersed in the scent of Jaxon. I was lying on my stomach with my arms stretched out underneath my pillow. He was laying his head on my bare back and had one hand cupping my breast. I felt like we had just gone to sleep when I began waking up. The two of us had been up late last night getting to know each other in this new way; it was the greatest night of my life.

I started flexing out my fingers underneath the pillow to get them to wake up. Pins and needles were running up and down my arms. Jaxon must have realized I was awake because he started kissing a line down my spine. I began thinking about last night, and it hit me that I had passed my three-times limit with him. I knew it was going to happen, but the thought shocked and frightened me at the same time. My body stiffened with my terror.

"Shh, baby, relax. Don't freak out." Somehow, he knew I would start to panic at this moment, and he was trying to tamp my fear down with his soothing kisses. "Just be here with me; don't freak out," he repeated.

My breathing evened out and my heart rate slowed to normal with each time his full lips touched my skin. When he was satisfied that I was calm, he grabbed my hips and flipped me over onto my back, and I couldn't stop the yelp from flying out of my mouth. He had a sexy, guilty smirk on his face.

"I've always thought it was the sexiest damn thing in the world to see you naked in my bed." Oh God, his voice only got better with the roughness of sleep added to it. I started to squirm underneath him, needing him in between my thighs. "But I was wrong."

I started moving out from under him. "Well, you sure know how to ruin one of the best moments," I grumbled.

His hands came down to hold me in place. "I was wrong, because you *waking up* naked in my bed is even more incredible and sexy. I want you to wake up here every morning." He bent down to start kissing my neck. "And I'm glad you think this is one of the best moments, by the way."

"I can't move in here," I said, in between heavy breaths.

"You don't have to move in; just sleep here every night," he replied with a huge grin on his face. "If it makes you feel better, we can sleep in your bed every once in a while, but I like seeing you here with your hair spread out across my pillow." When he dipped his hips down to move against me, I closed my eyes at the wonderful feeling. With Jaxon, there was no effort required for my sex drive to flip on. All he had to do was look at me with those blue eyes and I was in full gear, ready to go.

I ran my hands over his chest and noticed a black mark that wasn't normally there. At a closer glance, I realized it was the mirror image of the writing on my hand. I giggled at the backward *Mine* on his skin as I ran my fingers across it. I must have slept with my hand right here last night. He dipped his chin down to see what I was chuckling about and he smiled broadly when he realized what it was.

"I kind of like that." I was mesmerized, tracing the backward letters. When he looked up into my eyes proudly, I whispered, "It's like you're mine as well."

After a second, I realized that the sun was already up, so I turned to look at the clock on the bedside table. "Shit! We have to be in class in thirty minutes." I started scrambling out from under him.

"So what, let's skip." He laughed at me. "Stay in bed with me today."

"Jaxon, I can't; I've already missed way too many classes. Patterson will drop me if I miss any more this semester, and then I'll lose my internship."

"Okay, it's not that big of a deal. We'll go. You're extremely adorable when you get flustered like this, though." He laughed.

When I got up, I noticed he stayed in bed, not attempting to get out. I gave him a questioning look.

"Yeah, you go ahead. I . . . kind of have a situation . . . I need to wait out." He gestured at himself under the sheets. "I'll be set by the time you're ready to leave."

I leaned forward with my hands on the bed and knew he was enjoying the view of my naked body. "Join me in the shower and I'll relieve . . . your situation." I winked at him.

I'd never seen him move so fast as he sprang from the bed. I bounded out his door laughing, completely naked, and ran straight into the bathroom. I knew no one had seen me, but at the same time, it didn't even occur to me to care if they had. When I reached the shower and turned on the faucet, I felt large hands on my hips from behind.

"Emerson, I'll be honest: Right now, I'm not going to handle guys seeing my girlfriend naked very well," he growled in my ear.

I spun around to look up into his eyes. "Girlfriend?" I gasped nervously.

"I don't care what label you put on it, but you're mine, regardless. I won't share."

When I just stood there with a shell-shocked expression on my face and not responding, I saw the worry shoot across his. He lowered his voice and spoke slowly. "Babe, when I asked you if you wanted only me last night, I wasn't talking about one night only. Were you?" he asked, nervously clinching my hips tighter, as if I might leave if he were to let go. The steam from the shower began engulfing the room. The mirror was already fogged up and all I could pay attention to was his blue eyes contrasting against the white steam.

I shook my head no and watched the relief wash the worry away in his eyes. "I can't be a girlfriend, though. I'll be terrible at it. I just can't . . . I'll hurt you . . . I just can't . . ." I started shaking my head back and forth with my rising panic and rambling.

He gently pushed me backward into the shower and shut the glass door behind us. The water poured down over both of us and I slowly started calming down as his hands ran through my hair. He softly tilted my head back to soak my hair under the spray of hot water. Without saying a word, he was bringing me down from my panic; without saying a word, he was making me feel safe and cared for.

I turned my face to the side. "You deserve someone better than me," I whispered into his arm.

"You deserve to know how great it can be for someone to care about you."

"I don't even know what a good relationship is."

"I kind of gathered that, and one day, you'll tell me why you're so afraid of them." He tilted my face up to his. "I'll show you how great we're going to be. Because you're the most beautiful girl I've ever met, and I'm not talking about your gorgeous face, your stunning hair, or your drop-dead sexy body. I never knew it was possible to be so attracted to your best friend." My breath caught at his words. I'd never thought about it like that before, but slowly he had become my best friend in all of this.

I wish I had the words to give back to him, but I didn't. So, I just leaned up on my toes and wrapped my hands around his neck and kissed him with everything I wished I could say.

We hurried through our shower and raced to school. Before we entered the classroom, my heels locked into the pavement. I wanted to be who he needed me to be, but being in front of everyone, I was starting to freeze.

He leaned down from behind me, over my shoulder, to talk into my ear. "Hey, if it makes it easier for you, I won't call you my girlfriend. Deal?"

My shoulders released their tension and I exhaled in relief. "Thank you, Jaxon."

Right before I could walk into the room, he grabbed hold of my shoulder and spun me around. "This doesn't mean you get to be with anyone else, understand? Nobody else gets to touch you. There's only you and me, no one else," he spoke in a deadly serious tone. I loved when his voice got all rough and serious. Then he picked up my hand and tapped the inside of my palm where he had written last night. "Mine," he whispered.

I slipped my fingers into the waistband of his pants and tugged him even closer to me. "I only want you." I reached up and nipped his bottom lip with my teeth.

I heard a growl roll through his chest. "Do we really need to do this today?" He tilted his head toward the classroom door.

"Unfortunately," I said as I pulled him into the classroom.

When I was finished with biology later, I walked out of my classroom and Jaxon wasn't out there. I didn't actually know which classroom in the science building he was in, so I decided to walk down to the cafeteria, where we always met up with everyone else anyway. This whole "dating" thing was strange territory for me. Was I supposed to call him or text him to tell him I would meet him? Or was I supposed to just act the way I always did? I decided to go with the latter, because I had no idea how to do anything else.

I didn't know if Jaxon would want to hang around to eat lunch here or go back to the apartment. So I decided to just sit down with everyone instead of going through the lunch line for a tray. Quinn and Cole hadn't made it here yet, either. When I got to our usual table, I waved to Garrett, Mason, and Micah. I sat down in an empty spot, and slowly more people started to join us. Right when I sat down, Micah slid in next to me and wrapped an arm around my shoulders. I tried, nonchalantly, to move away from his hold. I didn't want to make this new change obvious, but I also knew how pissed Jaxon would be if he walked in here and saw Micah's arm around me.

Surprisingly, Jace slid in on the opposite side of me, eyeing Micah. He never ate lunch with us; I usually saw him sitting with a couple of other premed students.

I took advantage of his appearance. "Hey, Jace, how was class?" I asked, sliding closer to him and dropping Micah's arm. "Thanks for saving me," I whispered into his ear.

"Just trying to avoid a fight." He nodded toward the lunch line and then leaned forward to eat his food. Jaxon was pushing his tray through the line behind a couple of girls, looking directly at me. He looked angry.

"Shit, shit, shit," I continued whispering under my breath. "I knew I would be terrible at this." When I motioned to get up and leave, Jace clamped a hand down onto my leg to keep me seated.

"Don't run away, Ems. He'll be fine. Just relax." Jace's reassuring voice kept me in my seat.

Jaxon walked up behind me and placed his tray down in front of me. He had gotten enough for both of us. "Move it, Woods, you're in my spot," he said to Micah.

"Dude, last time I checked, we didn't have assigned seating," he replied, scooting closer to me.

"Micah, just move . . . please," I said, trying to move away from him and bumping into Jace.

Micah shoved his tray to the opposite side in front of me and got up to walk all the way around the table and benches. When he came back around and sat down, he eyed me curiously. Jaxon sat down in his vacated spot and, with his arm behind my back, gripped my hip and scooted me closer to him. Then he brought his arm back and started eating like nothing had happened. Quinn and Cole finally came to join us at the table as well, moving in next to Micah.

I leaned into Jaxon. "I didn't know if you wanted to stick around here or eat at home, so I didn't grab any food," I told him.

"Do you want to leave?" he asked, motioning to get up.

"You just bought all this food. We should at least eat it."

He situated himself back into his seat and shrugged noncommittally. I didn't like that I felt as if I was in trouble for something, as if I needed to explain my actions. I hadn't even done anything wrong. I placed my palms down on the table so I could push myself up taller. I gave Jaxon a quick peck on the lips and I watched as the tension left his face. He looked down at me and smiled, then gestured for me to eat as well.

With a mouth full of food, Micah pointed his fork at the both of us. "What's going on with you, Emmsie? You never dole out the affection." Apparently, the extent of my nicknames at this school was never-ending; I hadn't heard that one yet. I wasn't a fan.

"Not for you, Micah," I responded vaguely.

"Don't call her Emmsie." Jaxon shot a hard look at Micah while speaking.

"What, you're the only one that can call her something special?"

"Just drop it," I said to both of them. I noticed Jace stiffening up beside me.

"I call her by her name, jackass. Not some cutesy nickname," Jaxon replied anyway.

"Emerson sounds like a dude's name," Micah retorted, and then a cocky grin spread across his face as he got an idea. *Uh-oh. I didn't like that face.* "When I'm pounding into her, I like to call out a chick's name." My mouth fell open at what he had just said.

First, I noticed Jace's fist clenching, and then I felt the air rush past my head as Jaxon's body flew across the table. He took Micah down with him during his flight. Both of them grunted from the impact of the hard ground, although Micah took the brunt of it with Jaxon on top of him. I sat up to look over the edge of the table at the two of them down there. Jaxon was pummeling him in the face with his fists repeatedly. Micah was trying to bring his forearms up to block the punches.

Jace swiftly scrambled over the table feet-first and grabbed Jaxon by the collar of his shirt. I realized Jace had been anticipating this, because he scooped him up way too fast to have been surprised. Cole jumped up and helped Jace move Jaxon away from Micah. Cole stepped on Micah's hand and twisted his foot to grind it into the ground on his way out. Micah didn't say anything, but I saw him wince from the pain. Quinn shook her head back and forth at all of them. As the three of them were walking out of the cafeteria, Jace and Cole had their arms wrapped around Jaxon.

"Fuck you, Riley!" Micah bellowed from his spot on the ground.

I watched as Jace's and Cole's arms flexed from the brief struggle Jaxon put up. Then they continued out the door toward the parking lot, without even a glance back. It all happened so fast that not many people even noticed in the loud cafeteria. I think the only people that saw were those at our table, and one of the other tables that Jaxon and Micah fell between. Micah's food was half on the table and half on the floor. He pulled himself back up on the bench and sat down in front of me again. His face didn't look that bad; it was mostly just red. I knew that if Jaxon wanted to, he could have done some real damage. He had his head bent forward looking down at his food.

His angry eyes looked up at me. "You should stay away from him, Em. He's insane."

"Only to assholes, Micah," Quinn said from beside me, glaring at him.

"I didn't say anything I wouldn't say any other day!" He lifted his hands in frustration.

Garrett and a few of the other frat guys slid down the bench toward us. "You know what you said, fucker. Just drop it." He eyed Micah.

I looked down at my food for the next couple of minutes and picked at the turkey and ham sandwich. Micah may have been a jerk for what he said, but at the end of the day, he was right. I had allowed all of the guys to openly joke about our times together; hell, I was usually the one making the jokes. They didn't know any better. I wanted to believe that Micah wouldn't have said something like that if he had known I was with Jaxon now.

"I'm sorry, Micah. That was my fault. You didn't know."

His hard eyes shot to mine. "Didn't know what, Em?" he angrily responded. He knew and he was trying to get me to say it out loud, but the coward inside of me couldn't even do that.

"You just didn't know." I sighed.

The others in our group had finished their lunches and vacated the building about fifteen minutes later. Quinn sat faithfully next to me the whole time, offering her silent support.

"I don't think I can do this, Quinny."

"You can and you will." She looked at me with a serious expression.

"Quinn, you can't force me to be in a relationship," I spoke through a laugh.

"I can and I will."

"Cute . . ." I replied drily.

"Em, I've never seen any of those guys look at you the way he does. I've never seen you look at any of those guys at all, really. You look at Jaxon though, and you let him in. Don't quit now."

I sighed in defeat. She was right. The fact was that I didn't want to let Jaxon go or even be away from him, period.

"Jaxon's never going to be okay with the fact that I've slept with practically everyone." I said.

"He'll have to learn, won't he? Besides, you haven't slept with *everyone*. You haven't slept with Jace or Cole," she said with a wink. "Let's keep it that way, okay?"

"Yes, ma'am." I leaned my head on her shoulder. Quinn was good for my spirits. She knew what I was thinking before I even had to say it, and she knew how to ground me when I was becoming a flight risk.

We walked out to the parking lot to get in our car when we noticed Jace and Cole standing by the truck talking. There was no Jaxon in sight.

"Where is he?" I asked them anxiously.

"He hopped on the bike and left as soon as we got out here," Jace said with a shrug, but I could tell he was worried about his brother.

"Do you think that was the smartest thing to let him do when he's pissed?"

"I think he's just pissed at himself," Cole said.

"At himself? Why? I figured he was mad at me." I was shocked.

"He thinks he scared you," Jace said looking a bit forlorn.

"The only thing I'm scared of is him out there riding that thing while he's got so much running through his head." I pulled my cell out of my pocket and brought up his name in my contacts.

Me: Come back, please?

Jace pulled down the tailgate and we sat on top of it next to each other. Cole pulled Quinn into the bed of the truck and tucked her into his lap. I heard him whispering into her ear, but I didn't know what he was saying. I sat there swinging my legs back and forth, hoping that Jaxon was okay and that he would come back by here soon.

"Em, I have a class to get to." Jace's voice sounded unsure. I knew he was wondering if he should stick around to make sure Jaxon was okay.

"Go ahead, Jace. I'll text you when he comes back." I patted his leg.

"Thanks, Em." He leaned and kissed me on my cheek right before he leaped down off the tailgate. "Go easy on him, okay?" I nodded my head at him.

After Jace said his good-byes, Quinn scooted out of the truck. "I have to be at my tutoring session in five minutes. I'll see you at home?" she asked.

"Man, I never got to finish my lunch. My stomach's going to be growling the whole time, Quinn," Cole complained.

"You know you don't have to sit through her sessions, right?" I teased.

"As long as Bryce is her student, I do."

"You guys are overprotective cavemen," I grumbled.

"Come on, babe, you can eat in the Tutor Hall Café," Quinn said, while grabbing his hand. "Em, you can take the car; you should go home. Cole has his car."

"He'll come back here. I'm going to wait." I watched as they shrugged their shoulders and walked off.

I was left alone on the bed of the truck. It's ironic that I was just here yesterday hiding from Jaxon, and now I here I was hoping to find him. I scooted further into the bed and lay down flat on my back. The weather was unusually warm today and the sun felt good on my skin. I noticed a shirt balled up in the corner, so I reached over to grab it. It was Jaxon's and I wondered when he had taken this off to toss it back here. I used it as a pillow under my head to help alleviate the discomfort of the ridges on the truck bed floor. The scent of his cologne helped me doze off in the comfort of the sun.

I woke up with a start when I heard the loud rumble of a motorcycle engine. Jaxon was parking the bike next to the truck and pulling his helmet off. His eyes were already on me before the helmet was all the way off his head. He snapped the helmet straps around the handlebars of the bike. His backpack swung around the side of his body and he reached in to grab his black ball cap. I sat up on my elbows to watch him. I adored when he wore that cap; he looked even more sexy than usual.

"I love when you wear that," I decided to tell him.

"The cap?" he asked, looking surprised, and I nodded to him. Then, as he thought about something, he frowned at me. "You're going to be sunburned if you've been lying out here the whole time."

"I knew you would come back. I wanted to be here," I said quietly. "Ready to go home?" I scooted out of the truck.

He gave me a confused look and then nodded his head. I got up and went around to the passenger side of the truck. I wasn't even going to ask if we could ride on the motorcycle, since I knew the answer to that one. Jace and Jaxon carried both sets of keys with them at all times now. They were always switching out on each other without telling the other one. I think by now, Jace knew that if I was with Jax, the truck would be occupied. Jaxon followed behind and lifted me up into the seat. He stared into my eyes like he wanted to ask me something or he was waiting for me to say something. I leaned in and kissed him softly.

The ride home was quiet. I couldn't read him. I still didn't know if he was mad at himself or me. His emotions were all over the place on his face. I took hold of his hand as we were walking up the stairs to the apartment. He pulled out his keys and let us into his place. He pulled me into his bedroom and laid me down on the bed. I started breathing heavily as he climbed above me. I was instantly turned on by his proximity. His body was the best kind of aphrodisiac. The only problem was that his face still held a lot of worry as he looked into my eyes. I reached up to smooth the lines under his eyes.

"Beautiful, please just get it over with. Yell at me; tell me how mad you are, so I'll feel a little better. Not that I deserve to," he said in a rough, beaten tone.

"Huh? Why would I yell at you?" I questioned.

He bent his head down into the crook of my neck as he spoke. "Because I acted like an idiot."

I shoved his cap off his head and ran my fingers through his soft hair. "Jaxon, all of that would have been prevented if I wasn't such a coward."

"No babe, I shouldn't have let that get to me."

"But it did and part of being your . . . just yours"—I had almost said the "G" word—"I need to find a way to get over my insecurities and make you feel more comfortable."

I felt the side of his cheeks pull up into a grin when he caught me stuttering over that "just yours" part.

"No, I don't want to make you move so fast that it scares you off again. I can handle it next time, promise. I just hate that they feel like they can touch you whenever they want and say whatever they want."

"I wouldn't hate it if you touched me whenever you wanted to, though." I wiggled against him.

"Hmm . . . damn, I'll never get tired of you telling me that," he said while lifting my shirt up. His head bent down to take me into his mouth and I moaned, writhing against him to find relief. His sweet torment was going to be the death of me.

Before I knew it, we were both completely naked and he was thrusting into me feverishly. It was strange being able to do this with him whenever I wanted to. I didn't have to worry about my stupid rules. I didn't have to worry that he was with someone else, because he was with me. I didn't care if anyone else liked him, because he was mine. Because of those things, I got to ignore my limit-of-three rule repeatedly.

He grabbed my wrists with one of his hands and held them tightly above my head. He was driving so hard and fast it was almost impossible to concentrate on anything besides the euphoria he was building inside of me. I pulled my legs up so they went up over his shoulders, and he turned his head to trail kisses up the inside of one of my legs. The contrast between his fast and hard movements, versus this sweet side of him, started pushing me over the edge. I clinched him hard inside of me and I heard him groan as his hand gripped me tighter.

"Fuck, baby, do that again," he panted. When I did, he let out a long groan.

"Kiss me," I gasped.

His lips slammed against mine passionately. I couldn't hold on any longer and I screamed out his name so loud that if anyone else had been home, I would have been embarrassed. Jaxon was able to hold on for a couple more minutes, slowly building me back up. No one had ever revved me up this much.

By the time he let go, I made sure my eyes were open to watch the ecstasy on his face. The pure pleasure in his eyes sent me over the cliff one more time. He had let my hands go in his release so I grabbed onto his back, sinking my nails into his skin with my back arched into him while riding out the waves. He finally collapsed onto the spot right next to me. I rolled over to lay my head on his chest while we both panted from exertion.

His hand ran up and down my back softly. The soothing motion made my eyes heavy. I sat up to look at the clock because I had work tonight and Jaxon pulled me back down to his chest.

"Shh, Beautiful . . . just sleep. I'll wake you in time." He leaned down to kiss my forehead.

- THIRTEEN -

The weeks until winter break flew by. I thought it was best if we stayed away from the parties for the rest of the semester. Jaxon didn't argue with me. I think he felt like he couldn't yet control the urge to punch other guys who got too close to me. It was nice to be able to go out without the added drama of other people. I also still wasn't able to admit we were in an actual relationship, so if we didn't hang out around others, I didn't have to define it. Jaxon never brought it up, either. We'd had a lot of time to open up with each other, and he finally told me about his dad dying and how hard it was for him to cope afterward. It seemed like a good time to tell him about my parents, but I just couldn't do it.

We hadn't seen each other very much this week, besides at night-time after one or the other got off work. We entered finals week and I realized it was too hard to study around Jaxon, so I forbade him from coming over to distract me. It seemed to work out for the best because we both felt extremely confident about our grades.

On Thursday after our last final, all five of us were hanging out at the guys' apartment watching movies and eating junk food. We had all planned on going out to a house party together later, but we still had a couple of hours until then. Quinn convinced us to finally get out and celebrate the end of the semester.

"Are you excited about spending the holidays with your mom and dad, Emerson?" Jaxon asked.

Quinn's head shot over to look straight at me. I knew she was shocked that I hadn't told him yet. She tried to act casual, moving toward the kitchen as if to get something, but it was obvious something had bothered her. Cole stood up awkwardly to join her.

"Uh . . . no, not really. I don't really like holidays." Actually, holidays were the absolute worst time of the year, aside from February 2, the day they were both killed. Coincidentally, that was also my birthday. Yep, happy birthday to me. I *never* celebrate it. It's forbidden. Quinn doesn't even mention my birthday anymore.

Completely oblivious to our odd reactions, Jaxon laughed a little and said, "What? Who doesn't like the holidays?" He was holding my hand and I had to release it.

I looked over at our audience; Quinn, Cole, and Jace all knew. I looked to them for help, for someone to distract him from this topic. No one stepped up and I was all alone.

I gripped my hands together tightly and murmured, "Umm . . . someone who . . . doesn't have parents." It was hard to get out of my mouth, but I couldn't lie to him.

He turned to look at me, a little more concerned now, but I could tell he still thought I was pulling some weird joke on him. "What are you talking about, Beautiful? Yes, you do. You've told me tons of stories about how you grew up."

"All of those stories stopped before I turned fifteen. They were both killed in a car accident," I whispered, wringing the blood from my pale hands.

"Emerson?" he asked, appearing stunned. "Why haven't you told me this before?" His voice rose to almost a shout.

"Dude, it's time to chill out and leave her alone," Jace said, looking up at him from his spot on the couch.

Jaxon looked at his brother and I watched as hurt and even frustration crossed his features. "You knew about her parents?" He then jabbed his finger at Jace and turned to look at me again. "Fucking *Jace* knew?" To others he may have appeared furious, but to me and everyone else in the room, we could tell he was just hurt.

"I'm so sorry, Jaxon," I said in a calm voice, hoping it would bleed into him.

"Jax, seriously, stop it. It was a weak moment; you guys weren't even together yet. She had just come back from home to see you, when she saw that Audrey was here. She got upset and it just came out." Great, yet another piece of information I hadn't told him yet. Girlfriend of the year right here. Although I guess I didn't even have that title.

Cole finally stepped up. "Jax, you need to lay off of her or I'm taking her out of here, away from you. You can see her when you get back from break." The protective big brother was coming out in him and I loved him for it. But this was entirely my fault; he deserved to know that about me.

When Cole talked about taking me away from him, I saw his expression snap from infuriated to frightened. He quickly came up to me and knelt between my legs. Jace got up and left. Once Cole and Quinn were satisfied that Jaxon wasn't going to yell at me anymore, they left the living room as well.

"Baby . . ." He laid his forehead down on my leg. "Don't leave. I'm sorry I yelled," he apologized, lifting his head.

"I'm not going anywhere, Jax." I rubbed my hands down the side of his scruffy face.

"Why didn't you tell me? I told you about my dad."

"When you were telling me about your dad, it seemed like your moment. I felt that if I were to tell you about my parents at that time, I would just be one-upping you. 'Oh, you lost one parent, well I lost two.' You needed that private time to tell me about your dad. I honestly never talk about my parents anymore because of the way everything happened. I don't even talk to Quinn anymore about it."

He came up onto the couch next to me and pulled me into his lap. I wrapped my hands around him and kissed his neck.

"What happened when they died?" I instantly stiffened at the question. "Tell me." his voice was kind but firm. No more beating around the bush.

This whole event is basically why I've become the way I have. My life since then has fixated on that moment in a vicious cycle. I've never been able to step away from it. It's why I created my rules, it's why I haven't been able to give myself fully to Jaxon, and it's why events like this continue to come between us.

"My parents were divorced. My dad was remarried to Ellie, Quinn's mom. That's how we're sisters." He nodded his head because he knew we were actually stepsisters and not blood relatives. "Everything was perfect. My parents didn't fight anymore, and I got Ellie and Quinn in the deal. Then one day, our principal pulled me out of class and told me my parents had died. Together. In the same car. My parents couldn't stand each other, the last time I had checked, and they certainly didn't just ride around in cars together." I took a deep breath and he rubbed circles along my hand. "That was the day that I learned that people always leave. If they aren't cheating on one another, they're dying. My parents did both in the same day. It hurts too much to get close to anyone; I couldn't risk feeling that kind of loneliness again. I almost didn't make it out alive, and if it happened again, I know I wouldn't." I spoke all of this to his shoulder, too afraid to see his judging eyes.

He placed his hand underneath my chin and lifted it up. I'm not sure I liked what I saw on his face, but it was better than judgment. He looked as if everything I just said made total sense, as if now he understood why I acted the way I did.

"Emerson, I would never cheat on you. You have to know that no other girl compares to you. There's no reason for me even to need anything from someone else, when everything I want is here with you." I nodded my head, even though I knew that he couldn't be one hundred percent sure. He hadn't come across every girl. One day, he would get tired of my crap. "You have to stop worrying that you'll lose me. There's nowhere else in this world that I want to be. I love *you*, beautiful girl."

I gasped at his exclamation. Love? When did we get to love? How could I possibly say that back to him? I had never said those words to anyone after my parents' death. Not even Quinn or Ellie. Those words were permanent.

He grabbed both sides of my face and looked into my eyes. "Relax. I won't say it again for a while. I just want you to get used to the fact that one day, when you're comfortable with it, I'll tell you every day, multiple times a day. I want you to know how much I love you every single damn day, but for now, I'll just let you soak it in." He kissed my eyelids, nose, and each of my cheeks. "Besides, I know you feel the same way even if you can't say it. It's not possible for me to feel this deep of a connection and for you not to. I can't be the only one feeling this."

I pushed him back down onto the couch and started kissing him hungrily, and he matched my fervor. "You're the most amazing boyfriend a girl could ask for."

From underneath me, I saw his eyes shoot wide open in delight. "Boyfriend?" he hollered excitedly.

"Yes, I can at least admit to this right now. Will you be my boyfriend, Jaxon Riley?" I laughed at him and my ridiculousness.

His face relaxed into a happy, contented look and he quietly responded, "Baby, I thought you'd never ask." He flipped me underneath him with one hand in my hair and continued kissing me. Our hands started roaming each other's bodies, enjoying this new step for me. For us.

"Em, can we come out now? I really want to see if Emma Stone and Ryan Gosling hook up!" Quinn yelled from down the hallway.

Still not letting go of Jaxon's mouth, I shouted back, *"No, go away!"* Although I don't know if they could actually understand me.

Jaxon chuckled into our kiss. I grabbed him through his pants. He instantly lost the grin, and lust immediately consumed his expression. He dipped down to grind against me and we both moaned into each other's mouths.

"Ew, guys, stop it. Not on the couch." Quinn was right next to us, batting me off of Jaxon.

"Oh, like we haven't gotten plenty of fluids on this couch already, sweetheart." Cole laughed from behind her.

"All of you are disgusting! Shut up, push play, and keep your fluids to yourselves," Jace complained.

"Y'all couldn't have come at a worse time," Jaxon grumbled.

"Quinn, you don't even care about Ryan Gosling. You just want to watch it because you think Emma Stone is hot," I added.

"Hell, yeah, that's my girl!" Cole shouted proudly. Quinn laughed and smacked Cole in the chest while sticking her tongue out at me.

"Hey Quinn, guess what?" Jaxon said, looking around Cole at her. "Emerson asked me to be her boyfriend." He was teasing me, but he had a huge grin on his face. I didn't realize it would be this easy to make him so joyful.

Quinn started clapping and jumping up and down. "Emmy, you finally put the poor guy out of his misery!"

I instantly turned to face Jaxon. I knew Quinn was playing with me, but there was also truth in her statement. I pouted my bottom lip out at him. "Misery?" I asked.

"Baby, there hasn't been a second of misery for me since you said you were mine and mine only." He leaned down, sucked my pouty bottom lip into his mouth, and nipped at it between his teeth. I started running my hands through his hair again.

Jace had turned the lights back off and resumed the movie. Jaxon and I sat stock-still in our spots, but I was still riled up from earlier and my need wasn't going away.

"Babe, I don't think I can sit here . . ." I started to say.

He was already standing up with me in his arms. "Oh, thank God!" he shouted.

"You two are so damn annoying sometimes. At least go to her place," Jace grumbled. He sure was frustrated a lot more lately.

"Good idea, bro," Jax said as he turned around from the hall-way and headed out the door. "Oh, and I swear to God, we are getting you laid when we get home. You're grumpy!" He pointed straight at Jace. Cole burst out laughing at the scowl Jace made.

As we were walking down the hallway, I frowned at him. "You're going to go prowling for girls when you get home?" He walked us over to Quinn's and my couch.

"Oh, Beautiful, is that jealousy I hear?" He nuzzled into my neck.

"What? No. I don't get jealous." It was true. I'd never gotten jealous of any other girls. Could I be jealous of the idea of another girl hanging around Jaxon while I'm halfway across the country? That idea had never crossed my mind before; I hadn't thought about him going home in a couple of days and spending time with all of his friends from home. Audrey would be there, no doubt. "Well, maybe . . . a little bit. But only because I've seen how gorgeous one of your exes is. I can only imagine what the others look like."

"Trust me; there will be no prowling on my part. I'll probably spend most of my time depressed because I'll be missing my girl-friend." He flashed all of his brilliantly white teeth at me. He was enjoying that word a little too much already.

"You'll miss me?" I asked, surprised.

"Emerson, I miss you when you go to the bathroom, and now I'm supposed to go weeks without you?"

The winter break was a month long. We all promised each other to come back before the month was up, because that was a long time to be separated. But a good majority of that time would be spent apart at our own families' houses.

"I know that I'll miss you too," I whispered into his neck. It was still hard for me to be this up-front and exposed about my feelings.

"Come home with me. Please, you can meet my mom. She's great and I know she's dying to meet you."

"I can't, Jax, I need to go see Ellie. I'd invite you back with me, but I know how much you miss your mom."

"Yeah, I can't leave her during the holidays . . ." he said sadly.

"Hey, I understand." I grabbed his face. "It's only a couple of weeks, then we'll come back here and lock ourselves in your room and not come out till we're forced to go to class." I laughed.

"Promise?" he asked sadly.

"Promise." I leaned in to capture his lips. We were going to enjoy our last couple of days together.

- FOURTEEN -

Jaxon and I had holed up in his room for the rest of the weekend. I'm positive Cole and Quinn did the same thing in her room, because Cole was leaving with the guys to go back home as well. I never saw Jace for the three days that Jaxon and I had together; he must have gone to stay at a friend's house because we were so "nauseating," as he had repeatedly reminded us. I was starting to feel bad for leaving Jace out so much. He must be looking forward to having time alone with his brother and best friend back home.

Quinn and I dropped the guys off at the airport before we left to go home. Jaxon gave me the keys to his truck, in case I needed it for any reason at all. I made it known that there was no way in hell I would even attempt to back that thing out of the garage, let alone drive it down the street. I could just imagine crushing some poor, tiny car. He just laughed at me. I did ask if I could drive the motorcycle around though.

"Absolutely not." All humor had left his face.

He grabbed the keys back from my hands and removed the motorcycle keys from the keychain, just in case. I never actually planned to drive it; I just wanted to rile him up before he left. Mission accomplished.

I'll never forget the look on his face when he was saying goodbye. I swear if he had stayed in front of me at that security entrance any longer, I would have seen a tear slip down his cheek. I tried to reassure him that the time would fly by, but I was equally upset about this separation. I believed we still had a lot of obstacles in our fresh relationship, and this was such an inconvenient time to be apart. I hugged him tightly and leaned up on my toes to kiss his lips.

"Bye, baby," I whispered on his lips.

"Bye, Beautiful, I lo . . ." He stopped himself and sighed. "I'll see you soon."

I gave him a sad look as I waved good-bye. I hated that he had to hold back his feelings for me, but I still wasn't ready to say those words back to him, no matter what my feelings were.

~

The next two weeks moved at a snail's pace. Ellie and Charles had so many events planned for Quinn and me to attend. Not the fun kind, either. The dull business-function kind that we had to get dressed up for, smile pretty, and make polite conversation. I tried to act as if I enjoyed it because it was good business for Charles and it was the least I could do for him after everything he had done for me.

Jace and Jaxon had been waking up extremely early every morning to help around their mom's land while they were there. It was really hard to catch Jax on the phone. The two-hour time difference usually wouldn't have been a big deal, but Jaxon was going to bed really early, while I was getting home late from the functions and then sleeping in late. I was becoming frustrated with the lack of communication we'd had lately. We originally planned to video chat every day, but we hadn't been able to catch each other once yet. The most fun I'd had so far was sending him pictures of myself all dressed up for the functions. Every time I got a chance to check my phone later in the evening, he had always sent me back a sexy message saying how much he enjoyed my pictures.

I know that the guys had gone out a couple of times to meet up with friends in their town. Quinn always got edgy when Cole would go out to parties with them. Being such close friends with Cole before he started dating Quinn, we got to hear about all of the girls he would hook up with when he went back home for visits. I think Quinn was worried about those girls. I'd lost count of the number of times I told her how ridiculous she sounded because Cole was absolutely crazy about her.

Recently, he had gone to a party and had gotten so drunk he ended up crashing on the couch there. When Quinn didn't hear from him until the next morning, she was livid. Everyone in the house could hear her yelling through the phone. I realized he was explaining what had happened and was trying to reassure Quinn that there hadn't been any girls in his vicinity when he crashed. She apparently didn't care and eventually just hung up on him.

That was four days ago, and neither of them had even attempted to contact each other. At first I wasn't worried because Quinn was complaining to me while Cole was complaining to Jaxon, so I knew they would eventually cave. After four days, though, I was starting to worry that their pride would get in the way and they might not be able to get past this.

Quinn had been walking around crying off and on. I was consoling her on the couch in the large living room when the doorbell rang. Ellie and Charles had gone out for breakfast together, so I knew that I would need to get up to answer it. I pulled the door open, completely surprised by Cole, who was standing there looking as sad and depressed as Quinn felt. He had bags under his bloodshot eyes, as if he hadn't slept a wink.

"Cole! It's a long trip from Texas for a surprise visit!" I asked, shocked.

I heard Quinn gasp in the background, "What?"

"Sorry, Emmy." He shoved past me, barely even noticing that I had spoken. He already had his eyes on Quinn in the living room. He reached her on the couch and pulled her up over his shoulder, her head hitting his strong back.

"What the hell, Cole?" she yelled. "You can't just come charging in here!"

"Enough, Quinn! You've been ridiculous long enough." He found the staircase and started climbing the steps with a squirming Quinn over his shoulder. I followed behind, giggling at the show. "Where's her room?" he asked me.

"Take the left hallway. It's the last one on the right," I told him.

When she realized where he was taking her, she stopped fighting him. "Thanks, Em," he called back, turning down the hallway at the top of the stairs. Thank God, he had come to work things out.

I walked up to my room to take a shower. I took all my clothes off and searched for ones to change into for the day. My phone started ringing, but it sounded different from my regular ringtone. When I found it, I realized that's not what was ringing, and then remembered that I had kept my laptop open in case Jaxon and I could actually catch one another online. I positioned the screen so it only displayed my bare shoulders and face, since I was already undressed for my shower.

I answered excitedly, "Hi, baby!"

"Damn, Beautiful, you're a sight for sore eyes." He looked tired, but he also looked really tan, and if it was possible he looked even more muscular. As if all he had been doing this whole time was working out in the sun. Which is probably exactly what he *had* been doing.

"Wow, you don't look so bad yourself." I winked at him. "So . . . I'm pretty sure Quinn and Cole finally made up," I told him.

"Oh, yeah? Why do you think that? I thought I would've never heard the end of it from him, if that was finally to happen."

"He just showed up here and dragged her upstairs." I laughed.

"What? He flew back? That bastard," he grumbled, sounding upset.

"Why do you say that? I'm honestly glad I don't have to follow a crying Quinn around anymore."

"No, I'm glad they're making up. I'm just jealous he got to go see his girlfriend. I'm about two seconds away from jumping on a plane myself, especially after seeing your gorgeous face again." He grinned at me through the screen. I loved that little smirk on the edges of his lips.

"I'm glad you caught me. I was about to jump in the shower."

"Yeah, Jace and I are wiped. Mom has a million things for us to do. We just came in for some lunch." He smiled at me and then I watched as realization hit him. "Babe, do you have a shirt on?"

I shook my head at him. "I was about to get into the shower," I reminded him coyly.

"So, you actually don't have anything on at all right now?" When I shook my head, he leaned forward and groaned. "Just move the camera down a little bit." He pointed downward.

I decided to do him one better and lean back in my chair so he could still see my face while he got a show of my chest. I loved the lust that engulfed his blue eyes. When I reached down to cup my breasts in both hands and push them together for him, I swear I heard him growl.

I was about to ask him to show me something, when I spotted Jace walking into the room behind him. His eyes shot wide when he saw me in my compromising position on his brother's screen. I rocked back forward so the camera was back on just my shoulders and face. Jaxon jutted that plush bottom lip out at me in a cute pout. I almost returned to my seduction, but I remembered how mad he would be when he realized Jace was behind him. Who, by the way, was still standing there with a big Cheshire-cat grin on his face.

"Uh, Jax?" I asked.

"Yeah, Beautiful?" he responded breathily.

"Next time we should do this with your bedroom door closed." I pointed behind him. His head shot behind him to look at his brother.

"Damn, Em, I knew you had a great rack, but wow . . ." Jace leaned over to look at me from behind his brother, who was now standing up.

Jaxon did not look happy. I saw his hand shoot up to grab his laptop screen. Before it slammed shut, I heard him say, "I miss you, baby doll!" Then the screen went black.

I got up to walk to my shower, laughing at the image of those two, who were probably wrestling with each other right now. I missed Jaxon tremendously, but I realized that I missed Jace too. He had become like a brother to me. Well, maybe not a brother, since brothers wouldn't tell you how hot your rack is, but definitely closer than just a friend.

When I stepped out of the shower, I noticed I had a text message waiting for me.

Jaxon: Don't be mad at me, but check your e-mail.

I hate when people start comments like that; my mind always shoots to the worst conceivable outcome. What could he have possibly done in the last twenty-five minutes that would make me mad? When I opened up my e-mail, I noticed that there was a confirmation for a plane ticket to Texas and the flight was leaving tomorrow.

Me: You bought me a plane ticket?

Jaxon: You don't have to use it, but I hope you will. I miss you like crazy.

Me: You better be at that airport bearing gifts for doing this!

Jaxon: YOU'RE COMING?

Me: There's a handsome hunk on the other side of this ticket. Of course I am.

Jaxon: I'd bring the world for you if I could.

Ellie and Charles were sad to see me off so soon, but I think Ellie was happier that there was someone out there who was worth it for me to visit. I laughed at Quinn, who could barely tell me good-bye because she was so far down Cole's throat. We'd be back in our apartment together soon anyway.

When I got to the arrivals terminal, I rode an escalator down to the baggage claim. Jaxon was the first person in the line of greeters waiting at the very bottom. I started laughing the instant I saw him because he looked like a little kid at Christmas. His excitement was contagious, and I noticed the other people around him smiling at his giddiness. I'm sure my face mirrored his as well. He grabbed both my bag and me before I even made it down the last two steps. I wrapped my legs around his waist and pulled his face to my lips.

He walked me over to a bench, kissing me, when I heard an elderly woman say, "Man, can I get a welcome like that one?" I laughed into his mouth.

He sat me down on the bench and handed me a silver wrapped box that I hadn't noticed he was holding behind his back.

"Jax, I was kidding about gifts," I said, while taking it from his hands.

"It's nothing, really. Just open it."

I slid my finger under the silver flap and peeled off the wrapping. When I opened the box, I instantly knew what was in it. Chocolate raspberry truffles. I don't know how he had found this, but this man was mind-blowing.

"You remembered?" I gasped in a whisper.

"I remember everything about you, Emerson."

"Wow, I'm in love with Texas already." That made him throw his head back and laugh.

We walked out to the parking garage and I realized I had no idea what kind of car I was looking for; with Jaxon, it could be anything. To my total shock, he walked right up to an old black muscle car that appeared to be in perfect condition.

I froze. "This. Is. *Not*. Your. Car." I could totally imagine him driving this and I was already turned on.

"Uh . . . yeah, my dad rebuilt with me," he said self-consciously.

"Why the hell didn't you bring this with you to California? This is so hot!"

Relief spanned his face. "My mom said I would only get in trouble with it. Little did she know, I would move right next door to trouble." He winked at me.

"Oh, I can show you all kinds of trouble in this." I rubbed the shiny black hood.

"Please, God, do." He came around to me and pushed me backward up against it.

"What kind of car is this?" I asked, while he was moving his body up against mine. "All I know is, it's hot."

He leaned down and whispered in my ear, "It's a '67 Camaro. Four hundred seventy horsepower."

"I have no idea what any of that means, but I can't wait to watch you drive it."

He laughed while opening my door for me and helped me into the seat. I don't know what it is about seeing a guy drive a manual transmission. Maybe it's the way they pull the shifter into each gear, the way the muscles in their forearms flex with the movement, or maybe it's the cocky smile Jax got on his face while driving it, but I was thoroughly turned on by the time we pulled up to his house.

I was still staring at him when he put it into park. "I don't think I can meet your mom like this."

"Like what?" he asked, smiling.

"Like I'm about to jump your bones, that's what." I shifted in my seat uncomfortably.

"Oh, Beautiful, there will be plenty of time for that." He winked.

Before I could tell him I didn't think I could wait, Jace came barreling down the porch steps. There was a gorgeous and surprisingly young woman who was the female version of her sons trailing right behind him. When I opened my car door, Jace scooped me out of the car and into a bear hug.

"Emmy! I missed you," he said, smiling. Someone was finally in a better mood; maybe he had gotten some over the holidays.

Laughing at his enthusiasm, I returned his hug. "I missed you too, Jace."

"Sorry about walking in on you and Jax yesterday. I got my ass kicked for that." He gave me a puppy-dog look that closely resembled his brother's.

"Don't try to pull that sweet look on her after you violated her privacy." His mom shoved him. She knew about that? *Great.*

"Oh," I said, mortified.

She pulled me into a hug once Jace set me down. "Oh, sorry, I didn't mean to embarrass you. These boys tell me everything. I've

heard it all. Trust me, it doesn't bother me." I smiled at her warmth.
"I'm Julie, by the way."

"I'm Em. Thank you for letting me stay in your home."

"Think nothing of it. So you like to be called Em?" she asked.
"Jaxon calls you Emerson." Jaxon had made his way around the car
and was smiling at the two of us.

"Yeah, Jax is the only one that calls me that. I tried to break him
of it," I said, shrugging.

"Come on, ladies, I'm hungry," Jaxon said while putting his
arms around both of us and directing us up the porch stairs.

"You're awful smiley, son," Julie grinned up at him.

"I've got my two favorite girls in the same place. What could
be better?"

"Ugh, gag me, please. When did you become such a pussy?" Jace
asked, while squeezing under Jax's arm and pulling his mom away
from us. These two were dangerously adorable with their mom.

Jaxon's mom didn't care that I would be sleeping in his room
with him and she didn't bat an eyelash at some of the stories they
were telling her about college parties. I learned that she got pregnant with them when she was seventeen, which was why she looked
so young. Their dad sounded like he had been crazy in love with her
and he had worked extremely hard to build a magnificent life for his
family. I had no idea how well off Jace and Jaxon were. Apparently
their dad had been the CEO of his own company, so when he died,
they were at least left with enough to live comfortably for years and
years. I didn't ask for specifics. I just enjoyed hearing all of their
family stories; they seemed to be pretty tight-knit. I had heard Jax
talk on the phone with his mom every couple of days back home,
but it was nice to see them all together in person.

I would only be out here for a short time before all three of us
would fly back to California. We spent most of our time together,
Jace and Julie included. Surprisingly, it wasn't lame at all to have

their mom with us the whole time. She was awesome, and she could joke right along with her boys. I could see where they got their charm. I can only imagine how devastatingly handsome their dad was.

This was the first time since I'd met Quinn that I wouldn't be spending her birthday with her, but I was glad that Cole was there. I talked on the phone with her the majority of that day, neither one of us liking the fact that we weren't together. I may hate celebrating my birthday, but I love being with Quinn on hers. Jaxon and I had a chocolate cake and flowers delivered to her and she made me promise to bring her something back from Texas.

Jaxon and I also went to a few parties in his town. It was nice meeting a large number of the people that he grew up with. Their parties were a lot more low-key and mellow than anything I'd been to on Fraternity Row. On New Year's Eve, we went to a bonfire out on one of their friends' property. I'd never actually been to a real bonfire before, so it was nice to experience it with him and his family. I could stare into Jaxon's blue eyes lit by a fire for the rest of my life. For the first time ever, I kissed someone at midnight and I was thankful it was Jaxon I was kissing.

His family showed me around their town. Jaxon ended up buying me a pair of leather cowboy boots that he said would look hot on me with a dress. Julie bought me a dress that she said would go great with the boots. In one of the stores we ended up looking through, we lost track of Jace. I eventually came across him in the back of the store. I was surprised to see him talking with Audrey. He was speaking in harsh, clipped tones to her and she looked incredibly sad.

"Hey Jace, are you ready to go?" I said across the aisle from him, afraid to go over there and get in between them.

She looked at me with a shocked expression, "What is *she* doing here?" she demanded, raising her voice to him.

"She's Jax's girlfriend; that's what she's doing here, Audrey," he replied sharply, walking away. Audrey looked upset by this fact. I really didn't like the girl, but I felt bad about the miserable expression on her face.

He came over and threw an arm around my shoulders, and we walked away from her. "You okay?" I asked, looking up at him.

"Totally fine, Ems. She just cornered me." He shrugged and we walked back to the front of the store to find my boyfriend and his mom.

On our last night there, Jaxon was cooking us all dinner. I was thrilled to see how this would turn out, because he had never cooked back home before. He had the surround sound throughout the house playing country music. Jace, his mom, and I were all sitting on the couch with drinks and talking. When a new song started playing, Julie clapped her hands together.

"Oh, I love Brantley Gilbert!" she exclaimed.

Jaxon came over to me with an apron on and reached out his hand for mine. "Dance with me?" he asked.

I smiled, placing my hand in his, and he pulled me into an embrace. I put one hand on his shoulder and one in his outstretched palm. I looked over to see Jace pulling his mom up to dance with him as well. Jaxon spun me around the living room. Man, these boys could dance; their mom had taught them well. There wasn't an inch of this living room that Jace and Jax didn't cover with the two of us. Jace kept switching his mom and me back and forth between his brother and him. Jaxon only allowed me to dance with Jace for so long before he would come steal me back. Jace and his mom were laughing hysterically at how he kept spinning her around in a circle repeatedly as fast as he could.

Throughout the whole song, Jaxon was singing along right into my ear. I closed my eyes and let his voice flow through me. The artist sang about how no one knew his girl like he did. When he sang that she was his best friend, I melted into Jaxon. This was the sweetest song. I had no doubt in my mind he was singing this to me on purpose, and in a way, no one *did* know me like he did. I gripped him tighter as he sang the last words of the song to with his intoxicating voice.

I opened my eyes when the song ended and realized he had danced us out of the living room away from his family. We were staring at each other hungrily.

Then he stepped back and shouted, "Ma, can you finish dinner for me?" He was hastily untying the apron from around his waist and tossing it on the ground.

"Yeah, sweetie, see y'all later!" she shouted back from the living room.

He hauled me out the front door into the night faster than my shorter legs could handle. We got all the way to the car and he opened the door and sat me inside. When he had my seat belt buckled, he went around to the driver's side.

I jutted out my bottom lip. "I was looking forward to eating a dinner you actually made."

"Mom's probably throwing it out right now and starting all over again. You weren't missing anything, I promise." He laughed.

I enjoyed watching him as he drove. He didn't drive off of their property. Instead, he drove off the dirt road into the fields. I was surprised this car was taking the bumps so well. When it was pitch black and it looked as though we were in the middle of nowhere, he parked the car. His fingers switched on the high beams, which illuminated a beautiful pond. It was fairly large with boulders and tall grass surrounding it like a hidden gem. In the night, the surface of the water looked like black glass.

"I had one more thing to show you," he said quietly. "Jace and I use to live here in the summers. It might be a little cold right now because it's January, but it won't be too bad."

"It's really beautiful."

I got out of the car and walked in front of the headlights. Jaxon came around the opposite side to meet me. Taking advantage of our moment of solitude, I pulled my shirt over my head and then slipped my jeans down over my ankles. I smiled up at Jax, who was watching me with wide eyes. I pulled my panties off next. When I reached behind and unsnapped my bra, I threw it up onto the hood of the car.

The look in his eyes screamed that he wanted to own me, and I didn't know how to comprehend that look. I walked over, stood directly in front of his hood, and stretched out on top of it.

"I think I promised you all kinds of trouble on this." I patted the hood, while eyeing him seductively.

I raised my hands above my head, almost reaching the windshield. He stepped in between my thighs, reached out to palm my breasts, and ran his tongue across them. My back arched at his touch.

"Fuck, baby, you lying on this car . . . I'm pretty sure I had wet dreams about this kind of thing when I was sixteen," he whispered on my skin.

He nipped his way down my stomach until he hit the spot he was looking for. I was so revved up from listening to him sing to me, from being wrapped up in his arms while dancing, and from watching him drive that car earlier; it only took a couple of minutes until I was screaming his name, thankful we were out in the middle of nowhere. He quickly removed all of his clothes and then slid his hands up my backside, picking me up. He walked us down to the water. I gave him a worried look when he stood up on a high rock above the water. My fingers clenched into his bare shoulders.

"Ready?" he asked.

"No!" I squeaked.

"Too bad, Beautiful," he said, right before he jumped into the water with me in his arms. This pond was deeper than it looked. We sank down below the surface and it took us a second to swim back up to the top. It was absolutely freezing.

When I came out of the water, I ran my hands over my face and hair to get the water out of my eyes. "Jaxon, it's freezing!" I shouted.

He came up laughing. "Aw, babe, it's not that bad." I swam over to him to wrap around his body for warmth. "I'll warm you up," he said, nipping my ear.

With one swift thrust, he was inside of me, and I cried out instantly. If I had more time to think about it, I would have been impressed with his accuracy in the water, but before I could be amazed, he was pushing me up and down on him. The water had me out of my element and I had no control over our movements. I decided then just to relish this moment with him and all the power he had over me. I threw my head back with my hair in the water, enjoying his thrusts. His forearms were cradling my back and his hands were laced through my hair, holding me as close as he wanted. He sucked on the hollow point of my neck down to my breasts.

All of a sudden, he started to thrust into me and then stopped. He slowly drew my body back up him and quickly thrust back in. I dug my nails into his back with this new delicious rhythm. I needed to hear that groan that I love so much, so I started clinching around him. Clinch. Release. Clinch. Release.

"I love when you do that, baby," he groaned into my ear, as I made him temporarily lose his rhythm.

"I love everything you're doing to me right now."

The water between our bodies and his movements were creating a wonderful friction building in between my legs. I wanted to hold this off as long as possible, and I never wanted this moment to end.

"Emerson, you're amazing. I still can't believe I found you. Promise you'll stay."

"I promise," I breathed. "Promise you'll stay patient with me." I trailed kisses down his jaw.

"I promise," he replied. "I need you in my life."

"You have me."

"I love you." When I tensed up, he started slowing his movements to provide comfort for me.

I placed my forehead down onto his shoulder, silently telling him I felt the same way. I was afraid that if I said it out loud, I would be jinxing myself. I feel as though I'd been doing so well, and I'd become an actual girlfriend. If I took this next step too soon, somehow I'd end up failing him. I needed to find a way to tell him, though. I just needed more time.

Shortly after, he started speeding up his movements. I'd never felt him this deep before, and it was heavenly. I couldn't help focusing on his handsome face. The lights of the car were shining on us in the pond. The shadows contrasted against his high cheekbones perfectly. I couldn't believe a guy this gorgeous could be so thoughtful and understanding. I began feeling that wonderful sensation of completion spiraling through me. When I called out his name, he followed behind me two seconds later.

When we finally walked back through the front door of his house, my teeth were chattering. We didn't have a towel to dry off with, so we had to put our clothes back on our wet bodies, and my hair had drenched everything that my body hadn't.

"Jaxon Riley! Tell me you didn't take her into the pond?" Julie yelled at him right when we walked in. "Look at her, she's freezing!"

"Don't worry, Ma, I kept her warm," he said, chuckling. I turned and smacked him in the stomach. "Umph!"

"Get upstairs, you two." She laughed and smacked Jaxon on the back of the head on his way up.

"Geez, ladies, go easy on me!" he joked.

The next day we were at the airport saying sad good-byes to Julie. I felt at home here and I absolutely didn't want to leave. Now I understood why both of them wanted to come home on every holiday break. When the guys went to check their luggage, Julie came over to hug me and I had tears in my eyes.

"Don't cry, sweetheart." She hugged me tightly.

"I'm sorry; I can't help it. I just like it here so much."

"Please come back. I've never seen Jaxon so happy."

"I really hope I don't screw it up," I whispered into her hair.

She pulled back but kept a grip on each of my arms. "Guess what, love, you will. So will he. It's what you do with it once you've screwed up that matters." She smiled at me.

"Thank you." It was all I could say.

She grabbed my phone from my hand. "Here, have my number, and call me anytime you need to talk or vent. Jaxon told me your parents passed away. Don't hesitate to call me if you need a mom's ear. I won't take his side, promise." Then she gave me one more long hug that really brought the tears streaming down my face. Besides Ellie, I'd never met someone so open and loving. I squeezed her back just as tightly.

"What the hell, Ma; I leave for two seconds and you have her crying?" His words were harsh, but his tone was playful. He reached over and pulled me into his body while kissing my temple. Jaxon and Jace each gave her a kiss on the cheek and a hug, and then together, we walked through security to go back to the real world.

- FIFTEEN -

Our classes had all started back up. I had two classes with Jaxon, one class with Cole, and surprisingly, one class with Jace. We had an English class that both of us had been putting off. I was excited about that; I never got to hang out with Jace by myself, so this class provided the perfect opportunity. We would often hang out afterward and study together. It was also nice to have someone save me a seat.

The school was getting hyped up over the upcoming championship game that the team was playing in. The campus was littered with spirit posters, and everyone wore the school colors daily. Jaxon and Cole were practicing with the team twice a day now to prepare for the big game. They both came home exhausted and cranky every night. Quinn and I always tried to have food ready for them when they finished practice. It didn't take us long to notice a connection between being hungry and extreme crankiness. I was excited for them, but I would also be glad when this game was over.

Honestly, I'll be glad when this whole week is over. February 2 is tomorrow, the six-year anniversary of my parents' death and my twenty-first birthday. The closer it had gotten to this date, the more I had become agitated with everything and with nothing at all. I've been trying to hide my restless behavior from everyone, but I don't know how well I have been doing with that. I figured Jaxon and

Cole were too busy with practice, and by now, Quinn has learned not to bring up my birthday. A couple of years ago, I believed she honestly just forgot about it. I think that's for the best.

The football players all decided to have a party tonight. They claimed they needed to blow off a bunch of steam, even on a Tuesday. Apparently, the coach has been exceedingly rough on them at practice. Since half of the players are in fraternities as well, the party ended up being on Frat Row. I didn't really want to go; it honestly sounded like a bad idea with my mood. On the other hand, maybe I could blow off some steam as well.

When we returned from winter break, Quinn complained to Jaxon and me that we were becoming an old married couple, not going to parties anymore. I freaked out when she said that, and ever since then, we've been going to most of them. It's nice to go and have a good time with my boyfriend. Originally, I thought it would be stressful, with guys thinking they could touch me or with the way girls are still always hitting on Jaxon. We eventually found our groove, though, and have been having a good time.

By the time Quinn and I had finished getting ready, I was completely on edge and fidgety. For some reason, I just couldn't stop thinking about what tomorrow was. I heard the tail end of my cell phone ringing from in the kitchen, but I figured I had already missed it, so I'd check it when we started to head out.

"You're acting so weird. Sit down and breathe, Emmy." Quinn looked at me through the mirror while she reapplied her eyeliner.

"I'm not acting weird. I think I just really need to drink tonight," I said while shaking out my hands.

"Uh-oh, what's wrong? Did you and Jaxon have a fight?" She turned to face me.

"Quinn, he's not around enough lately for us to fight. Besides, there's nothing wrong with a college student just wanting to go out to drink." I shrugged my shoulders at her.

"Are you upset that he hasn't been around? It's almost over," she responded quietly.

"No, it honestly doesn't bother me. *I'm okay*, Quinn." I said the last part deliberately slowly so she would understand and, at the very least, recognize that I wasn't going to talk about it.

I really wasn't okay, but the last thing I wanted to do was have a therapy session. Tequila doesn't ask you to talk about your problems. Tequila and I have always gotten along. When I heard her sigh, I knew she wasn't happy about my response, but I also knew I had at least gotten her off my back for a little while longer.

There was a short tap on the front door and then it opened and closed. It had to be one of the guys, although they usually didn't even bother to knock. I heard boots shuffling on the carpet in the living room.

"Girls!" Jace called out down the hallway.

"In the closet," I called back.

When Jace came into the room, he was dressed to go out in a short-sleeved black button-down shirt; his dark, faded blue jeans fit him perfectly. His hair was styled in the signature Riley boy messy style and he was carrying his leather jacket, which meant he was probably riding the bike to the party tonight. I think he liked the option of being able to escape if he wanted to instead of having to ride with us.

"Geez, Em, stop checking him out so noticeably." Quinn elbowed me.

I watched as Jace's cheeks turned red. Oops. "Sorry! It's just so hard. I mean he's my boyfriend's identical twin. Obviously I like this brand." I gestured with my hand up and down, indicating Jace.

Jace and Quinn both started laughing at me. "Anyways," he started, with a shy smirk on his face, "I just left the field a little while ago and Coach was still running some of them. Apparently a couple of guys got in trouble, so they're being punished. Jax and

Cole included. When they stopped for a water break, they told me they could just meet us all at the party later. I'm sure half the team is already at the house."

"Uh-oh, why'd they get in trouble?" Quinn asked nervously.

Jace shrugged his shoulders. "I think they just weren't running plays correctly. Coach is anal like that."

"Great, now they'll be in delightful moods. It's probably best we meet them there," she responded.

I actually liked this plan better. I could get in a few shots before Jax even got there, without having to explain why I was taking them. Then hopefully, this crazy negative energy charging through my veins would chill out in time for me to act normal around my boyfriend. I hoped it worked, because I needed these memories out of my head. Last night, I dreamed about the last time I had spent with both my mom and dad, before they got divorced. We had gone to this little amusement park a couple of hours away and I had fallen in love with the only roller coaster there. I swear they rode that ride with me a million times that day. I just kept remembering how hard my dad was laughing when we rode through the upside-down loops. I needed to drown out that laugh. God, how do you stop missing someone? Especially someone you were so mad at?

"I'm going to ride the bike there; is that cool? Or do you ladies need me to drive you?" Jace asked while walking toward the door.

I was still stuck in my flashback, so Quinn responded for us. "Go ahead, Jace, we'll be right behind you." When he closed the door behind him, she turned and stared at my face. "Are you sure you're okay? Your face is pale."

"I'm fine, Quinn; stop mothering me. Let's go." I shouldn't have said that; it was cruel. She had always been my support through everything, but just for today and tomorrow, I didn't need anyone prying.

I grabbed my phone off the kitchen countertop and noticed I had actually missed two calls. One was from Jaxon, one was from a number I didn't recognize, and they had both left voice mails. I entered in my voice mailbox code and listened to what they had to say.

The first one was from Jax: *"Hey, babe, we fucked up at practice today, Coach is keeping us late. I'll meet you there tonight. Love you."* It was still strange to me how he would just throw in that last little line now. His voice had sounded stressed; looks like he was joining the crowd that would be blowing off some steam tonight.

The second message was from a voice I didn't know: *"Yes, I'm calling for an Emerson Moore. This is William Gordon calling from the Law Offices of Gordon, Simon & Bates. I have an urgent matter pertaining to sensitive material set up by Robert and Michelle Moore. If you could call me back at your earliest convenience, I would appreciate it."*

Thank God Quinn was in the bathroom and had left me alone in here. I'm positive if my face was pale before, it was downright colorless now. My stomach had hit the floor when I heard my parents' names. No one had said either of their names to me in years. What could this lawyer possibly have to tell me? It's not like my parents were out there stirring up new situations. They were dead. Mr. Gordon would have to wait until tomorrow. Tonight I was getting wasted.

There were two things wrong with this party already. The first being that there wasn't any tequila, only beer. I could get drunk off beer, but it was taking me longer to get there. The second problem was that Devon Ryan was here, the only other guy I came close to dating. I never expected to see him again after he transferred to some school up north after freshman year. If I were smart, I would have just left after discovering the first problem.

When I arrived, I went straight for the kitchen to find the hidden liquor. To my disappointment, all the bottles were empty. When I slammed the last cabinet above the fridge in frustration, I felt hands reach up around my waist and help me off the counter-top. The mysterious hands set me down and I turned around to face Devon.

"Devon?" I gasped when I saw his golden brown eyes and blond hair. He still looked as handsome as ever. He had a long, lean body like a swimmer, which I had appreciated freshman year. Now that I've had Jaxon's body, though, nothing could compare.

"Hey, little lady. How's life treating you?" He smirked at me, assuming I was checking him out. I wasn't, though; I was just surprised to see him.

"Well, I plan on spending today and tomorrow drunk, but then everything will go back to being great after that." I popped open a beer.

"Uh, okay. What's today and tomorrow?" Shit, why had I just said that out loud, especially to him?

We needed a subject change. "Don't you have a cousin down here?"

He laughed at my avoidance. "Yes, that's why I'm here. Well, that, and for the championship game. You guys got lucky with that Jaxon Riley guy; he's killing it out here."

"Yeah, my boyfriend's pretty great." I finished the beer and went for another.

"Is that what you're calling those poor suckers these days?" He laughed.

"Nope, I'm a one-man kind of woman these days, Devon."

"Holy shit, this guy must walk on water to get Em Moore to settle down." He pinched me in the side and I laughed.

An hour and a half later, I had finally reached wasted status and I was on the dance floor trying to sweat out this frantic energy

I still had inside of me. I was hoping I could drink it away, but I swear someone in this room had the same exact laugh as my dad, or maybe I was just hearing things. Devon was dancing next to me in the middle of the dance floor. I wouldn't say we were dancing together, just dancing in the same vicinity. I didn't feel like dancing with anyone; I just needed this feeling to go away.

I stepped away from the dancing to get another drink out of the kitchen when I was scooped up into strong, familiar arms. He started raining kisses across my eyelids, nose, and then finally my mouth. I smiled into his kiss and enjoyed the clean scent of Jaxon.

"I missed you, Beautiful. Sorry it's taken me so long to get here." He smiled down at me, although he still had some tension in the corners of his eyes.

"S'okay." Damn, I was smashed and I knew I was slurring.

"Are you drunk?" he asked, shocked. I couldn't tell if he was upset about that or not, so I just shrugged my shoulders.

All of a sudden, Quinn came barreling through and grabbed me by the arms to take me in the kitchen. Jaxon followed behind, along with Cole.

"Emmy, tell me I didn't see you out there dancing with Devon Ryan?" she screeched at me.

"Okay, first of all, I wasssn't dancin' with anybody." I hope they couldn't tell how bad I was slurring. My head didn't feel drunk, but my actions showed that I was. "But ya, thas him." I placed my forearms down on the countertop to steady myself. This room was spinning faster than I cared for.

"Shit, Em, you're hammered," Cole said, laughing at me.

"Who the hell is Devon Ryan?" Jaxon stepped in to ask Quinn.

"No one," I said.

"The only guy besides you that came close to being her boyfriend," she decided to offer.

"Shut the hell up, Quinn; I never had a boyfriend before Jax."

He continued giving Quinn a questioning look, deeming me too drunk to be accountable, so she continued, "He was the reason she created the limit-of-three rule."

I groaned at how they were talking about me as if I wasn't even here. They were also starting to sober me up with this conversation. I really couldn't deal with them right now. I hadn't done anything wrong here. I stood up to leave the kitchen in search of another way to get these memories out of my head when Rachel and a couple of girls came into the kitchen smiling right at Jaxon.

She came over to him and placed her hand on his shoulder with a perfected pouty look. "Are you really dating her exclusively now?" She said "her" as though she was disgusted with the idea. I figured she was up to something, because by now, I had no doubt she knew damn well that we were dating.

He removed her hand and stepped back. "Sure am. Sorry, Rach." I'm not sure whether I should be glad he used a nickname for her or not. It seemed too personal, but then again, he never called me by my nickname and we were about as personal as I knew how to get with someone.

Her pouty routine was grossing me out, when she continued, "Aw, boo, does that mean I don't get any more rides on the motor-cycle? It's so hot the way I could hold tightly onto your waist as we took those twists and turns."

And . . . I was sober. *Thanks a lot, bitch.* I was trying to find my words as I stared at the two of them. Rachel stood there smiling at me, knowing exactly what she had just said.

Quinn stepped in before Jaxon could comment. "You've been on the motorcycle with Jaxon? Are you sure it wasn't Jace?" she gasped.

She turned her saccharine smile toward Quinn. "Oh, I know who I had between my thighs; it was definitely this hunky guy right here." She patted his chest, while I heard him groan and I wanted to rip her arm out of its socket, but I was completely frozen.

When had this happened? If she was just now bringing this up, was it while we had been dating? Even if we hadn't been dating yet, I've been asking to go on that motorcycle since the first day of school and he always told me no. Why would he take her?

"You remember, silly, it was that night after the game." She turned toward Jaxon. "When we were all at that party. Actually, it was at Quinn and Em's apartment. You came up to me to ask me to leave with you. We had so much fun." She smiled brightly, while pretending to stare off at a fond memory.

I was going to be sick. On one hand, I had no room to be mad. I had pissed him off that night and told him to back off of me. I remember him leaving with Rachel. He told me that he had just taken her home. Rachel made it sound as if a lot more had happened. Why take the motorcycle, though?

"Shut up, Rachel; I took you home and that was it," Jaxon growled at her.

She shrugged her shoulders and walked out with her crew following behind. Her damage had already been done and she knew it. I started backing out of the kitchen toward the patio door.

"Don't do this, Emerson. Don't you dare start running from me. I get to at least explain the situation." He looked at me angrily and came toward me.

"What's there to explain? I think I understand pretty clearly. I told you to back off from me that night, and anything that happened after that, I deserved." He didn't understand that this was my fault, not his. I continued my retreat slowly. He stepped around me to block the patio door.

"When I left with her that night and got all the way down to the garage, I only had keys to the motorcycle. I was so angry with myself and with you; I needed to get out of there as soon as possible. So I got on the bike with her. I'm sorry, babe." I couldn't look at him, even though there was no reason for him to apologize. When

I didn't reply, he continued. "Let's go home so we can talk, please." I could tell he was trying his hardest to calm his voice down for me.

"Oh, I definitely can't go home yet; I have way too much alcohol to consume before this night's over. And seeing as how Rachel just sobered me up, I'm not too happy I have to start from square one now."

Getting away from everyone before I ruined everything was priority one. If they could all just leave me alone until after tomorrow, I swear I'll be back to normal. I just needed them to leave me alone until then, but I couldn't explain that to them. I stared at all three of them, urging them to understand me without making me say it.

"I'm not mad at you, Jaxon." He needed to know that, even though I hated that he had taken her on his bike. I really was only mad at myself.

"Of course you are, babe, why else would you be trying to run away from me right now? You're always running when we should be talking!" He panicked and reached for me and I took another step back toward the door to the living room.

"I'm not mad. I just . . . I just need to be left alone. I swear I'll be okay after tomorrow. I just can't deal with this for the next two days," I pleaded. "Please. Just trust me. Do this for me."

"What the hell does that mean?" he shouted. I turned and ran when he was distracted, looking at Quinn for guidance.

When I reached the living room, I heard Quinn say, "Oh my God, what is today's date?"

Leave it to Quinn to put it together because of my big mouth. I ran faster out the front door. She'd explain the whole thing to Jaxon and he'd pressure me to talk about it. I felt like I was going to hyperventilate. I never wanted anyone to ask me about it. I know Quinn won't make me talk about it, but Jaxon knows how to push every barrier I have. I just want to deal the only way I know how and then go back to normal when it's over. Everyone always thinks we should talk about our feelings, as if that would make it better. Guess what, it doesn't bring back my parents and it doesn't change that my dad cheated on Ellie with my mom.

I reached the side of the house because I obviously couldn't drive, so I just hid in the shadows of the large house. I heard footsteps following me around the side. I squeezed my eyes shut and ignored them, while trying to control my breathing so I wouldn't have a panic attack. *Please, let them just go away.*

I felt whoever it was lean up against the house next to me. "Shh, just take deep breaths, in and out." It was Devon. I didn't know whether I should be happy or sad about that. "You want to get out of here, go somewhere else?" he asked in a calming voice.

"I won't sleep with you, Devon. I'm with Jaxon," I said with my eyes still closed.

"Well, it's a good thing I didn't ask you to sleep with me then, huh? I have a fiancée back home that I love. I'm just trying to help you out. Call me crazy, but it seems like you don't want to be here."

"Understatement of the year." I sighed. "I would actually really appreciate it if you could get me out of here." I finally looked over at him.

"Cool, I'll run down and get my car; meet me out front in five."

I stayed in the shadows hiding from everyone while I watched Devon jog off toward his car. I hoped Jaxon wouldn't see me leave with him, but he'd understand later. Especially when I tell him nothing happened. I was committed to him and Devon was committed to his fiancée; I just needed a breather.

After I hopped into his car without being stopped by anyone, he started driving up the highway that ran along the coast.

"Want me to take you home?" he said after a while.

"I don't, but if you don't want to hang out, I'll understand." My head was leaning against the headrest.

"You want to go out to bar or something? Do you have a fake ID so you can get in?" he asked.

"Actually, since it's after midnight, I can now legally get in without a fake." He turned to look at me with a smile and I knew he was about to say that dreaded "happy birthday" statement. "Don't. Forget I said that, please. Don't mention anything birthday related." His mouth snapped shut and he shrugged his shoulders.

The first bar we walked into was pretty quiet, so we were able to grab a spot at the bar. I ordered my own drinks and he ordered his. Separate tabs made it known we weren't together. I watched as he texted on his phone for a while.

"Texting the fiancée?" I asked.

"Yeah, I figured I should tell Ally what's up before she hears from someone else I was out with Em Moore," he said with a little laugh.

"She knows who I am?" I was shocked.

"The girl who broke my heart? Yeah, she knows."

"Broke your heart? Don't joke about that kind of stuff." I chuckled.

"Whatever you want to think, Em," he replied. "Ally's cool, though. She understands."

Could I really have broken his heart? I hadn't thought it was that serious. "That's nice of you to let her know what's going on."

Exactly what I should be doing right now with Jaxon, but I had left my phone in the car since it wouldn't quit ringing. He'd understand too when I explained it all to him in a couple of days. Jaxon was the most understanding person I know and I was crazy about him. He'd understand when I finally had the guts to tell him what tomorrow was. But for now, I drank.

We ended up going to three more bars after that one and I was able to dance to try and forget as much as possible. Devon stayed close enough to keep me safe. A couple of times he tried to ask me if there was anything going on that he could help with, but I just shook my head and continued the destruction of my liver. Around our second bar, I looked down at my hand and gazed at the small hearts that Jaxon had drawn all over my palm this morning when were lying in bed. I remember relaxing on his chest as he drew each one of the hearts. Some were big and some were so tiny you could barely make out that they were even hearts. All together, it made a beautiful collage on my hand. This morning seemed like light-years ago.

Finally, right before the sun came up, Devon dropped me off at the apartment. He had to walk me up the stairs and to my door because I could barely function on my own anymore. I inserted my key as quietly as possible into the lock and walked in. Right away, I noticed Jaxon passed out on our couch. He must have been waiting for me to get home. I had about thirty missed calls between him and Quinn on my phone. They weren't going to go easy on me once we finally talked. I tiptoed past him and went straight for my bed. I made sure to lock my door before going to sleep. The last thing I remember is my face hitting the pillow before I crashed hard.

- SIXTEEN -

The next day, when I started coming back from the dead, I rolled over to look at the clock on my phone. It was already after three in the afternoon; so much for trying to make any of my classes today. Not the way to start a new semester. At least this day was almost over already. The less of this day I had to endure, the better. I had the hangover from hell and the only thing I was going to do about it was drink some more to dull the pain. I noticed I only had two missed calls, one from Jace and the other from Devon. I'd have to call them back tomorrow. I didn't have any more missed calls from Jaxon or Quinn since I had gotten home last night, so they must know I'm here by now.

I walked to my door and quietly opened it. My plan was to hole up in my room drinking until this day was over, since I still didn't want to talk to anyone. I needed to go to the bathroom, though, and grab some essentials from the kitchen. Once I got out into the hallway, I realized that there wasn't anyone here. Jaxon must have decided to go to class, and I knew he still had football practice this afternoon.

When I got back to my room, my phone was ringing. I answered it when I noticed it wasn't Jaxon, Quinn, Cole, or Jace.

"Hello?"

"Yes, is this Emerson Moore?"

"Yes, sir, can I ask who is calling?"

"This is William Gordon calling from the Law Offices of Gordon, Simon & Bates."

"Um, okay." I had forgotten about calling him back and now I was wishing I hadn't answered my phone at all.

"Sorry if this call seems out of the blue. Your parents actually set up a trust fund for you when you were born. Six years ago, they came to me to control it and I am supposed to contact you on your twenty-first birthday to relinquish the funds to you. They have grown quite dramatically since your parents first set them up."

"I'm sorry, I'm really confused about what you're saying right now."

"I can understand the confusion. I tried to get a hold of Mr. or Mrs. Moore first, but I haven't been able to locate a working number for them."

"Um . . . my parents actually passed away six years ago today, Mr. Gordon." I can't believe I had to talk about this, today of all days. The very reason I ran away from the people I love, and I was now being forced to face it anyway.

"What? They were just in my office that morning setting up this account for you; how is that possible?" *Well gee, I don't know, why don't you ask the lady who thought it was okay to drive while barely being able to keep her eyes open.*

I couldn't feel my fingers anymore, and I'm pretty sure all of the blood was rushing out of my body. "What do you mean they were with you that morning, Mr. Gordon? My parents were having an affair and they died in a car accident when they were going back home."

"Oh, that's not possible. There was no way Robert and Michelle were having an affair of any kind. I distinctly remember they could barely stand being in the same room together when they came in. I overheard him getting mad at her for being irresponsible with her car, which was the reason he had to pick her up that morning."

"I think I have to go, Mr. Gordon, I . . . have to . . . be somewhere . . . else." *I'm also freaking out, but you don't need to know that.*

"I'm really sorry if I've said something to upset you. Please just come by my office anytime and I'll get you to sign the paperwork for the account. It's quite a significant amount of money."

The only thing I remember the rest of that day is hanging up the phone and taking shot after shot until I passed out in my bed.

∼

I was being jostled awake and I was about to punch the person responsible for doing it. My stomach wasn't appreciating the movement, either. I remember finally waking up sick at one point last night. I'd never been this drunk, so it figured that it was time to pay the price. As I became more and more aware of my surroundings, I realized I was hugging the toilet. *Yeah, now I remember spending the night on the soothing, cold tile floor.*

"If that's you, Quinn, back away; I don't want to have to punch you. If that's you, Jaxon, you have three seconds till I do punch you," I moaned into the bowl.

"Yeah, if you can ever get Jaxon to talk to you again," Quinn said.

"Shut up, Quinn; go away so I can shower."

"Are you done being a colossal bitch? Are you finished drinking yourself stupid?" She was pissed at me. I'd have to sweeten her up later and apologize.

"Geez, Quinn, lay off. I'm sure by now you know what happened." I moved to sit against the wall with my hands over my eyes.

"Take a shower, Emerson; you reek." She slammed the door on her way out. She just full-named me. That means she's extremely pissed.

I tried to take as long as I possibly could in the shower. I hated a pissed-off Quinn, but standing for too long had proven to be too difficult. The shower walls were spinning around me, so I had to get out. I brushed my teeth and walked out to the living room to sit on the couch. Cole was lounging across it when I entered.

"Oh great, have you come to view my lashing as well, or are you going to be joining in, Coley?" I noticed Quinn was in the kitchen smashing pots and pans around.

"I'm here because I'm worried about you, Emmy," he said, looking at me sincerely.

"It's just a bump in the road. All is well now, I promise."

Quinn walked in and slammed a plate of bacon and eggs on the coffee table in front of me. I was starving, since I hadn't eaten in a day and a half.

"Thanks, Quinn," I mumbled.

"All is not well, Emerson!" she yelled at me when I reached for the plate.

"Sure it is. I'm better now, I promise. Those are just bad days for me and you know that. Now I'll go back to normal. I think I'm finally feeling better about opening up more to Jaxon." I started eating my breakfast and then I remembered that phone call from Mr. Gordon yesterday, before I drank myself into a mini coma. "Shit, I forgot . . ."

"What?" Cole asked.

"I found out my parents weren't having an affair six years ago."

"Em, people think tequila tells them things all the time. I'm sorry, but everything is still the same with your parents." Quinn still sounded agitated with me.

"I'm being serious, Quinn. Stop making me feel childish. A lawyer called me yesterday saying six years ago my parents were in his office transferring a trust fund that they set up for me to have when I turned twenty-one. He said they were arguing the whole time, and my dad was mad that he had to give my mom a ride there. The lawyer didn't know that my parents had died."

I heard Quinn gasp and bring her hand up to her mouth. Tears instantly filled her eyes. "Why didn't you tell me this was going on?"

"Quinn, as much as you want me to talk about this stuff, it's been too hard. I just had my world rocked yesterday. Everything I thought about what happened was a lie. My parents weren't having an affair. My dad wasn't cheating on Ellie. Every wall I built up was because of what I thought they had done. I have no idea what to do now. All I know is that I just want to find Jaxon and tell him how sorry I am for the way I acted, and how much I care about him. I'm such an idiot for continuing to let this get to me like that."

Quinn and Cole just gave me a sad look. "Emmy, Jax was really hurt by what you did . . ."

"I know, but now I'm going to apologize," I said, looking at both of them.

"I don't know if it will work this time. He looked entirely defeated the other night."

"We'll be fine, Quinn. Stop being so dramatic. Once I talk to him, he'll understand what happened."

"I agree with you, Em; you just need to find him and apologize. He really loves you."

"I really love him." The second the words popped out of my mouth, my hand shot up to cover it and my eyes widened to see if Quinn and Cole had actually heard that.

They had, because they were both staring at me as if I'd just admitted that I would be giving them a million dollars later.

"*What?* This is so great, Em! You have to tell him. He'll definitely take you back then," Quinn shouted.

"Take me back? You say that like we broke up." I frowned at her.

"Em, I'm telling you, he was really upset with you, and then when he found out you left with Devon . . . I've never seen him so wounded," she answered.

I looked at Cole to see if this was true and he nodded his head. "Shit. Well, I'll think of something really good. He'll forgive me; he loves me." I smiled and got up to go back to my room.

I decided I needed something really good to get his attention and let him know that I loved him and I was sorry—something besides just walking up to him and saying it. I opened up my laptop and started creating a mixed CD for him. He loved music. He sang along with every song on the radio. He worked at the radio station last semester for his internship, and my best memory of all was when he danced with me at his mom's house to that country song.

I started the CD off with a song by the band Of Monsters and Men, about a guy that loved a girl even though she couldn't love him back. It seemed fitting to begin this story of songs for him like that. The CD flowed into other songs about how I wouldn't be the same without him, and then finally, the last couple of songs spoke about how much I loved him. I planned on telling him I loved him in person before he listened to it. He deserved that. The more songs I would come across, the more excited I had become to see him. I decided to call him to find out when he would be home. I knew that he had practice soon, so I had to wait until later in the evening. The phone rang twice and went straight to voice mail. That was weird, so I sent him a text.

Me: Hey, I know I upset you the other day. I want to make it up to you ;-)

By midnight, there was still no response from Jaxon. Neither he nor Jace was answering the phones or coming home. I had gone out to the parking lot numerous times to check to see if either the motorcycle or truck was back. I was starting to look like one of those crazed, jealous girlfriends. Quinn told me she had talked to Cole, but he wasn't with the guys. I hoped that they were okay. I tried calling two more times before I went to bed, but then my calls just started going directly to voice mail sometime after ten o'clock. I'd just have to catch him tomorrow between classes, since we didn't have any together on that day.

SEVENTEEN

The next morning I woke up and decided to curl my hair in loose waves and leave it all down. I put on a little bit of mascara and lip gloss. I'm not going to lie: I was trying to look good for Jaxon. Neither he nor Jace had come back last night, so I was just hoping that he'd actually be at school that day. Then I remembered Jaxon saying that if they missed even one class, they would be benched for the championship game tomorrow. I knew he wouldn't risk something like that.

I didn't see him until near the end of my lunch break. I was sitting at the table with our regular group. Quinn was telling Cole about the new students she was tutoring this semester, which, not surprisingly, were all female. I had almost given up on the idea of seeing him at school that day at all. When I saw him through the windows of the cafeteria coming across the courtyard, I decided to go and meet him. He was walking with two girls I had seen only a few times before. They seemed to be animatedly talking to him, while he just nodded his head. I could tell he wasn't paying attention to what they were actually saying.

I turned and smiled at Quinn. "I'm going to go talk to him, 'kay?"

She nodded her head, but she looked unsure. She wouldn't be this weird if it was Cole out there and she needed to apologize. I should be the nervous one: I was going to tell him I loved him. I jogged out into the courtyard and met up with him in the middle.

"Hey, I've been trying to call you." I smiled up at him.

He didn't smile, just nodded his head back at me and said, "I noticed."

I looked at his two groupies and said, "Okay, you ladies can run along now; I'd like to talk to my boyfriend." They huffed and looked up at Jaxon to say something different, but he didn't, so they walked away, sulking.

"Em, I don't think we should be together anymore," he finally spoke.

"Why do you have to do that? Why do you have to purposefully call me Em whenever you're mad? Don't be childish, Jaxon," I replied angrily. This is not how I wanted to begin this conversation.

He took a deep breath. "Emerson, I don't think we should be together anymore." His voice sounded flat and lifeless.

I decided to ignore his nonsensical statement. "Jaxon, I've been trying to get a hold of you so I could tell you how sorry I am. I always get freaked out and weird around that day. I tried to keep it inside, but it was eating me alive, and I just didn't know how to cope. I'm really sorry. I realize now how ridiculous I was being." I grabbed onto the waistband of his jeans while I looked up at him. I grabbed on as though, if I just held tightly enough, he wouldn't even consider leaving. He tried to step back out of my grasp, but I just stepped closer to him, giving him a puzzled look. "I made you a mix CD. Just listen to it, please."

I bent down to pull the CD out of my bag when he finally spoke again. "Emerson, I tried to talk to you four days ago. I asked you not to run from me and you did anyway . . . again. I can't handle this anymore. I tried to be strong enough for you but . . . I'm just not." He took the CD from me, but he held it out as if he didn't really want it.

"Jaxon, stop saying all of this. It's not necessary." I grabbed his waistband again. "I'm going to be better now, I swear. Let me apologize." I took a deep breath and said, "I love you." I watched as he winced in pain at my words. That was definitely not the reaction I was hoping for. Just then the gravity of the situation started to hit, so I lowered my voice to a whisper as I looked up at him. "Don't do this. I love you."

"I asked you not to leave the other night, and you did anyway."

"You promised you would stay patient with me." My voice rose to a panic level.

"And you promised you would stay." The fact that the lifeless tone of his voice hadn't changed at all was scaring me.

"I never left, Jaxon. I just needed a breather from my life. It wasn't you, it was my parents' death." I was almost yelling now. I needed to reassure him that what had happened wouldn't happen again. "Look, I know it never made sense for you to like me. I was never meant to be in a relationship with anyone. But you forced your way in, pushing past every barrier I had. Don't give up on me now!"

I could feel the pain streaking across his face. "I don't think we should be together anymore," he repeated for a third time.

I stepped forward while he stepped back and I screamed, "No! I love you. I'm here! *Just forgive me!*" Tears were streaming down my face now and I knew I was making a complete fool out of myself in the middle of the courtyard, but he needed to know. "You can't do this!" He hadn't moved a muscle from his position; he just kept that aggravatingly unyielding face. When I reached for him again, he stepped backward away from me.

Suddenly there were strong arms wrapping around my body, lifting me away from Jaxon. "Shh, Em, just stop. Don't do this here. This isn't you," Cole whispered into my ear.

"Cole, you said all I had to do was apologize! You said he loved me!" I yelled at him. Then I finally saw it: No matter how minuscule,

I saw Jaxon take a step forward toward me. I almost breathed a huge sigh of relief, but then he caught himself and took two steps backward. My face twisted with the pain I felt surge throughout my entire body.

Cole started carrying me away when I screamed again. *"Jaxon, don't do this!"* I was fighting with Cole to get down and my legs were thrashing violently. If I could just get him in my arms again, he would realize what a huge mistake he was making. "You promised! I told you I wouldn't survive this kind of heartbreak again! *Jaxon, look at me!*" My frantic screams were causing a scene, and he was just standing there looking at the ground with his hands in tight fists.

Before we got out of earshot from him, Cole turned back for a second to face him. "I fucking told you this would happen, you asshole. This is the exact fucking moment I told you about, and you promised you could handle it. If you're smart, you'll stay away from her," he growled.

I went lifeless in his arms; there was no reason to fight it anymore. Jaxon didn't even try to keep me there with him. This was entirely my fault in so many ways I'd lost count. I was disappointed in myself for throwing my rules out the window for him. From the very beginning, I said that I wouldn't be able to handle being a girlfriend, and then he convinced me otherwise. Lesson learned: Always follow your gut. But I was mostly disappointed in myself for letting that day get to me so much that I ruined the best thing that ever happened to me. I never imagined that relationships were like that. I never imagined the extreme joy you can experience. What I did know was how it felt when someone you love was ripped away from you. How gut-wrenching it could feel. I should have stayed away from any possibility of ever feeling that again.

Cole had to carry me up to the apartment. When my head hit the pillow on my bed, I immediately pulled my knees up to my chest and let out all the pain that I felt. I cried for losing my relationship with Jaxon, for losing a best friend, and lastly, for losing Emerson. Quinn had once said how she was enjoying Emerson, and I now realize that I had begun to love her as well. Now I needed to learn only to be Em. Em didn't let her heart break.

I lay in my bed staring at the ceiling for countless hours. Eventually that evening Cole and Quinn came in to join me. They each lay on opposite sides of me. I loved having their comfort and support, but I also wanted to stew in my own mistakes alone.

"Emmy, you're still coming to my game tomorrow, right?" Cole whispered in the dark.

"You know I can't do that, Cole."

"You have to. Fifty years down the road when people talk about how our school went to the championship and your best friend scored the winning touchdown"—he nudged me with his elbow and I knew he was talking about himself—"you'll regret not going."

"Well, I'll just let seventy-one-year-old Em be mad then."

"Please, Em, you've been talking about how exciting a championship game would be with Cole since freshman year. I know you'll be sad you missed it," Quinn said, squeezing my hand.

"I'll think about it."

For some reason, I would get bouts of crying at the most random moments. I could lie there talking to the two of them, when all of a sudden, a wave of immense pain would nail me in the face and I wouldn't be able to breathe. While we were lying there in the quiet and darkness, a wave hit me and I gasped with a face full of tears. Cole reached for my hand while Quinn rubbed my arm and snuggled real close. I would get through this. I may not be the same on the other side, but these two people would get me through this. Then the realization that I had just lost Jace as a friend as well hit me with a fresh new round of tears, because how would I be able to look at him and not see Jaxon?

~

I had to work the early shift at the bar the next day, but Ed promised that I could make it in time for the second quarter. Last week, I was devastated that I would miss even a little bit of the game; this week I was just devastated, so I couldn't really care less how much I saw. Quinn made me swear that I would come, and she even packed a bag with an outfit, shoes, and makeup for me. I didn't even think about what I would wear, but it was probably best not to show up to a stadium packed with guys, wearing a too-tight shirt that says Nice Rack across the chest.

When I finally did arrive, they were about ten minutes into the second quarter, so I hadn't missed much. To my dismay, Quinn had packed the dress and boots I had gotten while in Texas. I knew what she was doing and I didn't appreciate it. I just wanted to be invisible, sit in some corner of the stands, and leave without anyone seeing me. Quinn knew I would try that as well, so she made me swear I would come over to sit by her.

As I walked up the stairs into the stands, I heard Quinn's, Jace's, and Jaxon's voices. I froze and took a deep breath in and out. I could do this; I needed to get over the fact that I would see him. I continued walking up when I noticed Jaxon leaning up against the stands barrier, talking to the two of them. Whatever they were talking about, it wasn't a pleasant conversation. Jace and Quinn looked mad at Jaxon, and he didn't look happy with them, either. Today the crowd was way too excited and loud for me to hear what they were saying.

When I stepped up onto the final step, Jaxon turned his head and looked right at me. I watched as he took a faltering step back and sucked in air between his teeth. At least I still affected him, even if he didn't want me anymore. I knew that this dress and these boots looked good on me. Jaxon had liked how the dress pushed up my breasts and dipped down just a little bit to show off my cleavage. I knew what he was looking at right then. I turned my eyes away from him and headed toward Quinn.

When I approached, I noticed that the only empty seat available was on the other side of Jace. There was no way I would sit next to my ex-boyfriend's identical twin. I was so deprived and needy of Jaxon right now that I wasn't sure I would be able to control my actions around a guy who looked exactly like him. I couldn't even look at him. It was too painful. I knew Jace was searching my face for me to acknowledge him, and I shouldn't take this breakup out on him, but I just needed time.

I walked up to the girl sitting next to Quinn and knelt down to speak in her ear since it was so loud. "Hey, how would you like to switch seats? You can sit next to that hunk right there," I said, pointing at Jace.

She looked over and I saw her eyes light up. "Sure!"

She got up and sashayed toward Jace and sat down with the most seductive motions I had ever seen a girl put into sitting in a chair. She turned her body to face him and stuck out her chest. I sat down in her seat next to Quinn, and Jace turned in his, putting his back to the new girl.

"Em, please don't ignore me."

"I'm not ignoring you, Jace; it just hurts too much right now to see you," I said, looking forward.

He sighed and leaned back in his seat. I noticed that Jaxon had already made it back to the bench and had his back facing us. He was leaning forward with his forearms lying on the tops of his legs, watching the game. I searched for Cole and finally spotted him on the opposite side of the bench from Jax, glaring daggers at him.

"He asked about you. If you were okay," I heard Jace say over Quinn.

"Yeah, and I told him to shove his concern up his ass. I'm not going to tell him anything about you," Quinn said, sounding frustrated.

That made me laugh. "Quinn, your moods are so confusing. Yesterday, you were pissed at me, and now today you're pissed at Jaxon."

"Yes, that was before Cole and I lay with you all night long while you cried your eyes out." She grabbed my hand and squeezed.

"You cried all night, Ems?" Jace looked at me with those puppy-dog eyes and I couldn't look away. "I've never been so mad at him, not even when he tried to steal my girlfriend in sixth grade by pretending to be me."

I wish they would stop making me laugh. "He did not do that!" I said while Jace nodded his head.

"Jace punched him in the courtyard after Cole dragged you off," Quinn piped in.

"Quinn, don't tell her that!" he said, looking sheepish.

"Guys, you can't be mad at him. This was my fault from the very beginning. I let him convince me that I could handle a relationship when I knew all along that I would be terrible at it. I just proved myself right in the end. At least it wasn't years down the road. I'm just trying to survive this the best way I know how," I said sternly.

"Please don't drink yourself into a coma again, Ems," Quinn protested.

"I'm pretty sure I'll never drink again; don't worry about that. If I hadn't in the first place the other night, I'd be sitting here cheering for my boyfriend right now. Instead"—I pointed behind me—"they're cheering for him." Quinn and Jace looked back to see Rachel and her annoying crew screaming Jax's name. "Apparently, word gets out fast."

Jace stood up and grabbed me; he lifted me into a giant bear hug in front of everyone. My feet just dangled down along his legs.

It was weird because his body felt like Jaxon's. I had to keep reminding myself not to wrap my legs around his waist and squeeze back.

"It's not just your fault, Emmy. Don't even let yourself think that. Please don't let this cause you to close yourself off again. You are the greatest friend that's a girl I've ever met. If Jaxon doesn't come to his damn senses, then some lucky guy out there will be thankful to be loved by you one day," he whispered in my ear. These boys were way too charming for their own good.

"Thanks, Jace, but I know I can't do this again." He gave me another squeeze and looked sadly into my eyes.

When someone shouted for us to sit down, he placed me back in my seat. I looked down at the field and saw Jaxon staring right at us from the sidelines. His eyes screamed, "Mine. She's mine and I'll kill anyone who touches her." But his actions said, "Just take her, I don't want her anymore." I turned to look somewhere else; I couldn't focus on what he was thinking about. I needed to remember that I couldn't think about him at all. I concentrated on watching Cole and cheering him on when he caught the ball. See, I could be perfectly normal.

By the end of the game, we had won, and surprisingly, Cole *had* scored the winning touchdown. I'd never seen Quinn jump up and down so hard. When the final whistle blew, Cole came barreling toward the stands. He hopped over the barrier with ease and scooped Quinn up into his arms. Their faces were attached to each other for the next few minutes without either one coming up for air. When he finally placed her down, he came over and hugged me as hard as he could. His excitement was infectious and I tried to share in it.

"Congrats, Cole; I'll remember this for at least the next fifty years. Thanks for making it worth it for me to come!" I yelled over the crowd's cheers.

He turned and gave Jace the brotherly hug/pat-on-the-back thing. I couldn't stop myself from looking out at the field one last time and searching for Jaxon. He wasn't celebrating or talking to anyone. I watched as he slowly walked toward the locker room. By the looks of him, you would have thought we had lost the game.

Cole asked all three of us to wait for him while he changed out of his gear and showered. I really just wanted to get home and back to my bed. I felt that I had done my friendship duty by coming, and now I needed to go cry some more in the privacy of my room. I'd seen Jaxon way too many times today already. I could feel the waves of pain getting closer and closer to bursting through. When Cole came out of the dressing room, Jaxon was walking right behind him. Both of them looked incredibly handsome, freshly showered and wearing their team polo shirts. Jaxon had thrown on his black ball cap over his wet hair. He knew I loved that cap on him. I couldn't stand here any longer.

"I'm out; I have plans. See you later, Quinny. Congrats, guys," I said while walking away.

"Emerson, just stay. I'm leaving. No one here wants to talk to me anyway," that intoxicating voice said.

I turned around to face the group, while continuing my backward retreat. "Like I told them earlier, this was all my fault; they don't have any reason to be mad at you. I hope you guys have a nice night."

"It's okay if we hang out in the same group. We were friends first, you know."

"It might be easy for you, but it's almost impossible for me." I continued my retreat and then turned to shout one last thing to him. "It's Em, by the way; Emerson doesn't exist anymore." Right before I turned around I saw his mouth gape open with surprise at my words.

I walked as fast as I possibly could while still appearing normal. When I disappeared into the crowd and knew he couldn't see me anymore, I took off running for my car. When I reached it and threw myself into the driver's seat, I laid my head down onto the steering wheel. I took off my stupid boots and threw them into the backseat. All the pain from seeing him started flowing from my eyes. A few moments later, there was a gentle tapping on my window. For the second time this week, I found myself wishing that Jaxon hadn't come to see my misery, and then I opened my eyes to find Devon.

I opened my car door so he wouldn't have to talk to me through my window. He squatted and sat down on the running board of my car, facing me.

"Still upset from the other night when we went out, Ems?" he asked.

"Nah, I've just had reality thrown in my face since then, that's all."

"Want to talk about it?" he asked kindly.

"I think I've done enough damage by running off with you once already, Devon. But I did want to thank you for watching over me that night, and making sure I got home safely. That was generous of you."

"Where's the superstar boyfriend?" he asked, looking around. When I winced in pain, his eyes widened a bit. "Wait . . . he didn't break up with you for hanging out with me, did he?"

"That wasn't the only reason. It was mostly a compilation of all my fuck-ups. Apparently running away from your problems isn't the right answer." I laid my forehead back down on the steering wheel. "I'm surprised you didn't hear about 'The Great Em Embarrassment' in the courtyard. At least that's what I call it. I made a fool out myself. For a guy. Who would have guessed?"

"I heard you guys had a pretty loud fight, but I didn't realize . . ." He was quiet for a few moments. "Well, he's just a douche and the biggest idiot I've never even met."

At that exact moment I spotted Jaxon and Jace walking across the parking lot toward the truck, and they were both looking right at us. I laid my head down on the steering wheel and groaned. Perfect, just freaking perfect. When I looked back up they were both already inside the cab of the truck and backing out.

"Thanks, Devon." I offered him a weak smile. "I think I'm going to head on home, though."

"All right. Well, you have my number if you ever need to vent. I'm heading back up north tomorrow. It was good seeing you, even under these circumstances." With my good-byes, I closed my door and drove home to my bed.

- EIGHTEEN -

I was proud of myself for not skipping out on any classes. If there was anything I wouldn't forgive myself for, it would be failing out of my junior year of college because I broke up with my first boyfriend. I was able to get seats in the back of the class away from Jaxon in our shared classes. I didn't meet up with Jace anymore after English, nor did I join them in the cafeteria after I noticed Jaxon sitting with them the day after the championship game. That was an awkward moment because as soon as I saw him, I backpedaled out of the room as fast as I could, and I know they all saw me do it.

I ended up finding this great big tree on the edge of campus that was an ideal place for eating lunch. Or in my case, just staring off into space, not wanting any human contact, and occasionally crying, although I'm not too proud about that. Julie, Jaxon's mom, attempted to reach out and contact me a couple times after she found out what had happened. I tried to be polite and talk to her, but it was just too hard, so I always found some excuse to get off the phone.

Ellie and Charles ended up going with me to the lawyer's office to read over the contract for the account my parents had set up in my name. Charles was skeptical that it was real, and therefore insisted on joining in on the meeting so that he could read over the fine print. The account ended up being legitimate, and I was basically set for the rest of my life. I guess I had my parents to thank for that.

I was still having a hard time dealing with the fact that I'd just spent the last six years of my life mad at the very parents who did everything to make my life better. My mom had always told me I should try for a career that makes me happy, not one that was all about the money. When I first started becoming interested in humanitarian journalism, I knew I wouldn't be making the best living. Thanks to my parents, I wouldn't have to worry about making my rent or any other payments while I was out traveling the world.

Almost a month had gone by and I was still surviving. I was almost back to a bearable state; I didn't cry as often as I used to. Jaxon would never be out of my heart, though. I'd always think of him as the only person strong enough to actually break through my walls. Why had I been so stupid? How could I have thought it was okay just to leave Jaxon that night, with Devon of all people? Jaxon was the best thing that had happened to me in years, and I had just walked away from him, even if only for a short time.

I'd become an expert at avoiding Jaxon and all of the places I knew he would be. Surprisingly, we never even ran into each other at home. Quinn would hang out with the guys at their apartment, and every once in a while, Jace and Cole would come over to our place to hang out. I was sad for our little group; we had been so close and then I had to go and screw everything up. Now, we couldn't even hang out together all at the same time. I never asked about Jaxon and I never searched him out in crowds. I knew I wouldn't be able to handle seeing him with a new girlfriend when he eventually started dating again.

Meanwhile, I was also having an eternal struggle with myself. I couldn't be Emerson anymore because she would forever belong to Jaxon. I also couldn't ever go back to sleeping around with every guy like Em did. I needed an in-between. Quinn and Cole had finally gotten me to go out again to a few parties. Once all the guys found out that Jaxon and I were no longer together, I constantly had to convince them that I wouldn't be going upstairs with them anymore. I honestly couldn't see myself being with anyone like that—I'd already had the best, and the rest would be second-rate. I was thankful that I didn't ever see him at these parties, because I wouldn't be able to handle them if I did.

It was hard enough staring at the back of his head in our journalism courses. Students would come up and talk to him; he even had two new girls that sat on either side of him, but I never really saw him actively engaging with them.

One day, as the professor was dismissing us and trying to add on more reading material, I watched as Tatum Johnson stood up in her seat next to him and kissed him on the cheek. Right then I thought I was going to be sick all over my desk. I scrabbled to push my papers and books into my bag. When I stood up, I saw that Jaxon was staring right at me. I slammed my chair in and darted out the door.

I ran across campus. I couldn't leave because I still had another class, and Quinn had the car today, so I couldn't go hide in there. I realized where I was subconsciously going: to my tree. I wish I had found this tree earlier in my time here at school. It was peaceful to lie under it and just look up at the swirling branches and intertwined leaves. It was so dense that the sun couldn't seep through, which created this beautiful glow around the outer edges of the leaves. This was the perfect place to hide and calm down so that I didn't hurl in front of all my classmates. The girth of the tree trunk was wide; I could sit up against it on one side and no one would be able to see me. I always sat on the side opposite from campus; I didn't want anyone to come bother me.

A few times Quinn and Cole had asked where I went for lunch and if they could come and join me, but I just told them I went to study hall. I'm pretty sure Quinn went to check on me one day, because later, she asked which study hall I was in. I eventually told her I had found a place to hide, but I couldn't tell them where I went because this was *my* happy place. I liked coming here alone.

I sat on the roots of the tree with my knees pulled up to my chest and my face in between them. I closed my eyes, pulled in long, deep breaths, and released them slowly, willing myself not to cry. I had known this was coming; I had told myself he would eventually get a girlfriend again. Warning yourself about something and then having it actually happen are two different things. At least I didn't see her full-on kiss him; it had only been a cheek kiss. It could have been so much worse.

"Hey, Emers—uh . . . Em."

Startled, I jolted backward and knocked my head on the trunk of the tree, once again embarrassing myself in front of Jaxon. I laid my head back down on my knees. Maybe if I kept my eyes closed tightly, he would go away.

"Oh, shit, sorry! Is your head okay?" He placed his strong, warm hand on the back of my head.

I winced and moved out of his hold. "Jaxon, please don't. I don't know how you even found me here," I said into my legs.

"I know that you always sit here," he replied, crouching down in front of me. When I finally looked up at him, confused, he continued, "I've been sitting under that tree over there"—he pointed across the lawn to another tree about fifty yards away—"for a while now. One day I noticed you walking over here and hiding behind this one. I started coming out here every day to watch you sit here. I just needed to know if you were okay. I hate when I see you cry over here by yourself. I almost told Quinn once where you were so she could comfort you, but then realized you probably come here to be alone."

All this time, I've come out here to release some of my most private thoughts, frustrations, and sadness. I've cried and I've screamed. All along, he was fifty yards away watching. This was about a hundred more times mortifying than my courtyard spectacle a month ago.

I stood up and grabbed my bag. "Well, I'm glad I've been over here putting on a show for you. I hope you've enjoyed my humiliation, but I think now it's time for the curtain call." I started walking away from him.

"Emerson, wait . . ." He came jogging up to me.

"It's Em! You don't get to call me that anymore!" I yelled at him. I was thankful we were so far away from the main hub of campus, because I really didn't feel like having an audience for another scene with Jaxon.

"Em, I didn't mean to make it sound like I've been enjoying your pain. I came over here to make sure you knew that I'm not with Tatum. I don't know why she kissed me on the cheek like that. I think she just wanted you to think something was going on. I told her not to do that anymore."

"You don't need to run anything by me. I don't have any hold over you or your actions." I continued walking away from him. What was he doing? Didn't he understand how much it hurt to talk to him?

This must have set him off finally, because he hollered back at me in the empty field. *"You think I'm not in pain? You think my heart wasn't ripped out of my fucking chest until I couldn't breathe anymore? You think this is easy for me?"*

"Isn't it, though? I mean, this was *your* idea. I certainly didn't choose this for myself," I quietly said, turning toward him.

Trying to throw my words back at me, he said, "Didn't you, though? When *you* decided to run away from me to go bar-hopping with Devon and get so wasted you couldn't answer your phone?"

"How did you know I was at a bar with Devon?"

"Oh, he didn't tell you?" he spoke with ice in his words. "Around three a.m., he started answering your phone to let all of *your* friends and *your* boyfriend, who had been calling you all night, know that you were with him!" he shouted. "I had to hear from some other guy that *my* girlfriend was safe. That *he* would take care of you!"

"If Devon answered my phone, then you know that nothing happened with us and that he has a fiancée he loves."

His surprised face showed me that he did have doubts whether I had done anything with Devon. No matter what he said, he still held my previous reputation against me.

"You are the most frustrating person ever! Don't you understand? It's not that I thought you were cheating on me. It's that you were *mine*! Not his. Mine, Emerson! But in your time of need, you chose someone else over me."

I felt as if I had been slapped. A slap I deserved, nonetheless. The thing was, I hadn't chosen anyone. I only went with Devon because I knew he wouldn't make me talk. He just sat there quietly all night, while I zoned off into my own world and my own problems. It didn't really matter if I clarified that for Jaxon anymore, though; the damage had already been done.

I turned around and walked away. "Don't follow me, Jaxon."

That semester I had to take a class in preparation for my summer internship. It was all about what to expect and making sure we knew exactly what we were walking into. I learned that I was going to need an insane amount of vaccines. Quinn was going to have to come along for that because otherwise, I might chicken out. We also found out that we needed to fund-raise a significant amount of money; there were a lot of supplies the school offered to provide us with, but currently the program didn't have enough funds to get everything. Professor Patterson was in charge of the internship.

Since I felt relatively comfortable with him by now, I asked to speak with him after class one day.

I told him how I had come into some money lately that I really had no need for, and that I wouldn't mind helping out the program. He was floored and very appreciative of my offer. He said that he wanted to try some fund-raising techniques throughout the rest of the semester first to see if we could raise the money. If we didn't reach our goal, I could come back and talk to him again about helping out. I hoped he didn't think I was trying to be a brown-noser, because that certainly wasn't my intention.

Every time my mom had passed a collection jar for a charity, or passed a homeless person on the street, no matter what, she always tossed in money. Once I asked her why she didn't just save that money for herself, since she could buy herself something nice if she just kept it. She had simply replied that she didn't need anything nice if there were still people out there that needed food or water. Every day she taught humbling moments and how we should appreciate every little thing we were given. I think she was the one who had inspired my future career choice. I was starting to understand why I never knew how well off my parents were—thus, my discomfort with having the amount of money I had in my bank account. I knew that there were people out there that needed it, and I had no idea how to begin to help them.

I asked Professor Patterson what his ideas for fund-raising were. When he told me a few of them, I realized that although they would bring in a decent amount of money, they would never bring in enough for us to be able to survive in Africa. I suggested we have a date auction, one where we find a bunch of guys or girls and we auction them off for dates. I had heard about other colleges doing it before. He loved the notion and brought it up in class the following day. The students instantly became excited about the idea.

The first thing after that class, I went and requested a meeting with our school's Interfraternity Council president. I explained to him our idea and how this would put out a good word about the fraternities and their generosity in helping out other areas of the university. He loved the idea but told me that some of the fraternities had been in trouble too often lately. He didn't want people to think that they were selling sex. I thought that was an obscene assumption, but I understood where he was coming from.

Professor Patterson suggested I ask Coach Chase if we could auction off his players now that they weren't bogged down with championship practices. However, the more I thought about it, the more I realized that guys would pay more money for girls than girls would for guys. So I decided to ask Coach Chase if we could get all of his players to go to a date auction to raise money for the journalism trip.

Coach Chase liked the idea of the auction and said that as long as we specified that the football team was sponsoring it, he would make sure all of his players were present. I ended up finding twenty willing females to be auctioned off. It really wasn't hard. When you post "Do You Want A Championship-Winning Football Player to Buy You for a Date?" all over campus, you have to start turning away girls.

Originally, Patterson suggested we just use the gymnasium for the event, but I convinced a local hotel to donate their beautiful ballroom for the night. The event was blowing up and I heard people talking about it all over campus. I'm not sure at what point I became the coordinator for this whole event, but it was nice to be able to throw myself into something that required all of my attention. It helped to keep my mind off of everything else, namely Jaxon.

Later that night, I pulled out my text to prepare for midterms next week. Typically, I would jump into a study group, but tonight

I didn't feel like being social. Professor Patterson always tried to make it easier for us college students when he could. With one of the journalism classes I had this semester, he let us use the same text we used in the prerequisite class, the one I had taken last semester with Jaxon. He and I had shared this text last time, but I assume by now that he had bought his own book for the class or that he was sharing with someone else. Why did my thoughts always stream toward him, no matter the topic?

The annoying thing about college textbooks is that, when you buy them used, they often come with writing and highlighting marks already in them. It's very distracting when you're trying to study. This text in particular had no rhyme or reason to all the marks inside of it. One word would be circled on a page and then you could go twenty pages to find one or two more words circled. I started to get distracted by the circled words. I started at the beginning and wrote down every word I came across. It took me two hours to find every word. I began thinking about how much time I had just wasted when I could have been studying, until I realized that all of the words together meant something.

I just met you and I'm amazed by you already.
Your beauty has me blind to all others.
My eyes will always find you in a crowd.
My favorite part of the day is when I get to hear your laugh.
One day you'll let someone in and he'll be a lucky bastard.
One day you are going to discover
how beautiful and strong you are.
I hope that I'm standing right next to you
holding your hand when you do.

My first thought was how impressed I was that he had found the word *bastard* in our textbook. My next thought was unimaginably heartbreaking. I couldn't believe what he had done in my book. I remember how he had borrowed it the night I came over to the guys' place after work. I'd fallen asleep on him and he'd carried me to my bed. Then he'd taken my textbook, the very same one we both studied in countless times after, and he'd written the most amazing love note I'd ever read. Never in my life did I think I would get something like this.

He had written that he hoped he could be standing next to me when I realized how beautiful and strong I was. There was a moment when I thought those things about myself: He brought them out and reminded me daily. In a way, he *had* been beside me when I comprehended it. He just didn't stick around afterward.

I knocked all of my notes and books off of my bed and crawled under the covers. I reached under my pillow and grabbed the T-shirt I had taken from Jaxon's room the first time we slept together. He knew I had it here, but he never asked for it back. I pulled my knees up to my chest and tried to fight off the tears.

As if to dig the knife in deeper, I heard music begin playing through the wall coming from Jaxon's bedroom. It took me a couple of minutes to recognize it as the mix CD I had made, which I had never heard him listen to before. In fact, he hadn't even mentioned it since I had given it to him, not that we had discussed much of anything since then. Why, now of all times, had he pulled it out? To increase my torture, he played the disc four times in a row that night. When it finally shut off, I succumbed to a restless sleep.

NINETEEN

Halfway through midterm week, Cole and Jace asked Quinn and me to come over to their place and have a couple of drinks. I didn't drink anymore, but it would be nice to just hang out with them again in a quieter setting than a loud house party. Jace reassured me that Jaxon was gone for the night. I tried not to dwell on where he was staying overnight. I can't say that the idea of his spending the night at some girl's house didn't enter my mind a dozen times, but I was strong enough not to ask.

We all had our textbooks out to at least pretend as if we were going to study together. Jace was the only one actually studying; he seemed a little more stressed out over his tests than the rest of us. I tried to help him by quizzing him from the back of his books. He was insanely smart; I don't understand how he could remember even half of this material. After hours passed with me stumbling over numerous medical terms and body parts I couldn't pronounce, he let me off the hook with an appreciative grin. I only had one exam tomorrow and it was in English, so I wasn't really worried at all about staying up too late.

Around midnight, we were all yawning. "Come on, Quinny, let's go to bed," Cole said, mid-yawn.

"Aw, I haven't been able to spend enough time with Em lately. In a couple of months, she's going to leave us for Africa. I think I want to stay out here with her," she protested. Lately, she's been bringing up my summer departure more and more. The most we had ever been apart was a week, so three months was going to be torture for both of us.

"It's okay, Quinn, we're all going to bed anyway. I'll see you in the morning," I told her.

"Come on, Ems, come get in bed with us too. I'd never say no to two women wanting to get in my bed," Cole joked, while Jace started laughing at him.

"I don't think I ever said I wanted in your bed," I said, nudging him in the ribs.

"Just grab her, Cole," Quinn told him. Before I could protest, Cole threw me over his shoulder and grabbed Quinn's hand with his free one.

He laid us both down on the bed, got up, and grabbed two of his large T-shirts from the dresser, tossing them at us.

"Y'all change. I have to hit the bathroom," he said.

After our jeans and shirts were thrown on the floor and we were in some form of pajamas, we lay down under the covers and Quinn held my hand.

"Night, Ems, I love you."

"I love you too, Quinn," I whispered back.

Then I heard her gasp and she sat up, looking down at me. "You've never said that back to me before."

I pulled her back down. "I know, and I'm sorry. That wasn't right of me, but I always have."

She snuggled in next to me, and not long after, I heard Cole come back and get in bed behind Quinn. He kissed her and told us both good night.

The next morning, before I even opened my eyes, all I could smell was Jaxon. I didn't want to open my eyes because I was too afraid it would disappear. I could stay in this dream forever. I rubbed my face across my pillow and could unquestionably smell him and his cologne. This was like the best dream and worst nightmare, all wrapped up into one. I reached over and knew that I wasn't in bed with him since the space next to me was empty, but I also realized that I was no longer in bed with Quinn or Cole. With my eyes still sealed, I skimmed my hand across the comforter and felt the pleats that I remembered were on his gray-and-white bed. For my final test, I searched for the left corner of the sheet and felt the telltale rip that my earring had caused once.

My eyes finally shot open and my sightless exploration was confirmed. I was in Jaxon's bed, but he wasn't here with me. How did I get here? Did I get up and get into his bed in the middle of the night? If so, I needed to get out of here before he came home. Nothing would be more embarrassing than being the ex-girlfriend that not only couldn't let you go, but also crawled into your bed in the middle of the night.

I stretched my arms out in front of me and noticed familiar handwriting on my palm. I brought it closer to my face to read, since my eyes hadn't yet adjusted to the morning light.

My rule still stands. My bed. Not Cole's or Jace's.

Was this seriously happening? Did he go in Cole's room last night and take me out of his bed just so he could come lay me in his bed all alone? Why the hell did he care where I slept anymore? "My rule still stands." Who did he think he was? He didn't have any right to make rules for me. He better not still be in this apartment, because if he was, I might rip off his head. What right did he have to take me away from my friends? I thought that I might even take a nap in Jace's bed later today, just to piss him off.

To my chagrin, I was only in Cole's shirt and my panties, which meant that he carried me with barely any clothes on. I know it shouldn't bother me because he'd known every single inch of my body at one time, but I think that I deserved to be awake if he was going to touch me again. I looked around the room and didn't see my clothes anywhere, so they must have still been in Cole's room. He at least could have brought my clothes with me when he kidnapped me.

While I had been looking around his room for my clothes, I did notice more framed pictures than I remembered the last time I was in here. There were pictures on his desk, on his nightstand, and lined up on his wall. I moved in closer to look at each of them, noticing that I was in almost all of them. There were pictures of me and his mom; me and Jace; me and some of his buddies back home that I met at a couple of parties; me, Cole, and Quinn; and finally, me and him.

My favorite picture of the two of us was sitting next to his bed on his nightstand. It was the night of Garrett's birthday party, when we weren't even together yet. I remember we were standing next to the counter in the kitchen right after I had taken the tequila shot in front of him. I was looking up at him as though he was the only person in the world. I was amazed that I was able to give anyone that deep of a look. My hands were, as always, grabbing the waistband of his jeans tightly.

I remembered that Mason, who was majoring in photography, had taken this picture. He was usually snapping away at every event. At the time, we hadn't realized that he was taking our picture—not until after we heard the identifiable click of a camera—and then he came over and showed us the image on his screen. I remembered we had both smiled at it, but I hadn't seen the photo since then. I wondered if Jaxon had gone and asked him for it, or if Mason had given it to him. If he had given it to Jaxon, why hadn't he given it to me as well?

I tried to think about the last time I was in Jaxon's room. It had been the day before that awful party where I freaked out and ran away from him with Devon. I remember he had the one picture of all five of us together, sitting on the couch, which I had taken by setting the timer on my camera. But all of these other pictures definitely hadn't been here. Why the hell would he frame all of these pictures of me and hang them up in his room? The more I sat here and thought about his actions, the madder I got. This was just hurtful. He needed to stop looking at pictures of me and playing my mix CD every damn night, where I basically poured my heart out to him through songs. He wanted this breakup; I didn't.

I left his room and went down to Cole's room. His door was closed, so I waited and listened outside the door to make sure I wasn't about to walk in on something I couldn't unsee. When all was silent, I entered the dark room. I noticed Quinn was still snuggled up next to Cole, sleeping. When the light from the hallway streamed in, they started shifting around.

"Em?" Cole's scratchy voice asked.

"Sorry, Coley, I just needed to grab my clothes."

"Emmy, where did you go? When I woke up last night and you weren't here, I figured you had gone home," Quinn asked, lifting her head up.

"That asshole Jaxon came in here, grabbed me while I was sleeping, and dumped me in his bed!" I shoved my palm in front of her face so she could read his written note.

"What are you talking about? Why would he do that?" Cole sat straight up, trying to read my palm as well.

"Months ago, he asked me not to sleep in your bed or Jace's. He left me this freaking note on my hand saying that his rule still stands. I don't know who he thinks he is. Now all I want to do is sleep in yours and Jace's bed every night." I paced back and forth.

Cole shook his head. "Wow, he's got it bad."

"He's about to have it real bad." I grabbed my clothes and stomped out of the room.

225

I actually hoped he was in the living room, because I was about to tear him a new one. Talking about it with Cole and Quinn had only riled me up more. Jaxon didn't have any right to break up with me—in public, no less—and then try to control where I sleep at night. It only made me want to go around and sleep with every guy he had ever spoken to at this school. I knew I wasn't capable of doing that, but he sure made me want to. I reached the end of the hallway with my hands in fists.

When I stormed into the living room, Jaxon was on the couch. Why would he put me in his bed, when he would just have to end up sleeping on the couch? He was lying on his stomach with his arms extended out under his pillow. On the rare occasion that I would wake up before him, I always found him like this. It became a game for me to see how long I could kiss his back before he woke up. Sometimes I could kiss a line up and down three times before he would start stirring. I had loved that uninterrupted time to explore his muscular back. With my fingers, I enjoyed tracing the lines of his tattoo that spread across the back corner of his shoulder.

I lost track of how long I stood there staring down at him sleeping. I hadn't allowed myself to really look at him this past month. Anytime I started to, he would catch me, so I forced myself to stop. My anger fizzled as I listened to the rhythmic in-and-out of his breath. I would get furious with him later. It didn't look as though he was sleeping peacefully anyway; he had a pinched expression in his eyes that I wanted to reach down and smooth out.

As I stood in the hallway entrance to the living room watching him, warm hands slid over my shoulders.

"Whatcha' doing, pretty girl?" Jace whispered in my ear.

I jumped at the sound of his voice. "I'm just heading out," I whispered back, but I didn't move forward.

"You were standing here when I went to the bathroom five minutes ago."

"Um . . . I guess I just zoned out. I'm still really tired," I lied.

"You two are like sad little puppies. I don't understand it," he continued, whispering so we wouldn't wake up Jaxon.

"This wasn't my choice."

"I don't think it was his, either."

I didn't want to talk about this with Jaxon's brother, no matter how good of a friend he was to me. "Hey, do you want to do a quick study with me later for English?"

"Sure, want to just do it now?" he asked.

"I need to shower first, but I'll be right back."

"See you in a bit, babe."

I hurried down to my place and pulled the T-shirt over my head. I balled it up and held it to my nose. It didn't even smell like Cole anymore. It smelled like me and Jaxon mixed together. I quickly tucked it under my pillow alongside his shirt that I'd never returned. Cole wouldn't be getting that one back for a while, either.

I rushed through my shower and wrapped my wet hair up into a messy bun. I had a busy day ahead of me; there wasn't time for blow-drying and styling. I needed to run through my review for the English exam today, and then after class, I would have to hurry over to the hotel and make sure all the preparations were done for the auction tomorrow night.

I walked up to the guys' apartment door and debated whether I should knock or just go right in. I used to walk right in when Jax and I were together. Besides last night, I hadn't been over here since our breakup. If Jax was still sleeping, my knocking would wake him up, and I didn't want to interact with him right now. I turned the knob quietly and slipped inside. The couch was empty and Jace was in the kitchen cooking.

"Hey, Ems, that was fast. I thought girls took showers for, like, hours?" he asked, laughing.

"I wish. I don't have time today, though. Do you mind if we study in your room?" I asked.

He shrugged his shoulders and handed me a plate of eggs and bacon. "Yeah, sure. This plate is yours, with the nasty chopped onions in it."

"You put onions in my eggs?" I asked, surprised. "How did you know I liked them like that?"

"Take a wild guess. He came in here, chopped them up, and threw them in without asking. Does he care that I hate onions? No. I had to start over and remake my plate," he grumbled.

"Jaxon did that?" He nodded his head and continued walking for his room. "You know he makes no damn sense," I said.

Jace and I walked into his room and I closed the door behind us. "You're trying to get my ass kicked, aren't you?" He nodded toward the closed door. "Why don't you just talk to him, Em? He's never happy anymore . . ."

"He wanted this. I messed up and now I'm paying for it."

"You're just making both of you miserable. Didn't we have this conversation with Quinn once?" When I didn't respond, he continued, "He is going to get pissed that the door is closed . . ."

"We aren't together anymore, Jace. If I want to go into some guy's bedroom, I can. He can get over it; that's what happens when you break up." I sat down on the edge of his bed.

Jace's room was just as tidy as Jaxon's always was. Their mom really had taught them well. Where Jaxon's bedroom was bright with light grays and whites, Jace's room was darker with a black comforter and black-and-white pictures on the walls. I noticed a pair of used boxing gloves hanging from the ceiling in the corner above his bed. On his desk sat a model car that was an exact replica of the one Jaxon drove around in Texas. Next to the car was a framed picture of him, Jaxon, their beautiful mom, and their stunningly gorgeous dad, all standing together in front of their massive barn.

Interrupting my inspection of his room, Jace asked, "You haven't been in many bedrooms lately, though, have you?"

I stared at him, wondering if I should answer that question, while he came and sat next to me on the bed. I decided not to. He would just relay that back to his brother and I would feel even more pathetic than I already did.

Instead, I pulled out my English text and began going over each subject area we needed to know. I quickly realized that Jace didn't need to study this at all. He knew everything by heart already; he was only doing this to help me out. I caught myself zoning out while he read from his book to me. I watched his facial expressions and his mouth moving as the words he spoke flowed from his lips— lips that were the same size and plumpness as Jaxon's. I spied that damn slightly turned-in front tooth that I had once told Jaxon was my favorite part of his face. My heart began to hurt from the sight of him. He looked too much like his brother and it was painful.

Before I could catch myself, I began leaning in toward his lips. In my mind, this had become Jaxon sitting on his bed reading to me, not Jace.

He immediately leaped backward away from me before I made contact. "What the hell, Em?" He looked at me with a stunned expression on his face.

I finally came back to earth and realized what I'd almost done when it wasn't Jaxon's deep, melodic voice I was hearing, but Jace's. My hand shot up to cover my lips.

"Oh my God, Jace! I'm so sorry!" I yelped. All of a sudden, tears were streaming down my face. What the hell was going on with me? I had stopped crying weeks ago and now this week, I couldn't stop.

"You really are trying to get my ass kicked," he said, trying to lighten the mood, and I loved him for it.

"No, no, no, God, that wasn't supposed to happen. I zoned out. You were . . ." I couldn't say it. I was humiliated enough. How could

I tell him that I had started thinking he was his brother and that was why I had almost kissed him?

"It's okay; I understand." He gave me a sad, pitying look, and I couldn't be in this room with him another second.

I quickly reached down and put all of my papers and books back into my bag and leaped for the door.

"Em, wait! It's okay!" he shouted.

When I ran out the door, I stumbled over Jaxon, who was sitting on the ground and leaning up against the wall. Reflexively, my hands flew out to catch myself but my face followed and my mouth hit my knuckle. I brought my legs in toward my body and crouched on the ground in that position for a second. If I ever hoped to get my dignity back in front of him, it apparently wasn't happening anytime soon.

"Babe, are you okay?" Jaxon asked, hovering over me nervously.

"What the hell did you do, man?" I heard Jace's voice from farther back.

"No, asshole, what the fuck did *you* do?" he barked at his brother. "I heard her shouting in there. Why would she be shouting when you said you two were just going to be studying?"

I couldn't let Jace take the fall for my embarrassing mistake. I stood up and faced them. "Stop yelling at him, Jaxon, he didn't do anything wrong," I scolded.

They both stared at me with wide eyes. Then Jaxon reached down, scooped me up, and started walking toward the bathroom before I had a chance to protest.

"Jaxon, you can't just pick me up whenever you want anymore. Put me down," I said angrily.

He ignored me and continued into the bathroom. He sat me down onto the counter and turned toward the linen cabinet. I watched as he grabbed a clean washcloth and brought it to the sink to run water over it. When he seemed pleased with the temperature of the water, he twisted the cloth to ring out the excess. I just sat there watching him, having no idea what he was doing. He finally looked up into my eyes, and my stomach dropped; I missed those eyes. He brought the washcloth up to my lip and gently pressed down. I winced at the pain. He lifted it up and with another corner, he wiped my chin. I looked down at the cloth in his hand and noticed it was covered in blood. My blood. I had had no idea I was even bleeding.

"Are you okay?" he asked, too much concern in his eyes.

I took the cloth from his hand and hopped off the counter, holding it against my lip. "I'm fine, Jaxon. Next time, try not to eavesdrop, and maybe I won't fall over you." I know my tone was filled with ice, but I hated how he was trying to be friendly now all of a sudden.

I reached for the doorknob and he slammed his palm against the wooden door to keep it shut. I didn't even bother trying to pull it open since he was a thousand times stronger than me. I just stared at the door, waiting for him to relent.

He came up close behind me without touching me, but I could feel the heat of his body. He started in: "What are you doing to me? You're ruining me. This isn't me. I don't drool after women, but I can't seem to get you out of my fucking head! Worst of all, we aren't even friends anymore. You were my *best* friend, Emerson. Now you've got me jumping down my own brother's throat because you're in his bedroom. You've got me taking you out of some other guy's bed just so I can see you in mine . . . just one more time."

"Jaxon, you ended us," I whispered.

"Why can't we at least be friends? Every time I attempt to talk to you it turns into a yelling match."

"It's impossible. I can't be your friend. It hurts too much. If I'm ruining you, then you've destroyed me. I finally trusted someone enough to love, and you proved that, all along, it wasn't worth it."

Tears were running down my face again. One day I hoped that these tear ducts would just dry up.

"Please, Beautiful, just come to my room and talk to me." I winced at his term of endearment for me. His arm came down from the door and I jumped at the opportunity by swinging it open.

"Just stop, Jaxon. Stop playing my CD at night, stop hanging up pictures of me in your room, stop taking me out of Cole's bed, and stop making sure I get my favorite food. You don't want me anymore; all of this stuff just confuses me!" I continued down the hallway to leave.

"Emerson, that's not—"

"Leave her alone, Jax." I heard Cole's harsh voice interrupt from the end of the hall. I walked out of their place and headed straight for my car to get to school.

≈

Everything was almost ready for the auction tomorrow night. Micah had actually been a huge help to me. I was surprised when he signed on for the internship at the beginning of the semester. I had no idea he was interested in this area of journalism. At least there would be someone I knew in Africa with me. I was still getting to know the others in the group.

When he saw my lip, he freaked out because it definitely looked as if I had been punched. It took a while to explain that I had actually managed to punch myself. After my ridiculous story, he laughed and told me that only I could accomplish that. Surprisingly, he hadn't hit on me once since Jaxon and I had broken up. Earlier, I had needed to call all of the girls that were going to be auctioned off to make sure they would all be here on time, and Micah volunteered to call all twenty of them. I don't care if he just wanted twenty hot girls' numbers; that was a lot of time that he was saving me.

While we were finishing up the ballroom, I turned toward him from across a table. "Thanks again, Micah. You've helped me out a lot. If it weren't for you, I'd have had to come up here at three in the morning after I got off work just to have this place done in time."

"Not a problem, Ems. I know I gave you a hard time last semester about the whole dating thing, but I think of you as a good friend. I realize you would rather have Jax here to help, but I'm glad I could."

"Right now, I'm glad it's you." I smiled at him.

"Wow, thanks."

"Hey, I have to head out to work, but you should come by tonight. I'll give you some free drinks for helping out."

"I just might take you up on that offer." He winked at me and walked me out to my car.

Later that night, I was cleaning off the bar top and talking to Micah about the schedule of events for tomorrow. I watched as Mark checked the IDs of Cole, Jace, Quinn, and Jaxon. They all smiled at me as they walked in, except Jaxon, who just glared at the back of Micah's head. I pointed them to the pool table closest to the bar, which I usually tried to save for friends. Cole and Quinn came in most often, and Jace would come every once in a while, but Jaxon hadn't been here in over a month. I wished he hadn't come tonight, no matter how much I liked looking at him. The way he was glaring holes into Micah's head gave me a pretty good idea that all he was going to do was cause me a headache tonight.

"What can I get you guys?" I asked as they approached the bar. Micah spun in his seat to see who was behind him. He tapped knuckles with Cole and Jace but just stared at Jaxon. They all gave me their drink orders. "I'll bring them out to you."

When they walked away to their table, I started prepping glasses for their drinks and pulling out bottles to pop the tops. Micah continued talking to me about the lineup for tomorrow, and I laughed out loud when he made a joke about one of the girls in the auction. He even made the annoying high-pitched noise she makes when she's upset. Then I noticed Jaxon making his way back up to the bar.

"Better watch out, Em. If you're not careful, you might pass your three-time limit with him," he jeered.

"What the fuck's your problem, man?" Micah spun in his stool to scowl at Jaxon.

"Leave, dude, before I kick your ass again," his voice was barely above a whisper, but I knew what he'd just said.

"If I remember correctly, you guys broke up. I'm pretty sure I watched you do it in the middle of the damn courtyard at school for everyone to see," Micah threw back at him. "If that's the case, you don't have any hold over her. She's my friend and I'll sit here and talk to her however long I want."

"Have you raised your limit, Emerson, and gone back to your old ways with this guy?" He may as well have called me a whore right here in the middle of my bar.

I turned my cold eyes toward him and I watched his face fall in horror as the weight of his words hit him. "Fuck! I shouldn't have said that. I didn't mean that at all, I swear to God."

"Leave right now before I ask Mark to escort you out."

I saw that my cold voice was making him panic, so I decided to escape into the back room. Before I could get the door closed to lock it, I was being shoved backward. Jaxon's giant frame took up the entire door as he came into the room behind me. He grabbed me by the hips and lifted me up, and my traitorous legs wrapped around his waist as if they had a mind of their own. They knew where they wanted to be, as much as my head didn't agree. My chest was heaving from my anger at what he had said earlier, and he just kept staring into my eyes.

Before I knew what was happening, he pulled the back of my head toward him and his lips were crushing mine, attacking them mercilessly. My body instantly responded to his fiery passion and the heat emanating off his body. I squeezed him tighter with my legs and threaded my fingers through his hair roughly. I needed this. I needed to release all of the pent-up feelings I still had for him. He walked forward until my back hit the wall of the storage room.

He pulled back too soon and stared into my eyes again. "Talk to me, Emerson."

"No," was my only answer. Then I pulled his head back to mine.

"I hate that I hurt your lip, baby." He pushed back and laid small kisses on my bottom lip. My mouth opened to allow his tenderness.

Not giving him a chance to stop the delicious feel of his body against mine, I reached down for the hem of his shirt. I needed to feel his skin and I needed it against mine. He didn't resist; instead he helped me by grabbing the back of his collar with one hand and pulling it over his head. My hands were instantly on his chest, feeling the bulges of his muscles. His skin was on fire and I instantly flushed from the feel of it. I wanted him and I knew he wanted me just as badly. His thirst was rolling off of him and it would have suffocated me if I hadn't been feeling the same thing. He may not have wanted me in his heart anymore, but for now, I could deal with the fact that he wanted my body. I could feel his need growing between my legs.

I wanted him to take off all of my clothes and remove his pants. I wanted to forget everything he had done to me that ripped my heart out. I just wanted to enjoy the one body that had ever actually pleased me. He started moving again, and this time I felt something hit the back of my thighs. I realized he had moved us to the big deep freezer. He lifted me up a little so I was sitting on the edge.

"Emerson, stop. I'm not going to do this till we talk."

"There's nothing to talk about besides the fact that I want you and I need you inside of me." He groaned at my words. What could he possibly have to tell me? I knew what this was. It was a weak moment. We both knew how good we were together in the bedroom and, just for now, we both wanted that back.

I could feel how rock-hard he was by now, and I couldn't stop myself from moving back and forth against him. When I looked up at him, his eyes were rolled back in his head and his mouth was open. A short gasp whistled between his teeth. I loved this man with everything I had; this was absolutely going to annihilate me after we were done. There would be nothing left—but then again, I don't know if there had been anything left in the first place. When he started his own rhythm of torture as he swayed into me, my back arched and I lifted my chest up toward him. The neckline of my shirt was already low, so he pulled it down farther.

"Do you have another shirt here?" he asked roughly.

"Uh . . . I don't think I have one like this, but I could probably find a T-shirt. Why?"

"Good. You shouldn't be wearing this so every dick out there can look at your tits all night anyway." At that, he ripped the neckline of my shirt and pushed my bra down as well, until my breasts were fully exposed. Then he took me in his mouth.

"Jaxon!" I gasped.

He rocked against me faster and I relished the moan that shot out his mouth. I was so close but I didn't want to end like this. I reached down for his waistband and pulled to let him know what I wanted. He moved back and I almost cried at the loss of his mouth on me. He quickly pulled my shorts and panties down my legs and tossed them to the ground. He unbuttoned his jeans and reached into his wallet for a condom before shoving them down his legs. Clutching my hips with his fingertips, he was instantly inside of me. Oh. My. God . . . Yes. How had I forgotten how wonderfully he filled me? How he completed every need that I had?

"Please talk to me," he said again. Who would want to talk during this moment? I don't think I could coherently express any thoughts right now.

"I know what this is, Jaxon. I'm not going to expect anything from you after this. I'm a big girl. Please, just go. Harder. I need you."

"Fuck, baby, don't say shit like that or I won't last."

He ripped the ponytail holder out of my hair, wrapped the length of my hair around his wrist twice, and tugged, so that I was forced to look up at him. His mouth came down hard onto mine and his tongue instantly darted inside. I missed his lips on me, anywhere they wanted to be on me, just as long as they were on me. His other hand traveled down my body lightly. The contrast between his rough pulling in one hand and the sweet caress of the other was invigorating. He knew I loved a little of both. When I bit down into his bottom lip, he picked up his pace again, pumping faster inside of me. I released his lip and he moved his mouth down to the spot under my ear.

"It kills me to see you writhing underneath me. I've never seen anything so beautiful." His voice dropped to a tone that I knew would make me come if he continued talking. "I love you so damn much." With that, my body went off and I cried out his name again. His head ducked into my neck as he quickly followed behind me. We stayed there for a couple of minutes longer, heavily breathing in and out. "For as long as I live, I'll never forget how your heartbeat feels against my chest," he whispered.

This statement brought me back to reality. I slid off the freezer, reached down, and pulled my shorts back on. I heaved my ruined shirt off over my head and found the shelves that held the extra T-shirts. I found one close to my size and pulled it on quickly.

When I started for the door, he called out, "Emerson, talk to me."

"I'm probably going to get fired for leaving the bar unattended. I need to get back out there."

"We aren't even going to talk about what happened here?"

"There's nothing to talk about. We got an urge out of our systems." With that, I walked back out to the bar, leaving my broken heart with him in the storage room.

Back behind the bar, I spotted Cole glaring at the back-room door from a barstool. I grabbed a rag and started wiping down the already clean bar top. I scanned the building to see if I could see Ed anywhere. Thank goodness, he must still be in his office.

"About damn time, Em; I had to cover for you while you were back there," Cole said angrily. "Are you okay, or do I need to go back there and take care of him?"

I came around the bar and collided into Cole with a big hug. "I don't think you will ever understand how much I appreciate your protectiveness or how thankful I am for you loving Quinn so much, Coley."

He wrapped his arms around me and squeezed tight. I felt him lay his cheek down on the top of my head. "You're like my sister, Em. I'll beat up any guy that does you wrong, even if he is my best friend." Speaking of the devil, Jaxon walked out of the back room right then. "I don't think I need to guess what you guys were doing back there. Just be thankful Jace went and turned on the jukebox right after he followed you, or we probably would have heard it all. Seeing your faces now, though, do you really think that was the best idea?" he whispered, still holding on to me.

"No, I don't. But I missed him so much." The tears were starting to come, so I began to pull away, but he just squeezed me in tighter.

"I hate seeing you hurt, Emmy."

"I'll learn to be okay."

"Get your hands off of her and let's go," Jaxon grated out from behind us. I stepped back from Cole and wiped my eyes, and he sighed in a frustrated tone.

I went back behind the bar and started getting everything cleaned up for the night.

"Stop being a jackass," Cole said, slapping Jaxon on the back of the head as he walked by. "And don't think I'm not going to kick your ass for what you said to her earlier, either."

Jaxon whipped around and looked at Cole with wide eyes.

"That's right, asshole, I heard it. I almost pummeled you into the ground right there, but I wanted Em to take care of it first." *And look at what a great job I did . . .*

"Don't worry. I already told Mom, and she'll do it for us," Jace laughed.

"Fuck . . . I'm such an idiot." He turned toward me with sad, apologetic eyes. I quickly turned away to tell Quinn good-bye and give her a hug.

He had started coming back over to me when Jace cut him off. "Come on, Romeo, you've done enough for one night." He grabbed his bicep and steered him to the door. "See ya later, Emmy," Jace called out.

- TWENTY -

We had everything ready and set up for the auction to begin. Micah helped me set up a stage with a runway coming out from the middle. Cole had agreed to be the auctioneer. I had asked him because he knew how to be loud and capture a crowd. Cole and Jace came early to finish with the setup and heavy lifting. Quinn was in the back helping all the girls finish getting ready to walk the stage.

I was lifting up a stack of three chairs to carry over to tables that still needed them when they were unexpectedly lifted from my hands. Jaxon stacked them onto another set of four chairs and carried all seven behind me as I showed him where they went. I didn't have anything to say to him, so he just followed silently. We kept up this silent exchange for four more tables and twenty-four more chairs. He didn't say a word and I didn't, either. I pointed to the banner stating that the football team was sponsoring the event, and he hung it up above the stage. He looked down at me from the ladder to check his work, and I just gestured my hand upward to indicate that the left side needed to be a bit higher.

After he fixed it, he looked at me for approval, and I turned to find something else to do. I heard his feet hit the stage as he jumped down off the last couple of rungs on the ladder. He came up right behind me and followed me around, lifting anything he deemed heavy, although I didn't think a box of napkins weighed too much.

"It looks good, guys. Thank you," I called across the room. "Might as well grab a drink from the bar before everyone else gets here." I pointed to the bar set up in the back of the room.

"Want something, Emerson? I'll get it for you." I shook my head at him. "Tequila? Beer? I'm sure I can find something you like."

"I don't drink," I replied, walking out of the ballroom. I shouldn't have been surprised to see him jogging up behind me.

"What do you mean, you don't drink?" he demanded.

"It means that anything that contains alcohol doesn't go into my mouth," I retorted, annoyed with his dumb question.

"I understood that part; it's the 'why' that I'm curious about."

I continued walking down the hotel hallway, looking for the closest bathroom. "I don't drink since it ruined the best thing I ever had." With that, I finally found the bathroom and walked in, leaving him behind. Thank God there was no one else in here.

Without missing a beat, Jaxon came in right behind me and locked the door behind him. He bent down to check for feet under the stalls, and when he didn't see any, he stalked forward toward me.

I continued walking until I reached the last stall. "Jaxon, this room is for women only. I'm sure you saw the sign."

He grabbed my waist before I could enter the stall and pushed me up against the wall next to the paper towel dispenser. He stared at me, inspecting my face. I needed to stay strong. I couldn't let him think that he could just seduce me whenever he felt like it now. Yesterday was a one-time thing to get each other out of our systems, no matter how much of a lie I was telling myself. He ran the pad of his thumb along my bruised bottom lip; the friction made me wince slightly.

"Sorry," he whispered. "It looks a little better today, though. Why do you only injure your lips?" His voice was reaching that dangerously low level that made me do things I would regret later, but I was frozen up against the wall. "These are my favorite; you should take better care of them." He bent down and started his spellbinding, tender kisses, back and forth across my lower lip. All I could do was open my mouth a little wider and let him.

"Would you rather I injured something else?" I gasped.

His lips moved down my jaw and across the edge of my neck. "Of course not. I'd rather you not be damaged at all, but I love to kiss it better."

At the word *damaged*, I pushed him off of me. "Stop doing this to me. I don't like to be teased."

"I'm pretty sure there was no teasing last night." He eyed me with mischief.

"You know what I mean. You can't keep kissing me . . ." Oh hell, the damn tears. I tried to sniff and wipe my eyes discreetly, turning away from him. "Please stop trying to 'talk' to me," I said, using air quotes.

"You think that when I kiss you or . . . make love to you, that's what I mean by 'we need to talk'?" He grabbed me and spun me to face him. "Shit, you're crying." He pulled me into his chest and rubbed along the length of my hair. "Please, Beautiful. Please don't cry. I really do want to talk to you."

I couldn't do this. I needed to leave this bathroom. He bent down and grabbed me around the waist to lift me up. I kept my legs hanging down, no matter how much they wanted to squeeze around his waist. He grabbed one leg and curled it around himself and when he reached for the other, I let that one fall back down.

"Please, Emerson, put your legs around me," he begged.

I stayed there, slack in his arms, with my feet dangling a foot off the ground.

"Please, don't do this," he whispered.

His familiar words hit me and I wiggled out of his hold. "I seem to remember saying, actually yelling, begging, pleading, those exact words to you a month ago. Let me respond the same way you did . . ." I saw him flinch right before I turned and walked out the door.

Halfway back down the hallway toward the ballroom I heard Micah say, "Dude, that's the chick's bathroom. Gents are that way." Jaxon didn't respond.

The ballroom filled up quickly. Professor Patterson was beaming ear to ear at all the attendees. Even the dean had made it tonight to donate to our trip, although obviously he wouldn't be participating in the auction. I was weaving through the crowd of people, thanking them for coming, when Cole's booming voice came through the speakers to welcome everyone. He handed the microphone to Professor Patterson, who explained our trip to Africa and what we would be learning. I noticed Jaxon walking in and taking a chair a few tables away from the stage. When Patterson began talking about the dangers of Africa and how we needed to be prepared, I noticed the stress on his face and his hands twisting the tablecloth. He looked over at me with a nervous expression, and I turned my attention back to the stage, where Cole had taken back the microphone.

"Okay, guys, I hope you packed your wallets because we have twenty beautiful women back there ready for you to bid on them. Cash only—pay before you leave or I'm giving them to someone else. Treat them with respect or Jace and I will pay you a little visit." He pointed to the back of the room at Jace.

I'd never thought of Jace as anything but a teddy bear, but he looked different with his tall body leaning up against the back wall. He had his muscular arms crossed over his wide chest. He looked dangerous and mean standing there glaring at everyone. I wanted to giggle at the apprehensive looks the other guys were giving him.

"All right, get your wallets out and raise your paddles high. If I can't see your paddle, then you aren't working hard enough for these beauties. Sorry, Quinn; you're still my number-one beauty!"

Someone in the crowd shouted, asking if Quinn would be auctioned off, and I burst out laughing at the face Cole gave him.

"I'll see you after, McAdams," he growled in a low tone.

Cole began introducing the girls, one by one, and calling out for the auction. Each girl had an admirer, and these guys came prepared to duke it out with their wallets. We were all laughing and having a great time watching the guys get extremely competitive over the girls, who were perfect. They were eating up the attention and taunting the guys from the stage. I was right to choose Cole as the emcee because he knew exactly how to egg on the guys. He knew what their weak spots were and how to get the most money out of them. When Tatum's turn came, I saw her eyeing Jaxon from the stage, silently begging him to bet on her. I was thankful he never bid on any of them; I wouldn't have been able to watch that. Each girl went for two hundred to four hundred dollars. With twenty girls, we were making a good amount for our trip, plus all of the donations we had gotten on the side. After the last girl was auctioned off to Garrett for two hundred fifty dollars, Cole thanked everyone for participating.

"I have a surprise for everyone. Don't put your wallets away just yet. I have one more pretty lady to auction off for you gentlemen."

I whispered up at him, "Cole, there are only twenty girls!"

"No, there's not, Emmy, because I'm going to auction *you* off! Emerson Moore, gentlemen!" he hollered into the microphone.

"*What?*" I whisper-shouted.

Jaxon shoved his chair back and walked right up to the stage where Cole was standing. "What the hell are you thinking right now, man?" he snapped in a harsh tone.

Cole ignored him and smiled. "I present the elusive Em. You guys had better take advantage of this opportunity, because I'm sure you won't get another. Em doesn't do dates, but I'm sure for a good price, she'll go out to a movie with you. She's beautiful and tons of fun!" Cole gestured for me to get on the stage and I shook my head back and forth. Micah came up behind me and lifted me onto the stage.

"Traitor!" I whispered at him.

Guys in the crowd began rising in their chairs and clapping their hands together. Jaxon was fuming. I decided to work with this because it was nice to see him getting riled up for a change.

"I hear she's been wanting to go for a ride on a motorcycle, if any of you riders are interested," Cole teased, knowing it was a weak spot for Jax.

Dalton Fisher, the quarterback, moved right up to the stage then. I happened to know that he owned a motorcycle. Jaxon's teeth were bared now. Dalton was a sexy guy and he knew it. He was almost the same size and build as the Riley boys.

Cole began shouting out for bids, and they were coming from all corners of the room.

"Two hundred fifty dollars!" Jaxon said.

"Three hundred," Dalton retorted.

Cole clapped his hands at the rising dollar signs. I gasped at the amount of money we had reached in less than ten seconds.

"Dude, I will kick your ass again if you don't back away," Jaxon sneered at Dalton. What did he mean by that? It seemed as though Jax got into more fights than I knew about.

"Four hundred dollars, Cole—call it," Jax said, sounding more pissed by the second.

"Stop it, Jaxon!" I yelled at him in a whisper. He continued looking at Cole.

"Four hundred fifty," Dalton countered, raising his paddle and smiling up at me. I gifted him with a brilliant grin in return.

"Fisher, if you don't back away from this stage right now, I will rip your fucking throat out."

"Five hundred dollars," a voice hollered from the back.

Jaxon slammed his fist on the stage in frustration. "One thousand! Cole, you better call it."

My eyes went wide at his bid. Cole laughed. "All right, let's put the poor bastard out his misery. Going once . . . going twice . . ."

Dalton stepped forward to raise his paddle, but Jaxon reached over and smacked it from his hand. Dalton bent forward, laughing at his antics.

"Sold! To the very possessive Jaxon Riley." Cole bent down and handed Jax his ticket so he could pay later. I watched as Cole whispered to him, "I'll make sure you never get within fifty feet of her if you hurt her again." Jax nodded his head once.

Instantly, he turned toward me and pulled me over his shoulder, so that my hands and face hit his back. I would kill him. This couldn't be more embarrassing. I was in charge of this event and he was dragging me out over his shoulder. I didn't fight it because I didn't want to create more of a scene in front of everyone. Thank God that I didn't wear a skirt today. He didn't stop until he got to his truck out in the parking lot, where he sat me down on the passenger seat and closed the door to walk around to the other side.

When he put the keys in the ignition I finally spoke. "I'm not leaving, Jaxon. This event was my responsibility."

He pulled his cell phone out of his pocket and began calling someone. "Woods, yeah . . . can you cover the rest of the event for Emerson? . . . Yeah . . . I fucking know . . . I understand . . . Okay, thanks, I'll owe you." I'm pretty sure I had entered the twilight zone.

"You just called Micah?" I said, shocked. "Why would you even have his number?"

"I had to call him today to talk to him about stuff," he responded, but I could tell he didn't want to talk about it. He drove past our apartments and I had no idea where he was headed.

"Why would you need to call him today?"

"Emerson, I don't want to talk about Micah."

"He's my friend, so I do. Why would you need to talk to him?"

"I called to apologize. Happy?" he grumbled.

"You apologized?" My shocked voice rose.

"If he's really your friend, and he's going to Africa with you, I needed to apologize. I'll need him to watch over you when I can't. It's pissing me off, but there's nothing I can do about that; the internship is full."

"You tried to get in the Africa internship?" It was one surprise after another with him. He nodded his head. "Why do you need someone to watch over me?"

"Isn't it obvious? Because I'll need at least an ounce of peace while you're away from me for three months. Because I love you so damn much. Because if something happened to you, I wouldn't survive."

"Why do you say that kind of stuff to me? It only hurts me, you know," I whispered. He pulled the truck into an empty parking lot at the beach and put it in park.

"I can't live without you. I'm done trying," he said, looking into my eyes while pulling me across the seat closer to him. He sat me in his lap facing him with my back leaning up against the steering wheel. I stayed quiet, not sure how to continue this subject.

"I ended things with us, Emerson, because I didn't think I was strong enough to be with you. When you went off the deep end that night before . . . your birthday, Quinn told me you usually got sad and became a little reclusive during that time. When she said you had never acted the way you did that night, I knew it was because of me. I was hurting you, somehow making you worse. I knew you deserved to find someone who could build you up, not tear you down. When you ran off with Devon, I figured that's what you were searching for as well."

"Jaxon . . . that's not it at all. I got a voice mail right before that party from a lawyer who spoke of my mom and dad. Hearing their names so close to the anniversary of their death set me off . . . I know I never should have left."

He nodded his head. "Quinn told me about the lawyer. I'm sorry I wasn't there for you during that; I beat myself up every damn day. After she told me that, it had already been a week since we broke up. You seemed sad at first, but then it seemed you were getting over me, and I didn't want to hurt you more by asking you back. I started going to parties you were at because I had to know if you had found someone new. It sounds awful, but I was elated every time I saw you just sitting down talking to Cole, Jace, or Quinn all night. You never left with any guys. I figured you would move on quickly. But week after week, you still came out to that tree by yourself and I started wondering if you missed me as much as I missed you.

"A smart lady," he continued, "once told me that I would screw up—we both would—but that it was how I handled it afterward that mattered. I didn't handle it the right way; I should have never let Cole take you away that day," he said and I smiled at his sweet mom's words.

"Jax . . . it's been a hard month for me. That day in the courtyard is high on my list of most painful days. I don't think I can put myself in the position to be hurt like that again."

"Since that day you walked out of the frat house with barely any clothes on, I've been calling you mine. Before I'd gotten to know you, I knew I had to make you mine. It only got worse the closer we got. When Cole carried you away from me that day, I realized you weren't mine at all. *I. Am. Yours,*" he avowed, while pounding his chest. "When I wake up in the morning, my first thought is of you, and every minute for the rest of my day is spent thinking about you in some way or another," he ground out.

"Jax . . ." I didn't know how to respond.

"I'm yours, Emerson."

"How do I know that if I panic again and need space, you won't walk away from me? I understand how hard I am to be with. I still have a mile-long list of issues with my parents' death, and I'm sure I'm not done freaking out."

He took my face into his hands and looked into my eyes. I loved being this close again to those brilliant blues. "You don't walk away from your heart."

I grabbed his shirt and pulled him closer to me. He stopped his lips from mashing into mine; instead, he stopped them right against me. We sat there waiting for the other, our breath intermixing. I could feel the softness of his lips on my mine, but he wasn't moving any closer.

"Please, Jaxon . . ." I whispered against his mouth.

Without moving his mouth, he brought his hands up and slowly undid each tiny button down the front of my blouse. When he finally had it open, he slowly removed it from my shoulders and tossed it in the backseat. I glanced out the windows to see if there were any people around. He caught me searching.

"Trust me, Beautiful. I'm not going to let anyone else see you."

With his reassuring words, I closed my eyes and let him take charge. I realized that five months ago, I wouldn't have cared if anyone else saw me. Now I understood that I wanted to save everything I had for this man right here. I couldn't imagine sharing any part of me with anyone besides him. For that, I'll always be grateful to him.

"You do make me stronger." I opened my eyes to look at him as he was freeing me from my bra.

"What?" he asked while trying to stay focused on my eyes.

I grabbed both of his hands and interlocked my fingers with his. "You said you thought you made me weaker, and that's just not true. You make me stronger. You make me appreciate what I have and make me want to be a better person for you."

I finally moved his hands to my breasts and he moaned. I couldn't handle it any longer, so I kissed him fiercely. My fingers moved to thread through his hair, which was longer than it was a month ago. I know we had just been together yesterday, but I hadn't been able to appreciate any of it. I had been full of angst and need, and I was too busy thinking about how destroyed I would feel afterward. This time, I could revel in the changes that had happened in a month, like the length of his hair. I pulled his shirt over his head, needing to press myself up against his skin.

I bent down and started kissing the lines of his tattoo, from his collarbone down to his bicep. If I hadn't been admiring it so closely I would have missed it, but there was definitely something different. I felt his body freeze when he knew I had found it. Wrapped in the already existing lines was a black heart with an "E" carved out in the middle. It was amazing how the artist could make it seem as if that heart had been there all along. It was perfectly tucked behind one wide sweeping black line. I traced the outline of it.

"You're my heart. You don't walk away from your heart," he whispered in my ear.

I looked at it in awe. This was permanent. This meant he wanted me in his life permanently. I couldn't stop kissing him; it was freeing to once again be able to do that whenever I wanted.

"Did Jace get one too?" I giggled as he pinched me in the side with a faux-angry expression.

His face turned serious again. "Emerson, have you . . . been with anyone else?" he asked nervously.

"Absolutely not," I responded with a disgusted face, and he sighed in relief with a chuckle. "Have you?" I continued.

He cupped my breasts and lifted them up so he could kiss the swells of them. "No, Beautiful, you've ruined me. No one else compares."

"Do you still want to stand next to me holding my hand?" I asked, thinking of the message I had pieced together from the textbook.

His eyebrows rose. "You found it finally?"

I nodded. "Not at the best time, either. It was after we had that fight by my tree."

"The night I started playing your CD out loud for you, instead of playing it through my headphones?"

Now this made *my* eyebrows rise. "You listened to it before that night?"

"Every night. I've listened to it every single night since you gave it to me."

~

Later that week, we had our official date that he had paid for at the auction. He came into my room while I was getting ready, handing me a huge present wrapped in light blue paper with a massive black bow on top.

"A black bow?" I laughed.

"It's fitting for the present. Open it," he said nervously.

All I saw was black at first. When I reached in to pull everything out, I realized it was a black leather jacket and helmet that matched the one Jaxon wore to ride on his motorcycle, only smaller. I looked up at him with wide eyes, considering what he was telling me with this gift.

"You're going to take me on the bike?" I asked excitedly.

"I may only be able to do it once, but you're going to wear all of this stuff. I don't want an inch of you exposed. It probably won't be any fun because I'm going to drive about twenty miles an hour. But yes . . . I'm going to take you," he said, taking in a deep breath.

"Let's go right now!" I squealed.

We walked down to the bike and he immediately went into education mode. "Don't put your legs down at all. Never touch this"—he pointed to some metal pieces—"because it gets really hot. Tap my shoulder, once to slow down and twice if you want me to stop. Always hold my waist and try not to lean against my turns; it'll make it harder for me." He was getting nervous.

"Jaxon, I trust you." I patted each side of his face.

"It's not me I'm worried about. I'm an excellent rider; I'd never put you in danger. I worry about the other idiots on the road."

"Jaxon, I trust you," I repeated and stood on my tiptoes to kiss him.

He mounted the bike and I swung my leg over to get behind him. I knew I would love this. The way I was molded against his backside was sexy already. He started up the engine and I could feel the vibration underneath me. He ran my hands along his sides and over his stomach until my arms overlapped. I hugged myself even closer to his back.

The ride was exhilarating; he wound up and down the road that ran parallel to the beach. Each turn he made with his body had me pulling in closer. Eventually, I tuned out the ride altogether and focused on the body I was holding onto. My hands started roaming across his stomach and chest, and he quickly pulled over next to an oceanside picnic area and turned off the engine. I slid off and he followed behind. He unsnapped his helmet and then did the same for me.

"Your roaming hands are a distraction." He nuzzled into my neck as he picked me up and walked us to a picnic table.

He sat up on the table with his feet on the bench. I laid my head down on his shoulder. We sat there, enveloped in a peaceful silence, while he rubbed my back softly.

"I love you, Jaxon."

"I love you, Beautiful, more than you can imagine." The feel of his lips on mine was heaven.

"I think we need to go back home now . . ." I whispered to him with a guilty smile on my face.

He leaned back to look at me, confused, until he saw the lust and desire in my eyes. It hit him hard and I saw the same flames in his. He picked me up and almost sprinted back to the bike, and I laughed the whole way there.

- EPILOGUE -

The longest three months of my life were finally coming to an end. If I had any say at all, I'd never let Emerson be away from me for that long again. But let's be honest, that girl had me so wrapped around her finger, I'd have done anything she wanted. I knew it would be difficult not to wake up next to her every morning, seeing that blonde hair spread out across my pillows or her smiling just a little bit in her sleep. She began doing that after I took her to her parents' grave before she left.

That day was brutal for me; I hated to see her in so much pain. But she got to say what she should have said to her parents long ago, and I could tell, when we left, that she had a little more peace. Damn, I missed that little, peaceful smile, but I never imagined how painful it would be just to be away from her for so long. The fact that I couldn't talk to her whenever I wanted made it even more difficult. So many times I would wake up in a pool of sweat just needing to call her to make sure she was safe and okay. I could never go back to sleep after those moments, so I got up and went for a run instead. I ran almost every night this summer; at least Coach would be happy.

During the entire three months, she'd only been able to call twice, because they were always far away from any kind of civilization. Professor Patterson had taken a satellite phone with him but could only let them use it on rare occasions because it was so expensive. About a month and half after she left, Ellie, Emerson's stepmom, got a call that they had been held at gunpoint while crossing the border of Uganda one night. They weren't supposed to be traveling after dark, but they ended up having to wait at a gas station for three hours just to fill up. Eventually, everything cleared up when the Ugandan police force showed up, but the second I heard, I started searching for tickets online to get to Africa. I didn't have a clue how to find her, but I was going to. My mom brought me down from that panic.

When she finally called to say she was okay, it was such a fucking relief to hear her voice. She said she knew I would do something crazy, so she bribed everyone with candy to let her use the phone first. I had a hard time believing anyone could deny her beautiful face, even without the candy. She told me that when they realized what was happening, Micah made her lie on the floor of the bus and wouldn't let her even attempt to get up until they were a mile away from the thieves. As much as I hated it, I was seriously indebted to him.

It had been a month and a half since I'd heard her voice and three months since I dropped her beautiful, tearstained face off at the airport. Jace called me a pussy for crying when she left. Hell, I didn't care what he called me: That girl drove me.

I tried to stay as busy as I possibly could this summer. I jumped on a plane back home with Cole and Jace immediately after Emerson's plane took off. Quinn had spent the majority of her summer in Texas as well. Every time I went over to Cole's to visit, Mrs. West, his mom, was treating Quinn like a princess and showering her with gifts. She looked like she was in heaven. I also noticed how Cole's mom was teaching her how to make his favorite meals. I laughed at how she was already prepping Quinn to marry her son. It was always nice to see Quinn, but every time I did, I expected Emerson to come bouncing out of the room behind her. Sometimes I caught Quinn looking at me with a sad expression and knew she was thinking the same thing when I walked in.

On the plus side, the more Quinn enjoyed Texas, the easier it would be for Cole to get her to move out here after graduation, which would practically seal the deal for my getting Emerson to move out here. If she didn't want Texas, though, I'd go anywhere. Hell, send me to any shithole as long as I'm by her side. I already had the rock that I would slide onto her finger one day, although I knew it would probably be at least another year until she was ready for something like that. In the meantime, I'd be on pins and needles until I could get that on her gorgeous hand. Just in case the opportunity arose, though, I'd have it with me in California.

Jace helped me put a new roof and siding on the barn at Mom's this summer. She complained that we should just hire someone to do it. I knew we could afford it, but Jace and I had built this barn with Dad when we were fourteen. If anyone was working on it, we were. It was tough work, and I admired my dad even more for dealing with the stress of building this thing from the ground up while having to teach two fourteen-year-olds, who knew nothing about building and were more concerned with their raging hormones. Jace and I got into a couple of fistfights over this barn throughout the summer, but I think it brought us even closer.

When we finished fighting, Mom would come out of the house with a tray of lemonade and look down at us, covered in dirt and lying on the ground, panting. She would give each of us a glass and say, "You two done being idiots? Did you get it out of your systems? If not, feel free to keep at it, but make sure you make up afterward." Then she would turn around and walk right back into the house, just like she did when we were eight years old.

After the first couple of fights, I noticed that Jace's swings were getting weak. He used to be able to knock my damn lights out, although that never stopped me from fucking with him on a daily basis. He was too easy to rile up. One day I brought it up to him, and he shrugged uncomfortably. Dad and Jace used to box almost every day. While working on the Camaro with Dad was our time, boxing with Dad was Jace's. After a couple of weeks, I finally got him back into some gloves and we were duking it out daily until after the sun went down. I could see how exhilarated he was; boxing made him happy. I'd have to remember to help him find a gym when we got back to California.

The day before we were flying back, I found Jace in the garage, polishing the Camaro one more time before we headed out for a couple more months. I tossed him the keys and he caught them in the air.

"Want to go for a ride or something?" he asked.

"Nah, I think I'm done with her." I rubbed the hood. "You should take her now."

"Take her where?" He was still confused.

"Wherever you want. She's yours," I said with a smile.

His eyes bugged out of his damn head and I couldn't help laughing my ass off at him. "What are you talking about, Jax? This was you and Dad's thing."

"Building it and fixing it up was our thing, but I've never appreciated it like you have," I replied, thinking about that model car it took him all summer to make when he was sixteen.

"You're fucking screwing with me, aren't you?" When I shook my head, his mouth dropped open and his eyes filled with moisture.

I started walking out of the garage to give him a moment, but shouted over my shoulder on the way out, "Who's the pussy now?" I heard his chuckle from back inside the garage.

Now I was standing at the gate, watching her plane taxi in and wearing her favorite black ball cap. The school had gotten all the family members and close friends security passes to wait at the gate for them to get off, since they had been gone so long. Charles, Ellie, Quinn, and Cole were all waiting right outside the gangway door so they could scoop her up the second she got off. I decided to stand farther back past the crowd of other waiting families so that they could all have their moment with her. The second I got my hands on her, I didn't want to have to share with anyone. Jace was bumming hard that he wouldn't be here when she walked off, but he had decided to drive the Camaro out to California. Mom had convinced us to ship the motorcycle back to Texas, saying we didn't need that many vehicles. I didn't mind because it still freaked me out to take Emerson on it, no matter how fucking sexy she was in her leather, grabbing onto me from behind. Mom was riding with Jace out here so that she could see Emerson as well, and then she'd fly back next week. I quickly shot both of them a text to let them know she had landed safely and I'd have her call them as soon as I let her breathe. I've always thought I had the coolest mom, but never have I had a girlfriend that got along so well with her before. Emerson just meshed right into my life like she was made to be there.

Slowly, students started wandering off the plane. They all looked really tan and tired, but happy to be back. I started getting antsy at the prospect of seeing her again. No matter how happy I was to see her, I was extremely proud of her at the same time. One of their assignments while in Africa was to write an article that related to the trip. They already had to have them submitted to Professor Patterson a couple of weeks ago. Ellie called to tell me that the school was publishing her article in the school's newspaper the first week classes resumed. The dean had called to tell her about it and he also told Ellie that Emerson didn't know about it yet, since communication was so limited. I was excited for her to find out, but I thought I'd try to hold off and surprise her with it the first week of school by showing her the actual newspaper. I had once told her that one day, we'd hear all about the great Emerson Moore: Humanitarian Journalist, and I wasn't lying.

Another reason I was excited to get her home was that I'd taken the liberty to go ahead and get all of her textbooks that she needed this semester. I found a new way to hide notes in each one. Hopefully I'd made it harder for her this time, but I had no doubt that she'd be able to decode them. I hope she didn't think I was just really lame and cheesy, but I guess love does that to a guy.

I spotted Micah first and recognized a girl from my economics class hugging him tightly around the waist; I think her name was Sophia. They started making out right in the middle of the crowd. He eventually began moving her out of the gate toward baggage claim. It made me feel ten times lighter that he had a girl; hopefully, it helped keep him away from mine.

As he was walking past me, oblivious to everyone around him except the girl on his arm, I intercepted him. "Hey, man, welcome back."

"I was wondering where you were. She's been talking our damn ears off about you. If I don't hear your name for the rest of my life, it'll be too soon."

I couldn't contain my cheesy-ass grin. I just prayed I wasn't fucking blushing. "I wanted to thank you for watching out for her, for me. She told me what you did that night. I don't care how annoyed she was; I sure as hell owe you one."

"I didn't do it for you," he replied.

"You still did it, so thanks, man. Sorry for all the shit I put you through when you were just trying to be a friend to her."

"No worries. I'm going to get my girl out of here now." He nodded toward the exit. Sophia was still grinning up at him like he was Superman.

We bumped knuckles, but before he even finished his sentence, I sensed her walking out into the gate. She was even more beautiful than I had remembered. Her hair had gotten longer and lighter from being in the sun all summer, and her skin had a golden hue that I was going to have fun running my hands all over later. She looked really tired as well. I just wanted to grab her and tuck her into my bed where she belonged and let her sleep for as long as she wanted, so long as she would let me lie next to her. Ellie and Quinn enfolded her in hugs the second she stepped out. I could tell she was happy to see her family, but it made me laugh when I saw her scanning the area for someone else over their shoulders. I prayed to God that it was me.

After Charles and Cole had their chance to hug her, I watched as she turned and spoke to all four of them. They all rotated and pointed their fingers right at me. She whipped around and let her bags fall from her shoulders when she spotted me. She took off in a dead sprint and hurled herself into my arms. God, this was paradise. This was where she belonged always. I breathed in her unfamiliar soap and shampoo, but I could still smell her comforting scent as well . . . the one that was unique to her. Her legs were squeezing the life out of my waist and I never wanted her to stop.

I never thought I would get this attached to a girl during college or even at all. I came out to California to get a degree so I could make my mom proud, and to play football. Back home, I was in a fight every week with someone different, I stole guys' girlfriends without care, and I was about two seconds away from doing something that would land me in jail. I never imagined that on the morning I met up with Cole outside of his frat house to get the key to our place, I would have my eyes practically bug out of my head at the most gorgeous girl I had ever laid eyes on. Clothed or not. The way she approached us—like she was embarrassed about not having clothes on, but she didn't want us to know—killed me.

I didn't even know her, and I almost grabbed her and threw her on my bike so that no one else could have her. I wanted to beat my chest like a caveman, screaming that she was mine. To my utter dumb luck, she lived next door to me. Cole still gave me a hard time about how I made him ask some random sorority girls to sit next to him in class that first day, so that I could get her to sit next to me. I never imagined how she would rock my world off its axis just in that first hour and a half. Almost instantly, she made me a better person just by flashing that mischievous, flirtatious smile at me, because I wanted to be worthy of her.

In class that first day, I grabbed her hand and wrote my number on it. The feel of her skin against mine shot electricity instantly throughout my body. I became completely aware of how beautiful she was inside and out. I've always tried to write on her palm because I enjoyed that moment of just touching her. I also liked having my mark on her in some way or another. I couldn't help it: I was possessive over her. I took every opportunity I could to get next to her from then on, and I'd never regret it.

We didn't speak or move for what felt like hours, but I think it was only five minutes or so. I just wanted to absorb her heartbeat into mine and reassure myself that she was actually back here in my arms. I needed to make sure I wasn't dreaming. I rubbed my hands up and down her arms, which were wrapped around my neck, just needing to feel her soft skin on my fingers. I slowly laced my fingers into her hair, inhaling the scent more. If I could get my way, I would carry her out of this airport and never put her down. I knew I would eventually have to, so I enjoyed the moment as long as I could. Her face was buried in the crook of my neck and I could feel moisture on my skin.

When she finally pulled back slightly, seeing her eyes full of tears made my heart plummet to the floor. "No, no, no, baby, what's wrong?" I asked nervously. "I thought you'd be happy to see me."

"These are happy tears, Jax. I just can't believe I'm finally back here with you. It's been so long since I've talked to you . . . anything could have happened. I didn't know if you would . . . be here," she admitted, nervously.

When I realized that she actually thought that I would leave her while she was gone, I squeezed her in tighter. It was hard for me to remember that she still had insecurity issues with people leaving. I'll never forgive myself for the way I handled our relationship this past spring.

"Nothing could have kept me away from being here."

I pulled her lips to mine and tried to kiss the life out of her. I would never get tired of these lips. I still couldn't believe she was mine, or rather, I was hers. I whispered in her ear how much I loved her and had missed her. She eased my heartache by returning it all back to me. I couldn't wait to tell her about the hot-air balloon tickets I had in my back pocket. I knew she was going to be excited, even though it was technically my gift from winning our first bet.

"Take me home," she whispered in my ear. Chills ran through my body at the possibility of having her all to myself again.

"Beautiful, I'll take you anywhere."

ABOUT THE AUTHOR

Photo © 2014 Zachery Parr

USA Today bestselling author Kimberly Lauren started out life as an avid reader. Inspired to challenge the more traditional relationship roles she came across while reading romances, she decided to write the scintillating and celebrated new adult series Broken. She currently resides in Texas with her husband, their son, and their three dogs.